Caleb Smith just happened to fall in with a deadly serious group, a team of Weatherpeople with bankrobbing as well as revolution on their minds. By the time they hit a small bank in Maine it's a little too late to leave the party.

Caleb is in a lot of trouble.

In fact, Caleb seems to have cornered the market on trouble and he gladly spreads it around to the unwary, including the couple who offer him shelter after a country cop puts a roadblock in the way of revolution. Then, when some people with nasty minds begin to suspect that Caleb is doubling with the cops, it is time for Caleb to retreat to the safety of New York City, where, in saner days, he moved a little dope and apart from that was a very law-abiding kind of guy. Operating on the theory that the Weatherpeople are a lot more anxious to get at him than the cops are, Caleb finds one way out of the box, a way that has just one chance to work right before Caleb is over his troubles for good.

This novel re-creates, with gritty authenticity, the atmosphere and reality of recent unsettled

(continued on back flap)

CALEB,

WHO IS HOTTER

(continued from front flap)

times. It also moves as fast as a speed-freak looking for a connection and is infused with a sense of humor which is always running just ahead of terror, desperation, and bad dreams.

THAN A $2 PISTOL

by Steven Ashley

David McKay Company, Inc.

NEW YORK

Library of Congress Cataloging in Publication Data

Ashley, Steven.
    Caleb, who is hotter than a $2 pistol.

    I. Title.
PZ4.A8263Cal [PS3551.S39] 813'.5'4 74-25718
ISBN 0-679-50536-9

CALEB,
WHO IS HOTTER
THAN A $2 PISTOL

1 / *Washington County and North*

Bank robbing ain't much fun. And Caleb Smith scratched his head nervously, glanced at the glass front door of the First National Bank of Bangor, and decided he liked dealing dope better.

You meet a much nicer class of people.

Oh, for a bankrobber, Willy was alright. Caleb checked for the third time that the stolen Dodge was in "Drive" and watched Willy through the door: short, lean Willy Ortez, directing some assistant teller who was stuffing money pretty fast into an A&P double-strength shopping bag. Willy was directing him with his huge chromium .45 automatic, and the teller was probably hoping that Willy wouldn't blow him away with that damn cannon and the nice thing about Willy was that he wouldn't.

If he could help it.

Chris, on the other hand, was not alright. Even for a bankrobber. He was tall and pretty—a thin kid with stringy golden hair hanging to his shoulders, and too smart and too icy cold. Not Caleb's sort of people at all.

They'd spent just three days together before the event.

Planning it all; sweltering in the steam heat of Willy's tacky Bronx apartment. They'd dropped acid together—so they'd know some of where they were and how they'd jump. Chris had told them all, in great detail, about cattle killing in the Minneapolis stockyards. He described the flaying alive, the boiling vats, the sounds the cattle made. When Caleb threw up, Chris laughed and told him that true revolutionaries had to know their enemy.

Chris would do you quick as a wink.

And if you were the president of the First National Bank of Bangor and if Christopher was sitting on the edge of your desk watching you over a Colt Python .357, with the gun waving around somewhat negligent and Chris's pale blue eyes examining you, bored and critical, you wouldn't like Chris very much.

Caleb didn't. But the bank-robbing business is not a business where you can freely choose your associates.

Not that kind of business at all.

The big Dodge was parked in front of the bank, smack dab in the middle of a No-Parking zone and brilliant two-tone blue in the January sun.

That parking place was Jeff's brilliant idea. And Caleb was sitting mother-naked and obvious, directly in front of the bank on Bangor, Maine's busiest street, waiting for some cop to come up and say,

"What's a matter, buddy. You blind?" or whatever cops said in this hick town in the hick state of Maine.

Another one of Jeff's bright ideas had gotten Caleb into the bank robbing business in the first place. Caleb had a low opinion of Jeff's brain, and he thought Jeff's personality left a lot to be desired.

Jeff was sincere and direct, and he'd read a lot of Marx and Marcuse and Fanon. He was the son of an immigrant Swedish fisherman who'd been some sort of Wobbly years ago, and Jeff was proud of being a second-generation revolutionary. He said, often, that the working classes were someday going to rise up and join the struggle. He said that a lot.

Meanwhile, Caleb hated him for putting him in this lousy parking place in this lousy stolen car waiting for three lousy bank robbers to come out, running, blazing-away, and all of them shot to pieces, bleeding their bellies out.

Caleb didn't want to die. Natch'.

He also didn't want to be hauled off in handcuffs, sentenced under the applicable laws and gang-shagged the first night in Portsmouth State Pen.

Cars streaming by him. Fords and Chevies and Plymouths and two Buicks crunching the packed snow, rattling chains, and the Maine residents sort of looking him over.

What the hell? Caleb lit a joint and watched the action inside the bank. Willy's chrome pistol shining like a new bumper guard. The teller was anxiously trying to stuff some rolls of change into the bag, and Willy's mouth was moving, "No thanks, man. I don't want the change."

And Christopher, dressed like a college kid, was herding the bank personnel into the president's office.

Caleb groaned. Hoping none of the citizens on the street would head for the bank with a thrifty expression and a mouth full of yells. Hoping that nobody would peer into the bank. Hoping. . .

The three robbers came out quick and nonchalant. Jeff was wiping his planky Swedish face with the back of his hand. Willy had the bag under his arm, and Chris jumped in the back and snapped, "Roll. We got three minutes. Maybe."

Caleb eased the Dodge into traffic and got the speedometer up to thirty-five, counting the minutes in his head. Three minutes went by pretty fast, but then, he was counting pretty fast.

Willy was sweating, stinking up the car with his sweat.

The first snow hit them just before the tollbooth on the

Maine Pike. Little gust of snow-filled wind brushed the windshield.

"Oh boy," Caleb said.

The blizzard had started in the artic somewhere and came wailing across the Canadian border as a Force-9 gale. It eased a little when it hit Maine, but not so much that you'd care to brag about it. Roofs that had been threatened all winter were being worried again, and telephone linemen were swearing, trying to get their cold trucks started. Electric and phone lines dead all over the northern half of the state.

They got through the tollgate OK, and once they were out of sight, Caleb tromped on it.

He got the Dodge up to 110 and turned the windshield wipers on.

"Man, I hate the cold," Willy said. And shivered.

"At least it's clean snow," Jeff said. "Not that crud we get in the city. Can't we go any faster?"

Five miles down the pike, Caleb swerved the Dodge off the road. No traffic behind them, and the Dodge bucked up the embankment and through the fence they'd cut that morning.

Tore a chunk out of the pan on a rock as they charged over the top of the bank, but God made a lot of Dodges, and he don't much care what happens to each individual one of them.

Caleb stopped the Dodge behind a screen of scotch pine that the State of Maine had planted to beautify their turnpike.

Heavy gust of snow whipped Caleb's face when he piled out of the car; but the same snow was already covering the marks they made up the embankment, so he gave it a grin.

They had another hot car—fat-ass Chevy—demurely parked along some farmer's dirt road which ran beside the Pike. Jeff said he'd drive.

They were twenty miles up highway 201, heading north,

by the time the alarm reached the turnpike; the alarm picking up speed, but heading south.

Caleb sat in the back beside Christopher wishing he'd never heard about the Weathermen.

Willy, in the front seat, was emptying the A&P bag and stuffing a whole lot of money into the money belt he was going to wear when they hit sleepy Canadian customs, forty miles north of sleepy Kennebec, Maine.

The snow was getting worse, filling the windshield, and already fewer houses beside the road and the trees getting thicker.

Northwestern Maine. Hundreds and hundreds and hundreds of miles of trees. The heavy woods divided only by highway 201 and checked only by the Canadian border, where a thin bulldozer strip declares the international boundary. In summertime, you can get a jeep along the strip. In winter, the only creatures who walk the border are deer looking for easier forage and shallow snow they can paw away from the frozen grasses underneath.

Grey-blue-green. Jack pine and Norway pine and white pine. With an occasional copse of white birch stuck in the snow like signposts—the black and white markers of some vanished religion. Twenty miles between people on highway 201 and off the highway, in winter, a hundred.

Big green Chevy rocking on its springs, slipping and sliding in the snow, hot-footing it toward the border.

Jeff, from New York, gunning it and swearing each time the rear end broke loose and slid towards the snowbanks on the sides of the road. Snow banks, snow cliffs—easy nine-, ten-feet high.

Willy wasn't saying much. His father's war souvenir chrome-plated .45 in his lap, and his hands resting on it, composed and protective.

Chris was quiet, too. His eyes were set at zero.

Caleb in the back, unhappy. Legs cramped up and squeezed by the bulk of his winter clothing. He shifted a shotgun off his legs and scratched his balls.

The car stank from their breathing and cigarettes and sweat, but a warm, good stink with all that cold whiteness whizzing by outside.

So they came sneaking through the tiny town of Kennebec, obeying the limit, radiating innocence. Two or three people saw their car through the frosted front window of Synder's garage but thought nothing of it. Thought they were crazy Canadians traveling when any fool would have known better. Here, a hundred miles north of Bangor, it had been snowing for three hours steady. And the Chevy's tracks filled and vanished within ten minutes on Kennebec's one and only street.

So, outside of Kennebec and wailing again and worried about the snow.

"I wish our Big Time Leader was here," Caleb said. "It'd really be nice if John suffered a little."

Christopher told him to shut up.

About five miles outside of Kennebec, and (as the newspapers later said) "a scant thirty-five miles from the Canadian border," the Chevy came wallowing around a turn, and two hundred yards ahead, a State Trooper car was broadside across the road, with its red and yellow police light flashing.

Jeff saw the roadblock about five seconds before the roadblock saw Jeff and the Chevy.

The police had been waiting, bored and cold, for nearly two and a half hours. Not enough traffic to keep one trooper occupied, let alone twelve of them, and as the snow fell heavier, they stayed inside their cars swapping lies, and nobody stepped outside except when they had to take a piss.

Sheriff Tom Holloway had a six-pack bet with the trooper from Rockingham. The sheriff said it would hit twenty-five below by nightfall, and at three thirty in the afternoon it looked like the sheriff was in for some free beer.

In the blockade car, Deputy Mackey was telling his story about the five-hundred-pound black bear he'd killed down near Moosehead.

Courtesy. The other three cops in the car knew the story by heart, but the deputy had a flask of rum (medicinal), and like gentlemen, the other cops sipped and listened.

Jeff saw the roadblock; he cramped the wheel hard to the left, and he bounced the Chevy into the snowbank.

One of the troopers looked up. "Jesus H. Christ," he said.

The Chevy was half on the road, half in the snowbank, and cutting the bank like the edge of a snowplow. Huge cloud of snow in the air. Snow explosion at the impact point and rooster tail behind the car and over it as it continued to slide. No sign of a car at all, just an avalanche of snow heading towards the troopers.

Inside the Chevy, dark for a moment and a punch to the heart and sudden stillness.

Willy was out first. Because he still had his father's pistol in his hand and because he couldn't think of anything else to do with it, he pointed it at the troopers' car and fired a shot.

The others crawled out real quick.

Chris had blood running from his nose.

Jeff grabbed the money belt and climbed on the trunk of the Chevy and started clawing his way up the snowbank. Caleb followed, swimming, digging, pulling the snow down past him, moving his feet faster than the snow could collapse beneath him. Shock of adrenalin.

Willy stood in the road and fired again.

Nobody, not even the cops, ever gets accustomed to being shot at. Some folks jump for cover, some start to argue, some grab for their own artillery; but most people don't do much of anything. They just stand there. Very surprised. When the snow cloud settled up the road and a little Puerto Rican nut jumped out of the car and opened up, the cops, at first, did nothing. The shot, in all that wind sounded harmless as a popgun muffled in a sack, and nobody understood that war had been declared. Just like Pearl Harbor.

All those bodies flailing and clawing and disappearing over the snowbank made it official, and the troopers in the roadblock car jumped out and layed down a barrage at Willy.

Bang, bang, bang, bang (boom of Deputy Mackey's shotgun), and the kid was still standing there and still shooting back.

Jeff was leaning over the top of the bank. "Come on, Willy. Get your ass up here. Run, damn it."

Caleb found a big pine tree and stood behind it, wheezing. He pointed the shotgun over his head and pulled the trigger. Boom.

A lot of heavy wet snow had collected in the upper branches of that pine tree and most of it fell on Caleb.

He said something rude.

"Willy!" Jeff was exposed twenty feet from the safety of the trees and the fire from the troopers was more serious now and a bullet cracked as it went by him and he wasn't going to stay there, in the open, forever.

He screamed, "Willy, for Chrissake!"

Willy saw the flashes from the troopers' guns. The snow was gusting and swirling, and from the middle of the vague bodies of those grey men came red flashes like teeth.

"Oh," he said.

Willy dropped his father's pistol, so those lunatics would stop trying to kill him, and ran for the snowbank. One step, two steps, a churning lunge and Jeff caught his arm and was pulling him up, light as a balloon.

Caleb couldn't see the troopers, and his hair was covered with snow and his jacket was wet, and his hands were cold on the shotgun. He fired his second barrel at the blizzard and hit it dead center. Willy slid behind his tree—classic sandlot slide.

"You crazy spic," Caleb said.

Willy looked like one of those statues of Don Quixote you can buy in airport gift shops. Except the eyes. Don

Quixote's vacant eyes being fixed on God and Willy's eyes being sharp, streetwise, and fixed on the main chance.

"Man," Willy said, "those pigs are trying to kill us." Willy stood up and brushed the snow off his neat striped pants' legs. He noted the mound of snow in Caleb's hair. "You look like the abdominal snowman," he said.

Bullets whizzing everywhere, seeking through the snow. A bullet whumped into the trunk of their tree.

"No good," Willy said. Scared breath coming in short hard gasps. "Let's split."

Caleb opened the shotgun, dropped two shells in the snow, and fumbled the next two into the chambers. He and Willy started to run, or wade, through the snow, in no particular direction, away from the road, herded by the firing behind them.

Under the trees, the snow was shallower and drifted, and they dodged through the forest running hard, with Willy in the lead.

Willy fell down. He fell hard and sudden and pulled an alder bush down with him, and Caleb's belly muscles clenched up.

When Caleb rolled him over, the front of Willy's throat was blood and two strands of purple cartilage hanging loose. He rolled his brown eyes at Caleb and a four-inch bubble of blood popped at his throat. His heels thumped once or twice in the snow.

"Hey Willy," Caleb said. The tone you use when you aren't quite sure if someone is putting you on. "Willy?"

Willy's foot thumped again and the shutters were sliding over his eyes. His face relaxed and he looked younger, dead.

Caleb felt like throwing up; but he didn't want to throw up on Willy, so he swallowed hard and looked away and fired both barrels of his shotgun in the air. He walked away under the smoke like a white man in a white world with a grey parachute.

They were all lost. The cops were lost; the robbers were

lost. Too much snow and the eyes were going blind, and ice was stacking up on the eyelashes and where to go anyway in this godforsaken country?

Caleb was getting adjusted to his own death, trying it on like a new suit and not liking the fit.

Or the style.

Or the manufacturer.

Snooping through the blowing gusts of snow, half-crouched, with the shotgun sticking forward—like a wand to ward off evil.

Boom. He shot a big old birch stump. Blew the snow off the top of it and pellets gouging out wood chips and splinters and Caleb half-glad it wasn't a cop.

The fusillade behind him had broken up into odd shots now and again; but the pressure was still real, pushing him on.

He was crashing through the snow now. Sometimes hip-deep. Caleb wished he had some gloves with rabbit-fur lining.

He wished he had any kind of gloves. The last time he reloaded, he had had a hell of a time.

He came into a little cedar clearing, and in the middle of it, Jeff was standing, calmly taking a piss.

"Hey," Caleb said.

"Hello," Jeff said. Quite calm, even . . . peaceful.

"Did you get any of them?" Jeff asked.

"Sure," Caleb said, disgusted. "Thirty-nine."

Jeff Svenigsun had lost control of his eyes. They were sparkling with tears, or great joy, or relief at finding himself doing what he'd always been meant to do.

"I got one of them," Jeff said. "With this." He held up his little grey automatic like it was a trophy. "The cop fell over when I shot him," Jeff explained. "He fell over on his side."

"Willy bought it," Caleb said.

Jeff dropped his automatic down to his side. "Shit," he said. "Are you sure. Are you sure Willy's dead?"

"Oh yeah, Jeffy, I'm sure. I rolled his body over myself."
After a decent interval, Jeff spat in the snow.

"Where's Chris?" Jeff demanded.

"Beats me," Caleb said. "Dead probably. Screw him."

Jeff rubbed his automatic between his hands. "Did you shoot Willy?" he asked.

"Huh?"

Jeff was almost apologetic. "I just wanted to know. How about Chris? Did you shoot Chris?"

"What's wrong with you, man? You freaking out or something?"

Jeff stuck his little automatic in his belt. "Sure," he said. "I was just kidding." He even smiled to prove it.

Caleb shook his head like a boxer who's just been punched. He decided to let it pass. "Yeah," he said. "You know, Jeff, I am really cold. I've never been this cold before."

Jeff, in his college-boy chinos and car coat, ankle deep in snow and that dirty fire guttering in his eyes.

"Yeah," he said. "I bet you were a lot happier back in New York dealing scag."

"I never dealt scag, Jeff," Caleb said, flat.

Jeff gave him one of those I-know-better smiles and said, "The pigs got snowshoes. Goddamned snowshoes."

He turned and not much caring whether Caleb followed, started to press out of the clearing.

Caleb said, "I wish I had snowshoes." But nobody else in the clearing now to hear him.

He didn't want to be alone, so he followed Jeff.

Caleb hoped that he might escape and not be shot in the spine and dragged back to the Highway Patrol cars with his head furrowing the snow and ice on his eyes like a deer shot out of season.

But the drifted snow made it hard for any hoping to be going on.

Every step now, his legs crashed through the snow until

his crotch stopped his descent. Under the powder a thin layer of ice; not enough to support his weight. The ice cut him up some, crashing through it and dragging himself out.

His pants were wet, or would have been wet if they hadn't been half-froze. They pressed against his skin like soft, irregular boards.

It was a little easier until he caught Jeff. Jeff left a trail like the wake of a speedboat permanently frozen.

But Jeff was bent over, gagging from exertion, when Caleb came up to him, so Caleb took the lead.

Was that a shot behind them? Was it close?

One foot down, then a jerky heaving motion forward—pulling his thigh muscles—and the other foot down, crashing through the snow crust.

Caleb's body working too hard and the smell of his own breath making him sick, and the two of them came over a little ridge and saw before them a vast plain of rocks and blowing snow.

Caleb's future died in his heart.

Some logging operation had cut that plain ten, twenty years ago. They took most of the big trees and broke most of the small ones. Downed trees and snags stuck out of the snow like a jumble of tinkertoys.

Caleb stopped, stock-still, and Jeff labored up beside him.

"Maybe. . . ," Caleb tried, "maybe we should give up."

Jeff inspected the tangle ahead of them.

"We're Weathermen," he said.

"No, man," Caleb said, angry. "You're a Weatherman; I'm just a damn fool. Remember? I just got sucked into this. John sucked me in."

"Oh." Jeff swiveled his eyes around to touch Caleb. Another obstacle, like the tangled forest in front of them.

"I don't think we should give up," Jeff said, reasonably. He patted the money belt. "We need this money. Look. . . ," he thought for a moment, "getting all this money will be quite a coup. John will be sitting on the Weather Bureau with this. And maybe you and me, well . . . who can tell."

"Terrific. Jeff, uh, I hate to tell you this when your mind is so full of important things, like the Revolution and all, but we—you and me—are going to die here. And John is never going to see any of this money. And if he's counting on it to make him a hero to the Weather Bureau, he had better make some new plans."

Jeff seemed to be listening. His ears were turned to catch the words. But when Caleb was done yelling he said, "Don't worry Caleb, it'll work out. Do you want me to lead for a while?"

"Jeff, we're finished!"

"This is a war, Caleb," Jeff said, seriously. He held the money belt out to Caleb. "Here, you carry the cash for a while."

"I'm carrying this shotgun."

Jeff tugged the shotgun out of Caleb's arms and raised the steel doors over his eyes so Caleb could see what was going on inside. Still smiling, he said, "I wonder how they knew we were coming up 201. I wonder who killed Willy and Chris."

The muzzle of the shotgun wasn't exactly pointing at Caleb, but it wasn't exactly pointing away from him either.

"Take the money belt," Jeff suggested.

So Caleb slung the canvas money belt over his shoulder and pushed off.

The going was about as bad as it looked. They avoided the bigger snags, but a thousand little snags under the mild surface of the snow caught at them, tripped them up, held them to a grotesque heaving crawl.

Not too much luck missing the snags and no luck at all walking on top of the snow.

For a few minutes it'd hold their weight, and then, abruptly, the crust would break and drop them through to their waists.

Caleb fell fullface, time after time, when his feet tripped on the under-snow obstacles.

It was getting hard to get up. Finally, the seventeenth or eighteenth time that Caleb fell, Jeff passed him.

Caleb raised his head from the snow. "I'd quit," he shouted. "If there was anybody to give up to."

Jeff's eyelashes were frozen and his hair was a haystack of snow. "I bet you wish you had some scag," he said.

Jeff plunged forward, heading vaguely uphill.

"I never dealt scag," Caleb yelled. But his words were blown back past his head, and Jeff didn't slow down.

Three shots behind them. The cops had found their trail.

Jeff was running through the snow, but not fast.

Ten, twelve minutes of gasping, hurting blindness and they made the top of a ridge. Walking a little easier here. But not much.

Jeff's face was pretty well gone, and he was falling every ten feet or so.

A shout behind them somewhere.

Jeff fell again, fullface. He pushed his white arms into the snow like sticks and propped himself up. "Screw this," he said, carefully.

Jeff got to his feet. He left the shotgun in the snow. He pulled the little automatic out of his pocket and stuck it under his arm. Pulled a clip out and dropped it in the snow. Put the pistol in his lap and pressed at the clip release with his thumb. Hooked two fingers around the old clip and pulled it out. Put the new clip in.

"What the hell you think you're doing?" Caleb yelled.

Jeff turned his broken face to Caleb and spoke to someone standing behind Caleb or maybe a thousand miles away.

"I'm going to die for the revolution," he said.

"You're nuts," Caleb said.

Jeff reasoned with the ghost behind Caleb: "Look," he said, "they're going to kill me whether I run or attack, and if I attack, I'm a revolutionary hero."

Jeff was shuddering. His jaw was having trouble forming words.

"You see," he said, "it's reasonable. . ." He would have said more, but his voice broke.

Caleb reached for his arm, but Jeff snatched it away and let Caleb see his weird, weird eyes.

"You're a witness," he said. "I'm not afraid of the truth." He bolted then. He ran right back down the path they'd made getting here.

Caleb didn't try to stop him. He bent over and picked up the shotgun and waded forward into the deep, cold snow.

He tried to remember his old lady's face. But Sara's features wouldn't come to him here.

A brief rattle of shots behind him. Jeff. Caleb neither increased nor decreased his pace.

A light-headed numbness, now. Less pain. Caleb wasn't afraid of dying anymore; he was afraid of stopping.

Caleb found himself on a long slope, dotted with black shark boulders. He stopped, resting his weight on his downhill foot. "Oh boy," he said.

Wind roaring again and louder now.

Halfway up the hill he started counting feet. He promised himself one hundred feet, but he stopped after half that.

He promised himself thirty feet, or just up to that chimney-shaped rock (whichever came first), and he made the chimney rock and stopped.

Nothing left in him. Not bile, or exhaustion, or anger. Just pain. Caleb was interested in the pain because he had never hurt so much before.

Ten feet at a time.

He passed near a lone cedar tree and pulled two needles off the lower branches and bit into them, and the taste reminded him of old clothes in his Aunt Helen's attic.

Sturdy little tree. He admired it. Irregular in shape and brawny where the north wind had tried to push it over.

He delayed by the tree because that would hold the cops behind him.

He didn't turn around because that would set them loose.

He didn't try to light a cigarette, because his hands

wouldn't work right and his slight fumble would bring them on quicker.

He wallowed with a certain slight dignity up the last ten feet of slope.

Something was roaring in his ears.

Nothing on top of the ridge but three windblown, black boulders. One of them was only a little taller than Caleb's belt buckle. He and the shotgun wiggled up on top.

Looking back down the slope at the earthworm track he'd made. Yes, it was getting darker. Definitely darker.

The roaring in his ears was enormous. So he walked over to the far side of the ridge.

The ridge stopped very suddenly. Land became air.

There was a river below. About as wide as Sixth Avenue. Boulders like tank traps in the middle and ice a couple of yards out from the shore. Cliff on the other side maybe three stories high with a few pine trees hanging on grimly; scrawny things with their roots in cracks in the rock and begging for a little more sun.

Some of the river boulders, half lost in spray, were as big as gas stations.

For some reason, Caleb had a picture in his head, maybe from a movie, of a tall railroad bridge collapsing (blown up), and the train cars tumbling end over end downstream in this very river, spewing guts and upholstery and unbelievable scraps of metal on the cold black monster rocks below.

Caleb shivered and sat down to wait for the cops.

> You know what they say about snowflakes
> ain't no two the same
> Well all those flakes
> look alike to me
> Every one is a dirty shame.*

---

* From "Snow" by Jesse Winchester. © 1969 Fourth Floor Music, Inc. All rights reserved. Used by permission of Warner Brothers Music.

Caleb hummed the tune and remembered the words.

The snow falling more gently now. And a shape at the far end of Caleb's vision.

Two shapes. As if behind a scrim, cautious and vague.

Caleb put his shotgun to his shoulder. He thought better of it and laid the gun back across his lap.

Now, a skirmish line of shapes coming noiselessly up the hill.

Caleb couldn't make out their faces.

"I wish I had snowshoes," he said, very quietly.

Ten men, maybe a dozen. Guns in their hands like scepters. Slow striding walk of snowshoes.

Caleb threw the shotgun to his shoulder and pulled the trigger.

Pain in his hands, too brittle with cold. Pain in his shoulder where the blood got started with a slam. Too much noise!

Caleb yelled, "Goddamn it!" and threw the shotgun away.

He slid backwards over the boulder, and half a second later the first rifle bullet exploded the ice where he'd been sitting.

And more to come. Shot after shot and shots on top of shots. The blunt roar of pistols and the heavier wham of big game rifles and the occasional boom of a shotgun. The top of Caleb's rock was a dancing mess of splinters and ice dust.

A trapped mouse. A squirrel in a corner. He dashed back and forth.

He floundered, or ran, down to the edge of the cliff. Ran out on the thin snow cornice which overhung the white water.

Heart jangling in his ears. The river canyon under his feet was a hall of mirrors. Each place the spume had touched, it had silvered.

Diamond boulders. Diamond stalactites. Diamond walls.

It looked like a mouth to Caleb.

He didn't feel so good.

He told his feet to jump.

"No Sirree."

He shivered so sharp it hurt him.

Decided he should quit. Decided he should put his hands over his shoulders and go face the cops.

But he shifted his weight and the snow cornice snapped, and he felt himself falling outward, arms churning for balance, into the river.

He would have screamed when he hit the water, but suddenly he had no breath for it.

2 / *Kennebec County*

Kennebec Rips—1.8 miles

The flow of water through this part of the Kennebec is controlled by logging dams upstream. In the short span of these rips, the river drops nearly 130 feet. The water is very fast, perhaps as fast as 40 mph. At low water, projecting rocks at Holden Point, the Two Maidens, and Houseboat Rock will gouge the bottom out of any canoe. If the canoeist should manage to avoid these hazards, he would still be caught by Hartley Falls at the foot of the fast water. THERE IS NO LANDING BEFORE HARTLEY FALLS. Hartley Falls divides into a "Y," and though, theoretically, a canoeist might negotiate the left prong of the "Y," most of the current flows over the right prong, with a 20-foot drop into a maelstrom pool. This pool, which combines a vicious undertow with hundreds of tons of falling water, can reduce the stoutest aluminum canoe to shreds in a few minutes.

If the canoeist does attempt the Kennebec Rips —and if he succeeds, he will join that small group of men who've survived a dangerous run, not by their own skills, but by the active intervention of the Lord. Grade 7—Impassable, even for experts." *

When Caleb hit the water, the river was high and that probably saved his life. Many of the smaller rocks, which would have gutted him, were well beneath the surface. And, his luck held.

The current snatched his body around the bigger boulders—boulders as big as two freight cars stacked on one another—instead of holding him under the bow of one of those grinders until his body was broken, stringy meat.

Caleb wasn't conscious. Or was only half conscious. He was being born again. A blood-red roaring inside him, and his diaphragm pressed until his heart almost popped. He was a sack of blood heading for the light.

He did not swim. He breathed only when his face was out of the water. His life had retreated deep inside and was sending simple weak commands to his heart and lungs.

He was swept in the left channel around Houseboat Rock and dragged in a serpentine between the Two Maidens. He passed under Holden Point in the slower water, and eyes closed, he never saw the eighty feet of slick basalt above him.

Cold. His body temperature was dropping—70 degrees now—he hadn't been in the water two minutes.

At Hartley Falls, a great Norway pine gave Caleb his second piece of luck. It had caught up somehow, jammed across the right hand prong of the falls, and it blocked the maelstrom pool. Like a crossing gate.

Caleb opened his eyes when he hit the log. Current was trying to suck him under it. His feet kicked once or twice, though he didn't understand anything and saw only an expanse of gouged, trembling wood which vibrated like a bow.

* *Field Guide to New England White Water,* National Sport Canoe Assn., Georgian Press, Boston, pp. 47,48.

It hurt in his chest where he'd hit the log, but only dimly like someone else's pain that you are trying to understand.

He couldn't breathe at all because the current had clamped him to the log and held his lungs flat. He blacked out, and the current rolled him sideways along the log and over the left prong of the falls.

Two and a half minutes. Caleb had been in the water two and a half minutes.

Below Hartley Falls, the Kennebec gorge widens into a valley, and for a few miles the river is slow, fat, and wide. At this time of the year, much of the river is frozen over. Only a channel near the right bank stays open all year round.

The ice is thick near the shore, and on their summer vacations, history students from Maine State University poke around the ruins of the nineteenth-century icehouses, which once lined this stretch of the river and supplied ice to New England and the southern states. At the peak of the business, clipper ships transported the ice in holds filled with sawdust to chill the gin and bitters of the English in India.

It must have been pretty amazing in those days. Farmers, dray horses, sledges, long ice saws. All gone.

Nothing here now, but a mass of clear blue ice, covered with snow and lining the bank of a forgotten river in Maine.

For the second time, Caleb opened his eyes. He was bobbing against the edge of the ice, the air trapped in his clothing was holding him up and some eddy in the river nudging him through the fragile rotten ice towards the thicker stuff near shore.

Someone was standing on that ice shouting something.

After a while something hit him in the face and he opened his eyes again.

The pole hooked under his money belt and pulled him through the rotten ice, and a couple of grabs and he was out of the water.

He lay on his back. It was night now, he thought. Arms picked him up. The snowstorm had quit and the sky was bright from all the stars there are. Big half-moon reflecting over a sea of snow.

Caleb, like a babe in arms, looked at his rescuer's face. Long stringy brown hair. Leather-faced country freak.

Caleb croaked. Tried again. "Got any dope?" he asked.

Minus 32 degrees.

By the time the tall man got him to the door of the little log cabin, Caleb's clothes were frozen solid and a film of ice had formed on both his hands.

A woman was standing in the kitchen, wearing two sweaters, blue flannel pants, and her blond hair drawn back in a bun.

"Good Jesus God!" she said.

"I fished him out of the river." The man set Caleb down in a narrow rocking chair in front of the stove.

"Is he alive? Here. Let's get him out of his clothes. Get the medical book, Denny."

She shucked Caleb bare, and Caleb didn't help or hinder because he thought he was in paradise.

He liked it when she started washing him with warm water. But when the heat started to penetrate his dead, frostbitten skin, Caleb cried.

"Hold still," she said. "Here, Denny, you keep on scrubbing him. Let me see the book."

Frostbite is very much like a burn of the skin. The outer tissues sear and die and the tender skin underneath is literally scorched by cold. Long before Caleb had fallen into the Kennebec, his face and fingers had acquired the red flush that marks the onset of frostbite. By now, the flesh on his ears and hands was dead white.

"I think we should get him to a doctor," Denny said.

"Now you see why we should have a phone," the woman snapped, winning a few points in an old argument. "You won't be able to get through to Kennebec on those damn bald tires."

"Maybe I should walk down to Stevenson's store and call."

Caleb had never hurt so much. His body was burning. An acid bath, as the warmth thawed his nerves and those nerves began to send damage messages to his brain.

He whispered, "No doctor."

"Man, you're in bad shape," Denny said, reaching for his gloves.

"No doctor. I'm a Weatherman."

The wind kicked up a flurry of snow which rattled like shots against the kitchen windows. Caleb coughed. The cold sat outside the door of that cabin like a child's monster come to life, and "Weatherman" made a small cabin in the Maine woods smaller and more rickety than it had been a moment ago.

"Oh boy," Denny said, and sat down.

"Oh Christ!" the woman said. She tossed the washrag to Denny. "Here, you do it for a while."

Caleb writhed and whimpered as Denny continued, and nobody spoke for perhaps half an hour. The splash of water, the creaking of the cane rocker, the hiss of wood in the big old stove.

Caleb's pain slowly faded and in its place a warm tingling came, as if someone had tapped his skin all over with a wire brush. Denny tossed the washcloth into the sink.

"I guess you'll live," he said. "I still don't like the looks of your left hand, but I don't know what else we can do about it. I'll get the down comforter."

Conference time.

Denny went into the other room of the cabin, and the woman followed him. The door between the two rooms was pretty lightweight, just a sheet of clear plastic stretched on a thin wooden frame, and Caleb craned his neck around. He could see them OK; but they were whispering, and he couldn't make out what they were saying.

The book the woman had been using was lying on a table beside him. *The British Ship Captain's Emergency Medical*

Guide—1943. Long journey to be in this cabin at this time.

Caleb opened it one-handed (his left hand still had no feeling in it) and read about frostbite.

When the two returned, the woman made Caleb a cup of tea. Caleb in a clumsy multi-colored down quilt, with a cup of tea in his hand, blowing the steam away and feeling very uncomfortable.

"Well," she said. "OK. I've got some questions. Are the cops looking for you?"

"Yes."

"The local cops, I mean."

"Yes."

"Damn it! Well, what do you expect us to do about it?"

"They may think I drowned in the river," Caleb said.

"Sure Karen," Denny said. "They'll think he's dead. Like that river driver last spring. Nobody comes out of those rapids alive."

She gave Denny a disgusted look. No doubt about it, this was Her Home. "Where did you go in the river?" she asked.

"I don't know. It was pretty dark. There were some high cliffs, I remember, and a lot of monstro rocks in the river."

Caleb wanted a cigarette bad. He wanted to put off the questions, but he didn't trust the woman enough to ask her to wait until morning. He was very tired, and the woman's face was an enameled pink balloon, yattering at him.

"Why are they looking for you?"

"Ah, shit lady," Caleb grunted. "Public Fornicaton. Indecent Exposure. Lubrication under unlawful circumstances. How 'bout that?"

"Don't give me any of your hippy-dippy punk answers," she snapped. "In case you haven't been able to get it together, I'll tell you. I think we should turn you in."

"Karen!" Denny exclaimed.

She turned on him, mocking. "We couldn't do that!" she whined. "Why this here Revolutionary is our Brother. See—he's got long hair and he smokes dope and he likes

rock and roll. We just couldn't turn him in." Her face was
mean as a speed-freak's liver. "But it would be alright to
lose our home and everything we have here. Wouldn't that
be alright, Denny?"

Denny's face was a charmer's face. The face of a man
who tickled the world to get what he wanted. Now he had to
be resolute and dignified. He tried, but his face had no more
dignity than a Salvation Army suit.

"Yes," he said. "What did you do? I think we have a right
to know." He assured himself: "We've got a right to know."

Under the best of circumstances, Caleb resented questions which would fix him to his past. He didn't think that
anybody had the right to make him pay up for his
accidental actions. Now, he was very tired. "I'm not that
person," he wanted to say. "I'm someone else now."

But he didn't say that. Instead, he put on his honorable
face and said, "It was a Weatherman action. Me and another dude were bringing ten pounds of hash across the
border. A little money for the revolutionary coffers. We
picked up the stuff in Montreal, and Kennebec was the
closest small border crossing we could find on the map. We
didn't make it."

"Oh," Denny said.

Karen looked him over, weighing and balancing. "Uh,
how did you get in the river?" she asked.

"I'm very thirsty," Caleb said. "Could I have some more
tea?"

"I suppose so," she said.

She went over to the stove to pour some tea. Caleb
appreciated her ass. Even under those baggy blue flannels,
it was small and tight and hard.

"What's your name?" she asked.

"Caleb Smith. What kind of tea is that?"

"Sassafras. It's good for what ails you. I'm Karen
Milanovich, and Denny, here, is my old man."

Caleb nodded, formally.

A gust of wind rattled the windows, and Denny went over and looked out. "Damn," he said. "It's getting colder. We'll have more snow before morning."

Karen shivered. "Just what we need."

Caleb knew he should leave. But wrapped up like a woolly bear and cup of tea in his hands, he couldn't.

"The pigs were waiting for us," he said. "We had the hash taped inside the spare tire, but forget it! There must have been ten–twelve pigs waiting at the border, and they were going to tear the car apart. As soon as my partner saw what was going down, he stepped on the gas and we crashed the border gate. We did alright for a while; but we had to abandon the car finally, and I got chased into the river. I figured that the river was better than jail so I jumped in."

"You should have been killed," Karen said. "Congratulations Pilgrim, you got more lives than a cat."

They listened to the wind for a minute or so. Caleb pulled the comforter up a little higher, and he stared at the white flesh on his left hand.

"Look," Karen began. "We're not really into your kind of politics." Denny started to interject, but she waved him down. "No, I mean, Denny is, sort of. He cheers every time you guys blow something up or raise a ruckus. But he doesn't *do* anything, any more than I do. We're the only freaks for forty miles, and we grow dope and talk to the neighbors about ecology, and we get along real well."

"They're straight, but they're nice," Denny said.

"I don't agree with what you're doing," she continued. "It's been a long time since Kent State. I'm down on the same things you're down on, but all this violence is just a cowboy trip, and so far as I can tell, there isn't much difference between the cops killing someone and you killing some cop. Either way, it's a dead person."

Denny jumped in, converting what she'd said into another chapter in an old private quarrel: "I still say it's a war, Karen. When some pig is shooting at you, only a coward wouldn't shoot back. I. . ."

She flared up. "Pigs! Pigs! You fathead. I'm really sick of all this revolutionary posturing. Because someone has long hair, he's groovy, and because someone else wears a badge, he's a pig! I wouldn't trade Buckshot for three bona-fide revolutionaries. And Mrs. Stevenson is worth ten of the far-out groovy freaks in the Weathermen. Ah, the hell with it." She walked into the other room, putting her heels down hard. Caleb could hear her crashing around in there.

"Don't mind Karen," Denny began.

"It's alright," Caleb said. "I know what she means. I used to deal dope in the Village, and I'd be a lot happier there than here."

Denny put his hand on Caleb's shoulder. "But you guys are doing really important things," he said. "You don't just talk about the revolution; you do it."

"Yeah, sure. Can I have some more of that tea?"

Denny put some more wood in the firebox and brewed the tea.

"I'll get Buckshot down here tomorrow to take a look at that hand," he said. He smiled with his own secret knowledge: "Buckshot is really far out. He's sort of our local homegrown north woods guru."

Karen was quiet in the other room, and the wind kept the air alive in the cabin.

"It must be ten o'clock," Denny said. "I've got to sack out." He opened a chest. "There's some quilts and stuff in here, and the fire usually doesn't go out before morning. You'll be OK here. They may stop by and ask us a few questions, but they'll probably concentrate on dragging the river. Dope smuggling isn't that big a deal. You'll be OK until morning. And we'll think of something then."

"Thank you," Caleb said. "I mean, thanks for saving my life and all that."

Denny had a nice-kid smile and he used it on Caleb, "My pleasure. Get some sleep. Goodnight."

Caleb sat in the rocker for a long time before he nodded out. One kerosene lantern, soft shadows on the walls, and the steady glow from the grate in the front of the stove.

Outside, the wind was looking for life to chill. But nothing moved. No small animal strayed from its burrow to tempt that cold wind's icy, deadly humour.

Caleb wished that Sara wasn't so political. He wished she and him were living together in a snug cabin in the Maine woods. He wished for a lot of gentle things that could never come true, because it was too late for the both of them.

Caleb tossed restlessly all night. Dull, repetitive, feverish dreams where he was busted by the narcs or the clean raincoats of the FBI.

When the cold blue sun snapped its light through the window at six in the morning, Caleb was glad. The fire was gone in the stove and he could see his breath.

Whisperings and rummagings in the other room. Creaks of an old house waking up.

Denny came in, boots unlaced, and pulling his jacket over his sweater. "Oh boy, oh boy, oh boy. Colder than a witch's titty," he announced. Went to the window, looked out, and shivered.

"I'll get you some dry clothes," he said. "Unless you want to stay inside and piss in a jar."

Caleb followed him outside and the two of them fumbling in the cold. The snow sloped up to meet the eaves of the cabin, and the place looked like a snowbank where people lived.

"Got a cigarette?" Caleb asked.

"Don't smoke," Denny said. "Gave it up a year ago."

Caleb's left hand had regained some of its color. But the little finger and fourth finger were still dead white, and he had no feeling in them.

Denny started the stove and put some water on. "What would you like for breakfast?" he asked. "Eggs, oatmeal, what?"

"Whatever," Caleb said. He was suddenly very hungry.

"How you feeling?" Denny pulling eggs out of the refrigerator and dancing around the stove.

"Better. Still a little shaky, but OK."

"Good. Good. A little breakfast will set you right."

"Good morning." Karen was head to toe dressed in a soft flannel nightgown. Soft breasts in soft cloth encased and moving. "How's the water?" She bent over a green jerry can beside the stove.

"I'll have to get some before I go to work."

Denny flipping eggs and hopping and explaining to Caleb: "We got a plastic pipe from a spring up the hill. But during the winter the pipe freezes, so I go down and get water from the river." He put a little salt on the eggs. "I thought you were a beaver when I first saw you. I only saw your hair and I thought you were a beaver. What time is it?"

"Seven," Karen said.

"Roll me a couple of joints, OK?" He set Caleb's plate on the table. "I got a four hour gig at Snyder's Mobil gas station, and I like to be prepared. I couldn't hassle it straight."

The eggs were better than any eggs Caleb had ever tasted. He ate four of them. He also ate five pieces of toast and two bowls of oatmeal. When he was finished, he pushed his plate back and belched. Karen raised her eyebrows.

"I always eat a lot when I'm worried," Caleb explained.

"Oh." First friendly grunt he'd got out of her.

Denny grabbed the jerry can. "Get a sleeping bag and put him in the dope shed," he suggested. "They may not come, but if they do, they'll never look in there. I'll find out the news and see if Buckshot is in town."

About four hundred yards behind the cabin was an old horse barn that, years ago, had been converted into a two car garage. Its sills were gone and the grey boards were leaning alarmingly and it wouldn't be too many more winters before the weight of the snow collapsed it altogether.

From the cabin, the barn was invisible. It lay in a slight hollow, in a clump of white ash, and when the leaves had fallen, you could see the roofline and one gable, but just barely.

During the summer, an old logging road—more a trail than a road—connected it to the house. And during the winter, Denny tramped a path through the snow.

He used half of the barn as a woodshed; the other half (the more decrepit portion) was filled with junk. An old Model T truck, twenty or thirty piles of magazines, a broken lawnmower, buckets with their bottoms rusted out, an intimidating ankle-turning pile of debris. Here, he kept his summer crop of dope.

Caleb followed Karen out to the woodshed. He had a mummy bag and a couple of books he'd snatched from their bookcase under his arm.

Inside the woodshed, she carefully unstacked about thirty pieces of cordwood and pulled a board aside.

"The snow's piled higher than the door on the outside," she said. "Climb over that junk. There's some boards on top of the rafters. You can stay up there."

Caleb crawled through the hole. He could hear her restacking the wood as he climbed awkwardly up to the rafters.

"Goodbye Karen," he said, sweet as he could. She didn't answer; he heard her crunching off in the snow.

There were cracks in the barn walls you could have thrown a cat through. And the winter cold strolled right in and made itself comfortable.

Caleb opened one of the dope baggies and sniffed and tasted. Surprised. "Not bad," he said to himself. "But it's too cold to get stoned."

He felt bad about lying to Karen and Denny, but he didn't figure he had much choice. He worried a little, wondering what Karen would do when she found she had a bankrobber in the woodpile. He was sleeping on their stash and that was, Caleb thought, some kind of insurance. He'd meet their anger when it came.

He put his face up to a crack in the boards to spy on the

wildlife, but except for a couple of starlings, which he could have seen in Central Park if he was interested in starlings, no wildlife.

The sleeping bag was very warm, and he thought about Sara and her nipples and how she always raised her legs and put her heels on his ass. Every time, she raised her legs. Not just some of the time.

The first time he saw Sara, he'd just been smashed in the head with a nightstick. Caleb sometimes thought (when he was being bitter) that their first meeting was symbolic of something.

It was the month of May. A foggy morning in May. Caleb and P.J. Black had been doing a lot of heavy dealing together. The night before they'd bought a hundred pounds and by hitting all the Village bars, they offed it by morning. With all that drinking, and all that polite sampling, they'd dropped quite a bit of speed just to stay on their feet.

Morning. 5 A.M. All the dope was gone, and the two of them had a lot of money to rustle in their pockets. Feeling pretty good, feet not too accurate, passing through Union Square.

"Here, my man," P.J. said, "take. Eat."

Caleb ate the tab. "What is it?" he asked.

P.J. chuckled. "Caleb, you have just done swallowed five hundred mics of the finest Sunshine. Your day is just commencing."

"Oh yeah? Dynamite."

They noticed a bunch of buses lined up in Union Square. And a couple hundred people milling around, drinking coffee out of paper cups.

Caleb remembered that he had read about some March on Washington, and he had an idea.

"P.J.," he said, "why don't you and me go to Washington?"

P.J. looked at him. Brown eyes in sharp black face. "I didn't know you wuz po-lit-i-cal."

Caleb, enthused, "Naw man, it'll be a groovy trip."

P.J. was doubtful, but the two of them got on a bus filled with medical students from Columbia. Some sort of student leader asked them what bus they were supposed to be on, and P.J. said "De bus to Washington."

Which flustered the student leader and he didn't ask them again or ask them for tickets, even.

The bus delayed. And it delayed. And delayed. P.J. stood up. "I'm going to get us some coffee," he said.

When the bus finally started off, Caleb was sitting alone, with the acid just commencing to come on. When the bus passed the entrance to Union Square on Fourteenth Street, Caleb saw P.J. talking to a couple of sprawled-out black winos. Caleb waved to P.J., and P.J. bowed.

The acid was as advertised, pure sunshine. And the normally dreary trip to Washington was a voyage through realms of joy and terror. At one point, Caleb decided that the medical students he was traveling with were very interested in him, as a cadaver. At another point the green grass of Maryland made him cry.

When they arrived, Caleb's head had been replaced by an interested, though dispassionate, camera. He walked through the sea of marchers, staring at faces.

One black man, a union delegate from Cleveland (according to his name badge), confronted Caleb after Caleb had been staring at him for nearly ten minutes. "What's the matter with you?" he asked.

"You have a beautiful face," Caleb said.

"What's the matter with you, you sick?"

Caleb walked away, with tears in his eyes.

In front of the Justice Department. Angrier here. Chants. Maybe two thousand people and a double-thick line of riot cops. The crowd surging back and forth. Photographers moving around, snapping pictures, protecting their equipment with their arms. Caleb snapping elegantly framed still photos with his eyes.

Smash of breaking glass. More breaking glass. Pop! Pop! of tear-gas cannisters. The crowd rushing toward Caleb, parting around him. Him, impervious to the rolling clouds of gas. Snapping faces. Holding them forever in his mind. A couple of cops ran by him.

Wham, up side the head, shattered his camera. Another in his stomach, and he sat down. Two cops had him by the arms and were dragging him towards the paddy wagon and a thin, fine-boned girl's face, maybe twenty feet away, was yelling, "What's your name?"

He yelled his name. And one cop wrenched his right arm and shouted, "Shut up, punk."

"Where do you live?"

He yelled that, too, and so they punched him in the nuts before they threw him in the wagon.

So Caleb spent the night in jail, and the next morning, very strung out, he pled guilty to "failure to disperse" and "resisting arrest," paid $250, and they let him go. He was lucky. They hadn't printed him, and they gave him back nearly half the money he'd made selling dope.

He took the shuttle back to New York, went home, had three shots of Tanqueray, moaned twice, and fell out for twenty hours.

His buzzer woke him up. Stumbled to the intercom. "Yeah?"

"Caleb Smith?" Thin, tinny voice.

"What do you want?"

"I'm the woman you talked to in Washington. Can I come up for a moment?"

"No. Go away."

He took two groggy steps toward his bed and the buzzer yelled again.

"Please," she said, "it's important. And it'll only take a minute."

"Alright. Alright. Sure thing. You come right on up."

He got a pair of pants on by the time she climbed the three flights of stairs.

"Hi," she said, standing in the doorway. "I'm Sara Rodgers. Can I come in?"

She was well-bred. Caleb could tell this because she did not vomit when she smelled his apartment.

"I'm in the movement," she said. "And I saw what that pig did to you."

"Uh-huh."

"I even got a picture of it."

"Terrific." Caleb noticed that the girl was maybe nineteen and had small breasts and wore no brassiere.

"I've got some really fine Afghanistan hash here," he said. He brought out his pipe and offered it to her.

"It's nine o'clock in the morning," she said.

"It's lit. Don't waste it."

They passed the pipe back and forth. When it was gone, Caleb slowly loaded it up again.

"We can get that pig," she said. "I got his badge number and everything."

"No good."

She refused the pipe. "Why not? I mean, you were just standing there, doing nothing and. . ."

"I got a warrant out on me in Detroit. I can't mess around with no policemen. No time."

"Oh."

While she was still surprised, Caleb kissed her. When she got over her surprise, she kissed back.

They were both very stoned and sensitive, and they slid on each other like two slippery playing cards. By the time Caleb pulled her underpants down, she was wet and musky and afloat in a dream. When he was inside her, she bucked her hips into him and twisted her face and called his name and put her heels on his ass and pulled him in deep.

Oh boy.

Caleb tugged the zipper of the sleeping bag and let some cold air in.

"I wish my fingers weren't so white," he said. "I wish I had a cigarette."

Karen didn't come back until dark. No flashlight, just bright moon.

When she pushed the board aside, Caleb was hunkered just inside, waiting for her. She had slick beads of sweat on her forehead and a few strands of her hair were hanging loose. Caleb wanted to pat them back into place but, of course, couldn't.

"Hi, liar," she said.

"I'm sorry," Caleb said. "I didn't know what else to do."

"I guess you better come up to the house."

So Caleb squirmed through the planks and followed her through the snow.

Denny was still wearing his grease-stained work coveralls. He had a cup of tea and another one poured for Karen. TWO, not three. Caleb sat down by the stove, facing them.

"Thanks a lot," Denny said.

Caleb nodded, but said nothing. Sat absolutely still.

"I hope you're rested," Karen said.

Caleb looked at her, blank.

"I wanted to turn you in," she said. "But Denny said you'd get us busted too."

"No," Caleb said. "I wouldn't do that."

"Sure." She made a face.

"I don't know," Denny said. "Nobody around here holds much with the law. There's a lot of poachers and a lot of the river logs disappear on the way to the mill. But you guys! You guys kill people!"

"Not me," Caleb said.

"God damned long-hair hippy revolutionary games!" Karen stood up and turned her back on them. Her body was shaking.

"You killed two cops. Two human beings. And another is in the hospital with a bullet in his spine, and they don't think he'll ever walk again. I knew those cops personally. The kid in the hospital is Bob Murphey's son who runs the planer at the mill. He was just a part-time deputy, that's all. Put the badge on Saturday night and the township gives you fifty dollars a month."

"I didn't kill anybody," Caleb said.

Denny picked it up: "And Ralph Snyder, my boss, tells me that I shouldn't come in any more for a month or so anyway, until the excitement dies down and half the damn town is combing the riverbank looking for you or that money or both. And Pete Cassidy's got his gun strapped on, and he's drinking over at the roadhouse, swearing he's gonna shoot the next hippy he sees."

They didn't want to tell him to go. They wanted the facts to do the job for them.

Karen took her solo: "I went into the store this morning for milk and Mrs. Ingersoll asked me, do I know you, because she assumes that all of *us* know each other. . ."

"Deputy Mackey drank coffee once at this table. He was OK. He was just a person.

"Until you noticed that big gun on his belt," Caleb said, softly.

Caleb couldn't make it easy for them. He didn't stand up. He didn't even look at his coat.

He idly scratched a piece of candlewax off the edge of their table. He stretched his legs like a cat stretches.

WHAM! He slammed his good hand on the table. The saltshaker fell on its side.

"Alright!" he shouted. "Fuck you people! I'll leave. I'll get out of your lives. But since I'm going to be deader than hell, half an hour after I leave this place, I got one or two things to say. I'd like a cup of tea. It's lousy tea, but I'd like a cup of it because I'm starving to death. You'd treat a dog better than you treat me."

Denny made a move toward the pot, checked himself, looked at Karen, looked away before he could read her, and ever so stiffly poured Caleb a cup of tea.

"Thank you," Caleb said. He gulped the tea down and put the cup on the table.

"Are any of my friends alive?"

Denny answered, "One of them. Someone named Christopher. The FBI came up from Bangor today to pick him up."

"Huh. Chris. I was hoping that Jeff. . . What a bummer."

He paused. "There were five of us in on it. Chris and me and Willy Ortez and Jeff Svenigsun and John. John was the planner, our general. He's a strange dude. He's got all these funny pointy teeth. Smart. Real smart.

"We had these meetings in Willy's apartment. John and Jeff had cased the bank, and there wasn't much to talk about. The plan wasn't very complicated. We were supposed to walk in, get the money, get on the Maine Pike going south, and sneak off it between exits and head the other direction. Simple. So we sat around for three days, bored, stoned, arguing with each other. Jeff thought it was very important we should have the Proper Revolutionary Consciousness. Willy didn't give a rat's ass. Chris was more interested in doing these exercises out of the *Canadian Air Force Exercise Book,* and I smoked a lot of dope to pass the time. Every morning, John would show up with some new danger he'd thought up the night before. At least he brought us coffee in the morning, so I suppose his heart was in the right place. Willy didn't pay much attention to him, and I'd bait him, and Jeff would get mad at me, and Chris would listen and not say much. It's funny. A long time ago, I was a Weatherman. When I was a kid, in Detroit, I used to fool around with stock cars. John's really logical. He thought it was very logical for me to be the driver in a Weatherman Action. Good old John." Caleb rubbed his head.

He opened his shirt. The canvas money belt was strapped across his belly. "This is it, kids," he said. "This is what all the excitement's about."

"For the revolution?" Denny asked.

Caleb grinned. "Sure. If it gets there."

"Uh, how much money is there?" Denny asked.

"I don't know. Want to count it?"

"Oh no, that's alright."

"They shot Willy in the throat," Caleb said. "It was horrible. I liked Willy. I never did understand how he got into this thing. He was too smart for it."

Karen's eyes hadn't changed an inch, so Caleb threw

something to her: "Did you read any of those magazine articles about the Weathermen?" he asked. He didn't wait for her nod. "And the Weather Bureau? I don't know any of them. I'm supposed to be a Weatherman and I never even met the cadre."

Denny was fidgeting. Caleb picked up his teacup, but there wasn't anything left.

"Man, you two people really blow my mind. You got enough dope in that shed to get twenty years. And if anybody ever found it, you think they'd say: 'Let's not arrest Denny and Karen. They're nice people'? Man, they'd throw away the key. And this Snyder cat fires you. And you blame it on me. Me! And some other dude's wandering around with a gun saying he's gonna get himself a hippy, and you get mad at me?

"Man, who in the hell do you think you are? Nice, clean-living folks who just happen to have long hair?

"You're illegal. You're immoral. You're dirty. You don't believe in God. You're broke. Man, to those folks, you're scum.

"And everything's OK as long as you keep on Tomming—'yassah' and 'nosah' and big friendly grin, and 'boss, can I give you a hand?'

"I never did want to be no revolutionary hero. It's shitty. Believe me, I'd rather be back in New York than hiding from the hick cops in some hick town in the hick state of Maine. I'm scared, and I wish none of this had ever happened."

Caleb let out a gust of air and took a couple breaths.

"I'm sorry I lied to you," he said. "I was tired and scared, but I shouldn't have put you in danger." He looked at their faces and guessed he maybe had them hooked.

"I wish Willy was alive," he said. "Ah, the hell with it." He stood up. "Thanks for saving my life. How much do you want for that rifle over there?"

The rifle was an old Winchester 94, and Caleb had seen a lot of them on late night TV. He picked it up and worked the lever.

Denny laughed. Explosive, snorty laugh. "Just what in the hell do you think you're doing, Wyatt Earp?"

And Denny laughed again, haw, haw, haw. "Half the cops in Maine . . . hell—three-quarters of the cops in Maine and almost every other plain citizen under eighty and over fifteen is looking, looking for you. And Wyatt Earp is gonna stride out of here, big as life, and stand on the only paved highway in fifty miles . . . he's gonna stand there . . . in his shirt sleeves and long hair and oh my God, a deer rifle slung over his shoulder . . . thumbing a ride."

He couldn't speak, even stutter. His laughter had him by the belly and eyes, and he was choking and coughing, and Karen was smiling, too (but timidly); so Caleb put the rifle back in the corner. Denny finally stopped himself and held it in check.

"I wish I had a cigarette," Caleb said. And that set Denny off again and this time all three of them were laughing.

Weaker, but cleaner, they all sat down.

"OK, you can stay," Karen said.

"I'm hungry. Anybody else?"

Nods of assent, so she started frying this and chopping that, and all the while, Caleb, with his feet up on the stove, was watching her ass, and Denny not noticing.

"Did you ever use one of those things?" Denny asked, pointing at the rifle.

"Nope," Caleb said. "But, I was hoping I wouldn't have to. After my number one revolutionary speech, I was hoping you'd let me stay." Caleb shifted his feet on the stove. "You had your chance," he said, complacently.

During the summer months, Denny and Karen were nearly vegetarians. Denny was an avid, though unsophisticated fisherman and, from time to time, brown trout or rainbow trout made part of a meal. They had chickens for eggs and the occasional tough old hen who could no longer produce eggs for their table wasn't, for that reason, neglected.

But in the winter, the hens stopped laying, and Denny went out and got a deer. Dried vegetables are OK, and the root crops will keep all winter; but cold thins the blood and venison thickens it, just fine.

Caleb had never eaten venison before. He liked it a lot.

After dinner, Denny rolled a couple of joints and they sat smoking.

"You cook good," Caleb said.

"Thank you. Denny is a little bit better. He bakes better bread anyway."

They cleared away the dishes and, obedient to the warmth, gravitated to the stove.

"Did you see Buckshot today?" Karen asked.

"Oh yeah, I meant to tell you. He was in town, getting his provisions." He rocked back on his chair and explained to Caleb: "Buckshot is a booze-head, and I've never seen him buy anything but 'Salt, twenty pound o' navy beans an' five quarts o' rum.' Anyway, he said he'd be over later. How's your hand now?"

"I'm afraid there's something wrong with it," Caleb said. "It really hurts. And I can't move my last two fingers. And it's starting to smell. Man, let's not think about it. It's a bummer. And I haven't been stoned in four days."

"Yeah. Did you deal heavy in New York?"

"Medium," Caleb shrugged. "It's good there. The cops don't care, just so long as you're not really outrageous. I had a friend who was dealing, and one afternoon he's on the street somewhere and a burglar breaks into his apartment. Climbs down from the roof. And this old Italian broad sees the burglar and calls the cops.

"Well, the burglar gets away before they get there and leaves the front door open on his way out. And when this friend of mine gets home, he finds two precinct cops in his apartment.

"And man, there's dope all over the place. He's got roach clips on the bookshelf and a big jar of clean grass on the table and a goddamned hookah right in the middle of the floor.

"Well, the cops are cool. They're walking around and

carefully stepping over the hookah—this is a four-foot by four-foot apartment—and my friend's scurrying around shoving things behind things and they're asking him if the burglar got anything and he's saying, 'no, no, I don't think so' and hoping they don't go in the kitchen because he's got fifty pounds in bricks, wrapped up, but obvious as hell stacked beside his refrigerator.

"The cops know him. They've seen him around. They know he ain't doing nobody no harm and ain't ever gonna give them no problems. So, they don't see anything. But as they are leaving, one of the cops sticks his head back through the doorway and shakes his head and says, 'You gotta be putting me on.' "

They are sitting in a log cabin in the middle of the Maine winter with snow falling outside—the only house on the road, a couple miles from town and two miles from their nearest neighbor.

Denny chuckles at Caleb's story.

The familiar sounds of the fire in the stove, the rustle, the occasional roar, the pop of the resin going up, the clunk in the firebox as a piece of wood falls over.

The familiar sounds of the creaking in the rafters and the tap-tap of the water from the icicles melting on the roof.

Denny says, "You want I should roll another one?"

A crunch in the snow outside the door. No mistake! Three more crunches. A footfall on the doorstep. Bang-bang-bang on the door.

The door handle turns. A head sticks around the corner. "Hello, hello, hello. Is anybody home?"

She was like one of those characters in those science fiction books where ordinary earth-folk are invaded by powerful alien intelligences who take over human bodies and direct their wills. But not like the science-fiction books portray them, not those vaguely fey walking zombies. But like such an inhabited person really would be, bulging and uncomfortable with an extra life inside.

Her eyes were too big; her ears were too big. She had

short, black scraggy hair. Chopped, not cut. Bones all over her body. Extra bones. It was hard to tell what size she was, though she couldn't have weighed a hundred pounds.

And very slightly drunk. Stepped through the door, sniffed, made a face, waved at Denny, "It's OK," she said. "You white men gave us booze for which we thank you." Turned back to the empty doorway impatiently, "Come on in honey. All the fire's getting out."

A little girl walked in, hesitating and anglo and pretty and coy.

"Come in here, and close the door," the woman said. "Plenty of time to be shy about that little ass once you can do something more with it than sit on it."

The Indian woman went over and sat beside Denny by the fire; the girl closed the door but stayed near it.

Pretty little girl. Somebody's picture of what a pretty little girl should look like. Flesh which had become someone's image of all the pretty little girls on TV.

Naturally the little girl asked, "Have you got a color TV?"

"No, Patti," Karen said. "We haven't got any electricity. So we can't have a TV."

"We have a TV," the girl said. "My daddy says he's going to get us a color TV for Christmas."

"Don't need one," the Indian woman said. "Don't need no crummy electricity either or no crummy telephone. Damn no good phone went out two, three nights ago. Morning of the big storm. Three snowflakes fall and my phone dies. All the phones in the town die. But next morning they fix all the town phones, but don't fix mine. I'll never pay them! Never."

"Our phone quit working at noon," the little girl said, precisely. "And the next morning when we heard all about those killers, we couldn't even call anybody. I was scared."

"You got any candy for the kid?" the woman asked. "She's driving me crazy."

"Would you like a butter cookie, Patti?" Karen asked. "I just made them yesterday."

"No, thank you. My mother made me salisbury steak for my dinner." She sat herself down near the door.

"Who are you?" the Indian woman asked Caleb.

"P.J. Black," he said.

"I'm Mary Two Hat," she said. "I'm twenty-nine years old, unmarried, and a high-school graduate. You drink?"

"Sometimes," Caleb said.

So she reached into her mackinaw and handed him a pint of Ripple. "They don't drink," she said, pointing at Denny. "They don't fart, either," she said gloomily. "But," she brightened. "Denny would be a wonderful lover."

She recaptured the bottle and took a hit off it. "Karen, don't get mad. I don't mean no harm. I'm just joking."

"You drink," the little girl said.

"Shut up," Mary replied. "Why do you follow me around? Why don't you go home to your Mommy and Daddy?"

But the little girl just gave her a knowing smile for an answer.

"Is it snowing hard?" Karen asked.

Mary peered into Caleb's face. "You live in California?"

"No," he said. "I'm hitching from Boston to Quebec."

"I'd like to live in California," she said. "Do you have a lot of oranges?"

"I live in Boston," Caleb said.

She turned to Karen. "When are you going to have babies? I like you. You should have babies."

"I don't want them, just yet."

"Why not? What do you think you're for?"

"Mary," Karen said, "you're too drunk to remember anything we say, so why should we say anything?"

Mary half closed her eyes and put her heels up on the stove with a thump. "That's true," she said, solemnly. "Poor Mary Two Hat. She just wants to learn and nobody will teach her." She handed the bottle to Caleb and waited until he took a drink. She started to say something, but stopped and looked at Caleb again. Peering close.

"Who are you?" she asked.

"P.J. Black."

"Pee-Jay?"

"That's right."

"Did you ever wear glasses?"

Puzzled. "No."

"You have funny eyes. Are you sure you don't wear glasses?"

"Sure, I'm sure. Don't hog the bottle."

Mary snorted and handed him the wine. Without thinking, he finished it, and when he handed it back to her, she shook it and held it up to the light.

"Empty," she announced. "Am I pretty?" she asked.

"Uh, yeah. Sure." And maybe it was the light, but Caleb was telling the truth.

"Do you ever make love?" She put her hands on both sides of Caleb's head and held him still and face to face. She dropped her hands. "You never make love," she said.

She walked over to the door and put the bottle on the floor beside the doorsill, like a milk bottle. "Patti," she said.

The little girl was already arranging her scarf.

Caleb couldn't see her eyes, but he knew she was looking at him.

"You never give nobody nothing," she said.

Bang of the door shutting, crunch of footfalls in the snow, receding. The wind, the fire, their breathing.

Karen sighed. "Well, that tears it."

"She won't say anything," Denny said.

"You fathead. Too much dope and the whole world is always rosy. Maybe she won't tell. But if she does, we're in the soup."

"What should we do?" Denny asked.

"Why ask me?" she said. "Why ask me anything?"

Scared. Silent. Scared. They heated up the tea, but that didn't help much.

By the time Buckshot showed, they'd run the fear up to 40, dropped it down to maybe 10 with a laugh or two, and let it grow again in the silence until it hit 30 and still climbing.

Denny let him in.

Buckshot looked like the spitting image of the statue of the Young David by Michelangelo, only not quite.

First off, make that statue come to life. Here he is now, a lovely young Italian youth, ambling toward St. Peter's, yawning, and wondering how he's going to get laid. Imagine further, that as our unsuspecting young man progresses, thinking rather simple pornographic thoughts, that a particular sardonic god sees him, and (bored with eternity) he decides to do what gods do best: to wit, meddle.

He removes this classic youth, snatches him away from his pussy and pasta and deposits him in a place so remote that we can't imagine it, like Madagascar.

Or Maine.

Next, he boils him down. So all the subcutaneous fat runs like yellow butter.

Of course, the lad shrinks a little, loses a few inches in height. And his skin tightens around his bones and muscles.

Very well, we have a young man, of stringy muscle; that's a start, but not enough.

We move him closer to the fire (or cold) and give him experience.

He is standing outside the gallows-frame of the Speculator Mine in Butte, Montana, with a lunchbox in his hand. The noon whistle blows. He drove 150 miles from Wallace when the Bluebird closed down, but the Speculator isn't hiring.

He is enlisting in the Great War. His best friend and the company dog are both gassed in the Argonne forest.

He gets the clap in Tucson, after hitching all night across

the desert and getting there on a big White Diesel at five in the morning, drunk, and the sky meets the earth about seventy sunrise miles away.

He gets jumped by four railroad stiffs in a boxcar outside of Bakersfield and gives an account of himself.

He gets his left arm broken because he was eating an ice-cream cone (strawberry) on Second Avenue in New York City and a Ukranian stevedore laughed at him.

He gets married in Reno late one night and divorced in Las Vegas two weeks later.

Model A. Hudson's Bay Rum. Acme Boots. Sorrel. Main Stope. Skidder. Mrs. Spencer Rolland. Winchester. Buckrake. Straight flush. Betty-Lou, Ann, Maggie, Mary (three Marys), Pocohontas, Georgia, Miss Junie, Sally, Sally-Mae, Lucille, Betty, Mrs. Jona, Margie, Patty, and Susie, the Greek, Maria, Judy, Melissa, Liz, Carlotta, Suzanne, Joyce, Estrelita, Elaine, Butterball, Pearl, Mrs. Winthrop.

One last change: the god exchanges David's soft brown eyes for Buckshot's glittering black ones and laughs until the other gods think he's gone batty.

Buckshot accepted the cup of tea with a nod to Karen and warmed his hands with it.

"Buckshot," Karen said, "has Denny told you about any of this?"

"Nope." Took a sip of tea.

"Well, I suppose I might as well, then. This is Caleb Smith. He was involved in that bank shootup, three days ago. He's . . . he's our friend and something's wrong with his hand. Will you take a look at it?"

Buckshot took his Red Devil chewing tobacco out of his jacket and fashioned himself a chew.

He put his hat on his lap and put his hands under it.

He spat in the fire.

"What's wrong with your hand?" he asked.

"I think it's frostbite," Caleb said. "No feeling in the last two fingers and it hurts when I touch it against anything."

Caleb was standing over by the wooden kitchen counter.

Buckshot went over to him, unhurriedly, took the hand, looked at the dead white flesh, held it to his nose, and sniffed deep.

"Gangrene," he remarked, casual.

Now, more delicately, he felt around the hand, pinching, judging the quick flesh and the dead.

"Not too serious," he said. "Set your hand flat." He pulled Caleb's fingers apart and pressed the hand firmly against the wooden countertop.

"Goddamn," he said. He rummaged through his pockets. Distracted. Terrible distracted. "You got tape and gauze?" he asked Karen. She nodded.

"Goddamn," he said again, still rummaging.

His eyes slowly came into focus and then unfocused again, as if what he was seeing was too slight for his attention. Then his eyes focused firmly and he stopped shuffling around. From his right eye, very slowly, a tear formed and streaked quarter inch by quarter inch down his cheek. The bones of his face were clear through his cheeks and his mouth formed that awestruck smile seen on portraits of great saints.

"Holy Jesus," he whispered, like ice.

Caleb turned his head to walk down Buckshot's eyes and for a millisecond, for a brush with something, he almost saw what Buckshot was seeing.

A distant thump.

"I reckon you'll be needing those bandages now," Buckshot said.

Caleb, still confused, looked at Buckshot and SCREAM OF PAIN.

Caleb's hand was still flat on the counter, but his two end fingers were shortened a joint each, and the fingertips were separate and winking at him like worms.

The blood came from the stumps and Caleb was almost sick to his stomach and Karen's hand on his and softness wrapping the pain. She led him, shaking, to a chair and sat him down.

"Damn it, Buckshot. You should have warned him . . . told him . . . told us."

Buckshot closed his heavy clasp knife. One-handed.

"Woulda hurt worst," he said.

Caleb giggled.

"What's so funny?" Denny asked.

"I was thinking that maybe you should put those things in your compost bucket," Caleb said.

"Funny, funny."

"They're my fingers," Caleb said, "and it would be pretty silly making them two little pine boxes and burying them somewhere."

But a gasp of pain and he wanted to throw up.

He didn't. And the sharp pain blunted and became a nag that he held close to his chest to warm.

"He shouldn't stay here," Buckshot said."You get too many visitors. He comes with me."

Oh, they argued and protested. (Denny protesting, not Karen), and Buckshot sat by the stove, mostly quiet, although he did say once, very formally to Denny, "I owe you a few favors."

And Denny pooh-poohed it and said they couldn't let him take the risk, and they sort of talked themselves down like a clock runs out, and their protests became bursts in a snowy field of silence.

"Alright," Denny said, finally. "But only for three days. When people stop thinking about him, we'll drive him in our van down to Portland."

He looked at Karen, and she nodded OK and that settled it.

They lent Caleb a sleeping bag and heavy clothes and long johns, and Karen let him borrow her snowshoes.

Caleb tied the money belt around his waist.

Denny slipped him a film can full of dope, on the sly.

Buckshot cadged a cup and a spoon from the countertop.

Caleb knew he was safer now, but his gratitude froze as solid as his eyebrows three minutes after they left the cabin.

Buckshot walked ten feet in front of him, walking sturdy, shuffling against the snow. Caleb's teeth were chattering.

He stuffed his damaged hand into his jacket pocket and bent his head lower against the driving snow.

"Maybe I'd be better off dead," Caleb said to himself.

The wind crept up his pants' leg and bit his knee.

"Naw," Caleb thought. "But I would be better off drunk. Drunk and warm. Warm and drunk."

3 / *Kennebec County*

The snowshoes were easier to use than Caleb had anticipated, and though he couldn't exactly imitate Buckshot's swivel-kneed shuffle, he didn't have any trouble keeping up.

The moon was three-quarters full, but under the clouds, on this earth, in Maine, the night was a dimly lit closet filled with wedding dresses, elegant, shadowless, and cold.

Buckshot used no light and made no sound except for the steady crunching of his snowshoes in the snow. A troll-like figure with a basket pack on his back and a fifty-pound sack of beans across one shoulder. Caleb came behind like a docile wife, with his arms cradling his sleeping bag.

Steady soft snow which melted when it touched Caleb's face. No wind. Cut off. A narrow space they inhabited, like two ghosts with no frame to fit it in, no referents, no fence-posts, no signs. They could have walked, that night, all across America in that snow, and though they might have passed within twenty yards of a diner on some lonely back road or walked through the orchard near some solitary farmhouse, no other living person would have seen them.

Traveling through some other world, not completely like our own world, with only the tracks in the morning for some kid to find, and those tracks blurred and running the fence-lines like a diary in the snow.

Directly it got flatter and they were on the ice of the Kennebec.

Buckshot's canoe, a white, regular burial mound, over-turned on the ice. Silently, Buckshot turned it upright, stowed his gear, and began pushing it ahead of him.

"We got far to go?" Caleb asked.

"Not far."

Buckshot walking more carefully now; setting less of his weight down at every step and the canoe hissing through the snow.

Caleb is careful to walk in his footsteps.

It would be dark under that ice. He vaguely remembered that there are supposed to be air pockets between water and ice; but swimming blind under there, in that cold, looking for light, how long could you last?

His hand hurt.

Big hummocks, at last, where the heaving frost had buckled the ice and Caleb could see the layers of ice, and there were small blue caves under them.

Buckshot stopped pushing on top of the ramparts and motioned to Caleb. Abrupt, windmill wave.

"In," he said.

And Caleb climbed over the stern and duck-walked for-ward, and Buckshot resumed his pushing.

Beyond the hummocks now, the ice was trembling under their weight, and Buckshot was walking forward with his weight over the stern of the canoe.

Quite suddenly, but not abruptly somehow, they were floating free in the water. Caleb turned his head, and the troll was seated in the stern, pulling a broad-bladed paddle from under the thwarts.

Moving easily, breaking the half-inch ice with their bow, until the canoe slipped out into the broad black band of main current and the bow started twisting downstream.

Rattle from behind him. The boat trembled a bit and then turned easily out into the current. They pushed upstream, paused, then pushed again. Heavy current: slush ran against their prow like a wave.

The river ran shallower here, but fast, and Buckshot was poling the canoe now, standing in the stern, shoving them steadily upstream.

Caleb's fingers ached. Or, more properly, the space where Caleb's fingers had been—ached. That empty space hurt like hurt fingers, and Caleb kept his hand tucked inside his jacket. He knew he should regret the loss of his fingers because now he could never be a concert pianist.

He watched Buckshot—steady shove and push to recover the pole and the canoe hung there obligingly, until he shoved again.

Caleb had never seen anybody stand up in a canoe before, let alone pole one like a goddamned Venetian gondolier. Steady. He never once let the pole tip skid on the rocky, irregular river bottom.

The shore was undifferentiated. A characterless line of snowy trees with no landmarks.

Caleb had been getting colder minute by minute, and when Buckshot pushed the bow between two rocks on the shore (Buckshot's landing), Caleb got out quick and hopped up and down, warming himself.

They hauled the canoe up, refastened their snowshoes, and their passage through the dead world continued.

"Is it much farther?" Caleb asked.

"No," Buckshot said. Then, as an afterthought: "You talk too much."

"Up yours," Caleb said, but under his breath as he bent over to brush some snow off the top of his snowshoes.

Between here (with the wind and the ghost trees) and Chicago, if he had to choose, Caleb would have chosen Chicago. Specifically, Caleb would have chosen a bar in Chicago, on the south side. Full of people and elbows and booze and a couple of black men—a guitarist and a harp player—playing Robert Johnson's blues.

Caleb had been in Chicago during the convention. Running through the streets and getting gassed and chased and Sara running beside him. Once they got separated, and Caleb went down to the south side and found a bar and got drunk and listened to music, and he liked that better than running through the streets, even though Sara had been running right beside him.

Buckshot's cabin was one of those simple affairs built for the logging crews in the woods. One room. Tar paper over the studs. Stove in the middle of the floor and a counter-sink arrangement beside the door. (The waste pipe emptied outside.) A bunk bed in the rear. Three windows with clear plastic stretched over them for storm windows.

It rested off the ground on wooden skids so it could be hauled from one cutting to another by diesel tractor.

Simple, practical, with no joy in it except its basic suitability for the woods and the needs of the loggers.

Caleb thought that the place looked more like a toolroom than a home. Everything hung on nails: crosscut saw, cant dog, traps, crowbar, drawshave, hammer, a pair of tongs that looked like icemen's tongs, three metal files, a sledge hammer, and a couple of metal wedges. Even Buckshot's metal cup was hanging on a nail.

A bucket of water on the floor, and a small axe leaning against the door frame. A row of rum bottles neatly lined up on the south window. Odds and ends of twine, tied into loops, and also hanging on nails.

Buckshot leaned his snowshoes against the wall and started to unlace his boots. "You take the top," he said.

Iron-framed bunk bed. Bare springs. Caleb took a couple of blankets from a pile in the corner and laid them down under his sleeping bag.

Strong animal smell, mixed with kerosene, wood smoke, and pine. Like breathing another atmosphere.

Buckshot was frying some beans in the skillet. Two

plates, a metal one and a porcelain one with a faded rose dead center. He gave this plate to Caleb.

Not good. Not bad. Beans and molasses. A little burnt. Food. Caleb ate it all.

After Caleb crawled into bed, Buckshot blew out the kerosene lantern. Dark, except for the vague white glow easing through the small windows.

Buckshot, seated four-square on the cabin's one wooden chair, meticulously pouring himself one metal cupful of rum after another.

Sometime after dawn Caleb woke up, wiggling and shivering. No Buckshot. Neat, empty, tidy cabin washed in white light and one more empty rum bottle in the row on the windowsill.

Quiet except for Caleb rustling around in the sleeping bag, trying to generate a few more calories of heat.

He leapt out of bed, pell-mell, stumbling, and rapidly grabbed his shirt, his pants.

"Goddamn!" His shirt was frozen. Not quite solid like a suit of armor, but semisolid where his sweat had frozen. Indecisive and naked as a jaybird, hopping around on the frozen wooden floor.

Wrestled the shirt, grunting and moaning, got it on, got into his long johns. Another shirt, his pants, two pairs of socks, and ZIP back into the sleeping bag.

"Oh, oh, oh, oh, oh," Caleb said, wriggling against his clothes.

"Sara is such a good lay," he said. And the clinical sound of his voice surprised him.

"Sara is an amazing lay," he said. "She knows what she wants and she takes it."

He lay back, warmer, and counted the two by fours over his head. "She is very sincere."

His left hand looked very strange to him, and he half expected it to heal up—to grow new fingers on the stubs of the old. He favored it though it didn't seem to hurt so much this morning.

He lay there, in his sleeping-bag cocoon, until he was long past ready.

The iron stove was bitter cold to the touch and only a couple big pieces of wood in the woodbox, so Caleb picked up the small axe and ventured outside.

Not much colder out there, but colder enough.

Fir trees covered by snow. Caleb felt like an ant in a sea of frozen grass.

Some kind of road (logging road?) cut by the cabin; the roadbed was under five feet of snow. The cabin itself was completely buried, a snowbank. Tunnels led to the windows and there were huge snow heaps on either side of the door.

A mound beside the cabin, which might be a woodpile, so Caleb pawed away the snow and sure enough.

Neat chunks of cordwood, about twenty-four inches long and six inches across.

He set a piece vertical in the snow and balanced a smaller piece on top of it.

Whack. The axe bounced and his construction fell apart.

He set it up again. Whack. And he got a sliver of wood.

He set it up again. Whack. Another piece of wood.

Set it up again. Thud. Overshot and hit the handle.

Set it up again. And sometimes he split a piece off and sometimes (not too often) he hit the wood with the handle instead of the axehead.

He built a neat stack of wood in the stove. A small pyramid like a Druid's funeral pyre and Caleb looking around for paper to get it started. No paper.

No cardboard boxes. No newspapers. No magazines. No writing tablets. No paper bags.

"Christ," he said.

He went through his pockets and wallet and peeled the wrappers off the bills in the money belt.

He lit his fire, he blew on it, the flames rose higher and higher, the wood scorched, and the fire went out. Caleb shivered.

He ate some cold beans out of the pot and felt bad.

So he put the snowshoes on and spent the rest of the day in a frozen picture of paradise.

He left the U.S. to venture in an alien land.

In this blazing country, Abraham Lincoln was never elected and the Titanic never set sail. A horned owl got a squirrel there! And here, a red maple, overburdened with snow, pulled its roots up out of the cliff and, in a great white flurry, unheard, lay over on the ground.

Oh sure, Caleb had trouble. At first he had the bindings too loose, so the snowshoes didn't quite point where his feet did, and later he had them too tight, so his toes lost all feeling inside his rubber boots. But nothing to it: just adjust the damn things and forget it.

Aloft, suspended in a land as strange as the dusty distant moon. And unavailable for conquest, shifting, living, becoming something else.

He could stand on the snow! Five feet above the earth on a thick white cloud. All the particularities—the special character of the ground beneath him—unavailable, quite frozen, cysted and buried under a shifting, dancing dune of white frozen water molecules.

Caleb tugged a small blueberry from a juniper tree. Dusty blue, about the size of a matchhead.

Caleb had always lived in cities. Spring meant one terrific day in May, when everyone was smiling on the streets. Summer was too hot even with air conditioning. Autumn simply didn't happen, and winter was, bluntly, too cold.

But here, what it was was *WINTER*. Before it was interesting or dull, or happy or sad, it was *WINTER*. A massive and dominant fact. Everything—all beings—related to it, served it; it was what life meant now and here.

Caleb was warmer, moving around, and unzipped his jacket.

And what a dance it was: here a branch caught lacy frozen, throwing itself outward like a dowager throwing coins from a taxi. Here, the snow whistling and rustling over the tumbled terrain, like a sandstorm in the Sahara.

Caleb stuck his hand into a snowbank and felt four different layers of resistance, and when he pulled his hand out, he'd created a pool of blue light at the bottom of the narrow cave.

Here it leveled out. Was this a meadow? A pond?

Underneath, there was life and unimaginable: wasp eggs in the thorax of a paralyzed, but still living, grasshopper. In the spring, the larvae would hatch and feed on him until he died. (This grasshopper was becoming a philosopher and perhaps had experienced a religious conversion.)

Surely this was a meadow—or was it a pond, disguised? Ten feet of still water under five feet of ice. Light filtering through, but curious, streaky light. Water plants swaying dead and brown in the current. Four brown trout, a few inches over the bottom, breathing about as often as you change your mind and dreaming of the sun.

Caleb followed some animal tracks (rabbit tracks, he thought) through a history of this morning, when the snow was fresh and unmarked. Nothing happened to the rabbit, so far as Caleb could tell; but who knows; the present often makes it seem like the past never happened, and Caleb was not seeing what the rabbit saw, but was four hours later and six feet higher in the air.

He hadn't thought to do any dope. The world that dope gave him was too predictable, and for the first time in five years, Caleb didn't want to be stoned.

As Caleb was trudging back to the cabin the sky turned purple, and great colored clouds, like the iridescent bellies of fish, were sliding one after another across the planet.

The cabin was empty and cold. Caleb tried to understand what he'd seen and felt, but he couldn't. He held Sara in his mind for a minute, but that vision started making him horny so he let go of her. He was cold. Just cold.

Buckshot came home an hour after dark.

Bunch of traps in his hand, he took a few minutes outside stretching a lynx pelt where the racoons wouldn't get it. As he brushed his pants' legs free of snow he half nodded to Caleb. Acknowledged his presence, established Caleb's right to be there.

Silently, he made a fire. Set Caleb's kindling beside the stove, went outside again, bang, bang, bang, bang, bang of splitting, and he returned with an armload of pine and rock maple.

Caleb watched, leaning quietly against the bunk bed.

Buckshot peeled layers from the bark of a piece of paper birch, thin shreds of parchment. He used those for tinder.

It got warmer quick.

"You do a lot of trapping?" Caleb asked.

"Some."

Beans again, burnt again. And the evaporated milk made Caleb's coffee taste like evaporated milk. But he was hungry, and so he found new taste marvels in the taste of evaporated milk, like discovering fine musical complications in a bad record when you're stoned.

"I go into town day after tomorrow," Buckshot said. "You aren't comfortable here, I expect."

"You wouldn't be comfortable in New York," Caleb said.

Buckshot sucked on his coffee. "No," he said, "I expect not. I went there once . . . in 1954, I think it was."

"I'll wash up," Caleb said. "I guess it's my turn."

It disturbed the old man's routine, having someone else doing something in the cabin, and he fidgeted with the chair before he finally settled himself upon it and opened the rum.

He sipped, strangely delicate, like an old lady with an heirloom teacup; and by the time Caleb fell asleep, the bottle was down a third.

Caleb's body missed Sara all night. He'd gotten used to her curled up against him.

Before Sara, Caleb had only had one old lady. A sweet little Grosse Pointe teenybopper speed freak who stabbed him two days before he got busted in Detroit.

As Sara put it: "Not a hard act to follow."

Not that Sara was any less lethal than his small-breasted knife-wielding sweetheart. Just not so crazy.

At first, Sara and Caleb only knew each other in Caleb's bed. All that was common between them, all of their history, was no wider than his old cotton mattress.

Caleb hadn't intended it that way, but he didn't have too many friends and hardly any close friends at all. P.J., maybe, and Long Jim.

He could run a tab at half a dozen bars and cash a personal check in three of them.

Sara, particularly as her politics got more radical, suffered from a similar smallness of world: informers.

They aren't much more than an annoyance when your political program includes marches, leafletting, and letter-writing campaigns. But they get bothersome when you start buying dynamite.

Both Sara and Caleb were illegal. And while that fact was supposed to make them ideological amigos, it meant in truth that their friends were mutually exclusive.

Sara thought Caleb's friends were nice, vague, music-loving, uncommitted, vacuous dopers.

Caleb thought Sara's friends were nice, hard, rhetorical, ambitious, unfeeling politicos.

So they met in bed, and their bodies loved each other.

You can live a lifetime between two bellies sliding on each other. That's what they thought, anyway.

Bitter first light, and rattle of bindings or random grunt woke Caleb. Turned a reluctant eye to Buckshot who was standing in the doorway with his traps slung over his shoulder.

Frosty breath around his head.

Picked up the axe and held it so Caleb could see the scars in the wood.

"Hope you know how to hang an axe," he said. Walked out, and took the axe with him.

"Son of a bitch!" Caleb yelled. But no response.

Hopped out of bed and banging around the little cabin trying to get dressed. Shirt sleeves inside out and frozen that way. Impossibly mouldy frozen socks. Snowshoe binding too loose and the snowshoe twisted as he was scuttling across the stoop, and Caleb toppled full face into a snowdrift.

"Son of a bitch!" he bawled. And he hadn't fastened his jacket and it was full of snow and Caleb's eyes were open now. Like two plates.

Sucked himself out of the snowbank, into his snowshoes. Fastened the bindings with resolute, shaky hands. Shuffled down the old man's track like a caboose.

Beating the snow off himself and already denouncing Buckshot: "Listen man. I didn't ask to come here to your little rural castle. . .

"Listen, old man. I didn't ask to come here, you asked me. Why, I don't know. No matter why. And you got some sort of totally complete life out here with your woodpile and your traps and your goddamned burnt beans and your frigging rum.

"You ever think to offer me a shot of rum? Huh?

"Man, you are about as hospitable as J. Edgar Hoover. . .

"Man, you are about as hospitable as an old grizzly bear.

"How in the hell do you expect me to not bust your miserable axe? I'm a city boy. I like those bright lights and to hell with this pastoral crap. You expect, maybe, I'm Paul Bunyan? You leave no wood cut for me, I bust your axe. It's that simple. . ."

When Caleb caught up to Buckshot, he was kneeling beside one of his traps skinning a beaver. He shot Caleb a quick look and then back to his work as Caleb came up all stiff and casual.

"Howdy," Buckshot said.

Caleb grunted.

"We eat tonight. Beaver tail. The old timers thought it was the best meat around. And they had their choice."

Deftly he freed the pelt from the carcass, amputated the tail, and rose to his feet.

Caleb pointed to the bloody carcass. "You just going to leave that here?"

"Coon 'll get him. Tried to eat it myself a couple of times, but couldn't hold 'er down."

"You dig this? Killing small animals?"

Buckshot shrugged. "We know each other," he said.

"You know how few of those animals there are? I mean, there aren't many beavers left."

"More'n there were ten years ago. Look, boy, I'm sorry about that axe. I should have showed you how to use it. . . You get set in your ways, living alone."

"Yeah."

Caleb shifted from one snowshoe to the other, all the steam hissing out of him.

"You want to learn what a trap line's all 'bout?"

"Yeah, sure. Why not?" Caleb snorted. "It's cold in that cabin of yours. Maybe you should get an electric heater."

"Well, I will, boy. A genuine mail order Monkey Ward's electric heater. But first, I got to finish paying for the TV."

So, two sets of snowshoe tracks in the snow, along the frozen creeks for the beavers, along the windswept ridges for the marten, lynx, and fox.

A steady path, lattice marks, one after another.

Now here's something—big old hole in the snow where someone tripped and went in and floundered—see it? And here's a second set of tracks standing nearby and rocking until the snow was shook off and all the swearing stopped.

Following them across a beaver dam (here the tracks overlap, moving careful), there's a little fast water running out of the base of the dam and we're three feet above the frozen pond and there's a few reeds sticking through the ice.

We walk safer now, but still cautious in a screen of jack pine and alder. Their tracks are deeper here where they hunker down on their shoes. Otter slide across the pond.

"I never could trap otter," Buckshot said, as a sleek, long brown otter whoopeed down the slide. "I saw one of the young ones take a duck, right over there by that snag last fall."

Two sets of tracks moving, pausing, moving again, through a barren, icebound wilderness that was no more a wilderness than the streets of New York or the space within us where we dwell.

No sense of dominance. Not much of a foothold. A tiny pride, perhaps, and that best kept under control. A responsiveness to the snow and the weather and the glare and the trees and animals that share this home. But mostly a riding along with, a bending, with only a few strokes when the current is right to turn it to advantage. Mother wit. And a sense of timing.

But the snow is already drifting over the tracks and the light is failing. Perhaps we hurry our own steps a little as the blue Norway pines go black-blue and close ranks against us.

Ah, here's the cabin and a thin crinkle of smoke rising from the stovepipe. Two pairs of snowshoes leaning against the stoop and Buckshot's querulous voice inside, "Not that way, boy, you got to get the skin off her before you fry her up. Here, I'll do it. You slice the spuds."

Air of nineteenth-century busyness and hissing of the kerosene lamp. Shadows shifting on the cabin walls and the two of them colliding, as Caleb blundered into Buck-shot's habitual paths.

Buckshot opened the top of the cast-iron stove and laid the beaver tail on the naked fire—first one side, then flipped it over.

"Boy," he said, "you're going to taste something that'll give your old filet Mig-nons a run for their money."

"You're burning it."

"No, I'm not Burning It. I'm just singeing it a mite. What about them spuds?"

Pulled it out, peeled and jabbed the skin off with a fork.

Pop of grease in the frying pan, and Buckshot muttering and prodding the meat as Caleb put out the plates and cups.

The meat was strong and good and greasy and unlike anything Caleb had ever eaten before. What is lamb like compared to beef? Much the same, but different.

They ate in silence, and when he'd finished, Buckshot pushed his plate away from him and belched. He poured them both a full cup of rum.

"Wash 'er down," he said.

Caleb took a sip. "Jesus," he said, "this is really horrible."

Buckshot chuckled. "Half creosote and half bear's grease. Warms you up though."

And it did. And after his second cup, Caleb went into his pocket for the little can of dope.

Buckshot watching the whole process, sharp-eyed.

"That marywanna?"

"Uh-huh."

"You a nar-cotics addict?"

"No." He poured himself a little more rum. "You a drunk?"

Explosive, "Haw!"

Two neat joints, looking a little effete, a little feminine, on the table. Caleb lit up.

"You ever try this stuff?"

Buckshot took the joint between his fingers and looked it over, trying to SEE it.

"No. Couple Mex's used to smoke it when we wuz building a dam out in Arizona. They wasn't much good with a single jack, but they were nice fellows."

Caleb took a long toke.

"I used to smoke opium," Buckshot said.

Caleb coughed.

"Before they made it illegal. I must still have the pipe around here somewhere. I was a hoofer in Cincinnati, and four of us used to smoke a pipeful in the dressing room before we went on. You ever hear of Everett Simpson?"

"No."

"Yeah, well, he's dead now. But he had the fastest feet I ever seen." He squeaked his chair back from the table and grunted. "I wasn't much good at it, but I was hungry enough to keep my feet bouncing. But boy, when we'd had a pipeful or two of opium, we really put on a dog-and-pony show."

"When did you quit?"

"When I got canned. I think that was in nineteen twenty-five."

"I mean, when did you quit smoking opium?"

"About the same time, I guess. The government was telling us how dangerous it was and it was illegal now, and besides, Everett Simpson's brother Billy, who used to get the stuff for us, got killed in a fight and I just guess I didn't care enough to look it up for myself."

He fired the joint and took a puff.

"Tastes like pepper," he said.

They smoked in silence for a while. Caleb ate his roach.

"Boy, that's quite a trick," Buckshot said. "What's supposed to be happening?"

Caleb smiled. "With all the booze in you, probably nothing."

"You get it from Denny?" Buckshot asked.

"Uh-huh."

"Yeah, well I figured they were up to something like that. Denny had a couple of strange looking plants growing down by the Kennebec, near them black rocks just before Lost Woman Rips. I guess he didn't think anybody knew, but I knew. One day, Pete Murphey, who runs a trapline on Moosehead, was mentioning them in the store."

"Nobody called the cops?"

"Naw. It was a good joke. Here's ol' Denny snoopin' and poopin' through the woods, and half the old timers in town sort of keeping an eye on him. Him hidin' all those plants in that fallen-down garage behind his house and a big innocent look on his face every time I ask him about those big city dope fiends. Haw!"

"They're nice people."

"Uh-huh. Good neighbors. Last winter when I got my leg broke, I laid up there for a spell. Sure made life miserable for them. Me bellerin' and bitchin' and Karen running in with more tea and Denny goin' out to buy me rum. I believe in speaking my mind, and those two folks sure got an earful."

"How'd you break it?"

"Damn fool carelessness. Dropped a big old birch for firewood and the butt kicked back on me. Drink up, boy, I'm gainin' on you."

Caleb topped off his cup and rolled another joint.

"No more for me," Buckshot said. "It makes me dizzy and I'm too old to change my poisons."

Caleb got up to put the plates on the sink, and he wobbled, bumped his hip against the table.

"I sure wish you had a radio," he said. "I'd like a little music."

"Wouldn't do much good," Buckshot said. "These mountains do something so you can't hardly pick anything up. The northern lights have something to do with it. You can get radio and TV in Kennebec, but they got a cable. Couple years ago, Sheriff Holloway decided he wanted to be all fancy and modern and put radios in the police cars. Dan Johnson, on the town council, is agin' it. Too much money. But Holloway buffaloes him and the council votes enough money for one car to try it out and everybody standing around down at Bronson's and Holloway ordering everybody to stand back and they've got this little set inside, right next to Bronson's cash register and Holloway saying 'Come in, Unit 1.' Deputy Mackey and a state trooper are 'bout twenty miles upriver on the road to the gravel pit. The set's howling and buzzing, and Holloway's getting redder and redder until he chased everybody out. Never did get the damn thing working."

"Sure wish we had some music though," Caleb said vaguely.

A little more rum.

"This stuff has got me going," Caleb said. "The music means a lot to me. I don't know if you old codgers can understand" (Buckshot snorted), "but it's the only way of keeping in touch. It's like knowing what's going on on the other side of town when the town isn't really a town but citizens here and there a thousand miles apart.

"There's somebody in San Diego down and out and broke and strung out on speed, and he's part of the town.

"And some fat teenybopper, mad at herself for how fat she is, in Scarsdale; she's in the town too.

"And some high-stepping black cat makes a fine move with his wrist, and he's standing on Main Street of our town even though he's still in Peoria, and his wrist move is to point out to a couple of Peoria cops how ignorant they are and stop jivin' him.

"And the music is the only word we get about what's shakin' and who's doin' what to who." He waved his hand awkwardly. "Anyway, I miss it."

Buckshot's calm eyes. "You ever see a buck and wing?" he asked. "Hell, I'll show you."

Twenty thousand four hundred and eight feet above them, an American Airlines 727, New York to Montreal.

The passengers have loosened their ties, and the junior executives are on the second of their two allotted cocktails.

Inside the plane, it's warm all around and the stewardess, awkwardly pushing a metal cart, coming down the aisle toward us.

Warm all around, an unnoticeable warmth, that makes you look out the window at the white-covered mountains, visible through a break in the clouds below, and almost repress a shiver and turn to me, sitting beside you, and smile that broad harmless California smile and say, "Brrrr. Man, that gives me the willies just looking at it. I hope it's warmer in Montreal."

And below, infinitely far below, a cabin stands in a clearing by a logging road. Both cabin and road are buried

in snow. There's a damp patch around the stovepipe about
ten inches in circumference. The roof has been shoveled
clear of snow. There's a wisp of smoke from the chimney
and a roar of a fire inside.

An old man is tap-dancing in front of the stove. Another
man, a young man about half the other's age, is lounging on
a chair.

The old man is pushing a song out past his lips, a song
with no notes, a ghost of a song or its essence, only with all
the notes removed.

The old man, himself, has a ghost within him. Of a 1920s
highfaluting dandy. And his feet flash patent leather, bright
as a spit shine by gosh. Bam. Bam. Buck and wing!

The younger man sits up, as if to protect himself, and a
tear is at the edge, hanging out at the edge of his right eye.

"Hot damn," he says.

Caleb woke up pissy-horny and hung over. The cabin
was empty. Buckshot had left for town hours ago.

Caleb got some wood and birch bark and splashed water
on his face. He stood on the stoop, shivering, waiting for his
fire to go. Thinking about Sara and the very best balls they
ever had. Thinking about Karen and wondering what she
and Denny did in bed.

"Too many damn secrets around here," he muttered, and
hunted up some oatmeal.

He swept out the cabin with a great flurry of broom, with
dust to coat him and clog his nostrils, but he skipped all the
corners and the dirt under the bed.

He dressed too warm and clambered up on the roof to
shovel the last snowfall and ended with both shirts and
jacket open to let his sweat out.

He wondered if Sara was making it with someone else.
He sat by the stove for half an hour, warming his feet,
thinking how Karen's breasts moved and the ways she had

of puckering her ass when it was going away from you with your eyes on it.

He went outside and chopped some wood. He set himself deliberately for each stroke and controlled his temper. It went a little better. It was a bit easier; he cut more wood, and he didn't bruise the haft of the axe.

He sat by the stove for a while, stretching and wondering if he and Sara and Karen could ever make it together.

Heated up some water and washed last night's greasy dishes.

Put the snowshoes on and described a circle around the cabin, looking for animal tracks. He found tracks, but didn't know what animal made them.

He and Sara once spent two weeks in the Weatherman commune in Boston. Heavy, intricate, revolutionary rhetoric and lives clashing in each pronouncement.

No dope. And that nearly drove Caleb out.

Talk, all the time. And that nearly drove Caleb out.

While they were there, the cadre came to the conclusion that "personal relationships distracted from political activity and encouraged the bullshit patterns of male dominance and woman dependence." No more monogamy.

At first, Caleb liked it a lot. Making it with whoever, satisfying his curiosity.

But he didn't much like it that Sara was also making it with whoever.

Caleb put his boots on the stove and recalled as much as he could about each one of the women he'd balled then. They were all in danger. They would, in the next months, separate themselves from their families, their connections, and the patterns they were intended to fit. And oh, how they shone, those beautiful kids!

It started to snow again—wet, heavy, deliberate flakes, with every intention of keeping it up for a while. Caleb just finished taking a piss when he saw Buckshot coming up the logging road, a little quicker than usual.

"How'd it go?" Caleb asked. But Buckshot, up close, just nodded to him and went inside.

He was rummaging through an old pack propped up in the corner. He kicked it.

"What's wrong?" Caleb asked.

"Don't worry boy. Nothing's going to happen to you. You're just unlucky for your friends."

Poured himself a cup of rum and gulped it down, standing indecisive in the middle of the room. Went over to an old cardboard trunk, dug under some blankets, and fished out an ancient Colt .38 and a greasy yellow cardboard box of shells.

"Holloway and his boys arrested Denny and Karen two days ago. 'Bout two hours after we left, I expect."

"Oh, Jesus."

"I'm sixty-six years old," Buckshot said, "but I'm as fit as I ever was."

"How did they find out? Did Mary Two Hat. . . ?"

"Naw. Hell, no. She's still got her wits. It was that damn little girl who follows her around all the time."

"Well, how are they doing, Denny and Karen, I mean?"

Mildly. "I expect they ain't pleased."

He set one boot up on the chair and laced it tighter.

"What's going to happen to them?"

"Now what in hell do you think is going to happen to them? They hid you and that don't set too well. And Holloway tore the place apart and found fifty pounds of Marywanna in that old garage. And that didn't set too well either."

"Are the cops coming out here?"

"Why should they? I'd guess they think you'll try 201. They're keeping the roadblocks up."

"Oh."

Buckshot stuck an old brass engineer's compass into his right breast pocket. He hung a skinning knife from his belt (after he'd tested the edge with his thumb). He went to the mirror over the sink, and for the first time Caleb could remember, he combed his hair. He sat down at the table and loaded the old revolver. He dropped the extra shells into his other breast pocket.

"What are you going to do?"

"What the hell you think I'm gonna do? I ain't exactly dressed for dancing."

"Many, you're crazy. You're out of your mind. You can't do anything."

Buckshot spat on the floor and stood up.

"Hey, wait a minute. Look, old man, ain't nothing going to happen to Denny and Karen. It ain't them they want, it's me."

"Waaal, boy, you just keep right on thinkin' that. Sheriff Holloway has a dead deputy to think about. And there's an FBI man come all the way up from Portland to 'consult' with him. And all the folks in town are madder'n hornets. Boy, you ain't half smart. This is the biggest thing that happened up here since the sawmill strike. They got your fingerprints off a gun you dropped; they found your fingerprints at Denny's house, and they done captured themselves enough narcotics to get Holloway's face on the front page of the *Bangor Herald.* Boy, I ain't glad I ever met you."

Caleb hurried after him, got his bindings half-fastened, and flopped through the snow by the old man's side, talking hard and waving his arms.

Buckshot paid no attention.

By the time they reached the canoe, Caleb had run out of words, and the snow was falling heavier. Buckshot turned the canoe over and slid it into the water.

"I, uh, I guess I'll go back to the cabin," Caleb said.

Buckshot pulled the broad-bladed stern paddle from under the seat.

"Uh, could I borrow your compass? The snow has drifted over our tracks."

Buckshot looked at him, slow, and handed him the compass.

He rearranged the gear in the canoe.

"Goddamn it!" Caleb yelled. "I don't know how to use this thing. I don't even know what direction that crummy shack is in."

He shoved the compass back into Buckshot's hand and sat in the bow of the canoe.

"How do you steer this barge?" he asked.

"Just paddle; I'll steer. And Mr. Smith. . ."

"Yeah?"

"I would like you to recollect that when you are running off at the mouth about a 'crummy shack' that that 'crummy shack' is my home."

Their paddles bit into the water, and the current grabbed the boat as soon as they were out of the shelter of the bank.

4 / *Maine—Boston— New York*

When Sheriff Tom Holloway came cruising down the main street of Kennebec, most folks gave him a wave, although some of them waited for his wave first. And, excepting only three people in town—three of nine hundred and twenty-nine, Tom Holloway always waved too, a careless lift of the wrist from the wheel; sometimes before the other person waved, sometimes after; the sequence strictly observed.

He never waved first at Canadians because he thought they drove too fast.

And he never waved first at downstate hunters, because he was prejudiced against them. When hunting season came each year, he girded himself for the only time he really disliked his job. For two weeks every year, the population of Kennebec nearly doubled.

The merchants made out OK. Two gross of red flannel shirts. Twenty-five cases of '06 ammo. Three thousand two hundred ninety cases of beer. Two hundred eighty cases of potato chips. Twelve cases of Coleman fuel. And every room in the town's three hotels booked up. And the rates half again what they usually were.

Hunting season was important to the town. So Tom Holloway never spoke against it.

But since Kennebec had no jail (no bank either), he had Bronson clean out his back room before the season started. And almost every night except Sundays, one or two or sometimes three drunken hunters would find themselves locked up in Chas. Bronson's storeroom, crying for their lawyers and (since the storeroom was unheated) shivering and trying to stay awake.

He didn't like them because they made him stay up until the bars closed, when he liked to be in bed by eleven.

He didn't like them because they were men who needed to be tough and obeyed none of his normal understandings.

Now Pete Balbour was tough. And every now and again he'd cut loose and fight somebody, and Tom Holloway had to come and make noises at the two of them and make sure they paid for the damages. But Pete Balbour was predictable. (And not a bad guy when you got to know him.)

But these downstate sportsmen, Lordy! As soon as they put on their hunting garb, they started talking hard and from the corners of their mouths. And the knives they had strapped on their belts! Some of them were easy a foot long! And though no one had ever been shot, all those screwy men, armed to the nines, getting drunk in three bars at once, and shooting tough glances at one another, made Tom Holloway nervous.

So he didn't like them. And never waved.

His dislike for Canadians was irrational, and he knew it and that didn't alter his dislike one whit. They drove 201 with a complete disregard for sense and a cheerful ignorance of the S curves, hanging over the river below. He knew it wasn't any of his damn business. But he had to pull bodies out of drowned cars from time to time. And he didn't like Canadians, no matter how birdlike and lilting their accents. Despite the fact that none of them had every done anything to him or the town except for the cost of the guardrails the town had to replace periodically.

Tom Holloway was one of the rarest of all Americans, and perhaps one of the most fortunate—a man in harmony with himself.

His abilities were not greater, or lesser, than the demands made upon those abilities. His powers weighed equally with what other people expected him to do. His desires were met, for the most part, and those that were unsatisfied, to his mind, would be satisified with the passage of time.

He'd never been outside of Maine except for Korea. Where he did about as well as he could, hated it, and came home on the earliest rotation he could make.

Every summer he fished for two weeks on one of the back country ponds.

Every now and again, he slept with Mary Beth McLaughlin, the eldest and unmarried daughter of the McLaughlin who had that split-and-baling-wire lumber operation outside of Augusta.

And everytime he went into Bangor, he found a whore.

But today this good man, this lucky man, was quite cast adrift, confused; and the solidity of his life, which had stood beneath him, unknown, was visible to him now, and seemed like rotting ice, bad footing, unsafe to trust your weight.

Not the least of it was the death of his deputy, Hank. A part of his life had been cut away and not replaced.

He sat in the Morning Star Restaurant with his cup of coffee and the chair across from him was empty and no one to flip for who paid.

And clearly, Hank Mackey's death was his fault.

He'd examined the matter, turned it over slow and reflective, and he thought, in all fairness, with no hysteria, he'd made the mistake that got Hank killed.

Little fat man, Hank, who always kept a pint in the glove compartment of the cruiser and continual chatter about his plans, his family, what was on TV.

They'd set up the roadblock with none of them believing anything would happen. First mistake.

Tom Holloway's mistake, alone.

He hadn't understood. Different ballgame. Different league.

These weren't kids like the long-haired town kids, who listened to music too loud and passed you on the street dreamy-eyed and stoned. These kids weren't kids at all; they were dangerous killers.

And when that crazy kid came busting out of the woods towards him and Hank, banging away with that little tiny pistol, Tom Holloway should have dropped him fast. Another mistake.

Because that crazy kid, charging them with his toy pistol, had got off one lucky shot that caught Hank Mackey in the jugular vein, and Hank bled to death promptly and predictably as Tom was pumping 30-30 bullets into the kid.

He missed Hank. He felt bad. He was mad as hell.

He wouldn't have been so angry if Hank had been shot in some fracas with ordinary hoodlums. But these were kid killers, or only a little more than kids. They should have been going to college. Or getting married and nervous-eager-nice in the way young people were when Tom Holloway was younger.

Tom, like most of us, didn't actually have any opinions about Hippies or the Military-Industrial-Complex or the Balance-of-Payments. Newspaper editors are paid to have opinions. But nobody gave Tom Holloway one thin dime for his views, so he didn't work up enough steam to invent "The Holloway Doctrine" or pronounce it.

When he did talk, to his credit, he sounded more like *Newsweek* than *Time*. And, more to his credit, he *acted* more like the former than the latter—generous, amiable, not terribly overprotective, a little vague, and mildly willing to Do the Right Thing.

But these kids were a sick joke, a bad memory, a terrible dream. He'd read about the Weathermen, but until now he'd assumed that they, like Charlie Manson, were the craziest products of a huge country, made crazier by the madness of Los Angeles and New York.

But the boogeymen were real.

They laid the bodies out, on tarpaulins, on the floor of Snyder's garage. Kids' bodies.

Greasy tools on the black greasy counters. A stack of old tires lying sideways next to the new tires on the rack. Pale-grey winter light filtering through the skylights overhead. Bare, big light bulbs steaming in the cold. And, so help me god, *kids!* lying on those torn tarpaulins and hardly a line on their foreheads. And blood like red tar in their hair.

The one they caught alive wasn't much better.

He wanted to call his lawyer. And when Tom told him the phone lines were down and had been for some time, he just said that he'd call his lawyer when they were fixed and not another word out of him. Pure gall. And only Holloway to cool down Pete and John Cassidy, who'd lost their brother-in-law to his friend's bullets. (Said brother-in-law being the only member of the Cassidy clan who had steady employment.) And Bill and John being oddball Birchers and waving their twelve gauges around wondering loudly what kind of sheriff would protect a commie-killer who'd just shot down three of the town's citizens.

Tom Holloway kept them from killing the kid, dead as a stuck pig, right there, and still the kid wouldn't say anything.

And he was a pretty kid. Not handsome, pretty. Tom couldn't tell what the others looked like; they were too shot up, but this kid was pretty as a young girl, with long blond hair hanging to his/her shoulders.

For some reason, he embarrassed Tom Holloway. Normally, the sheriff was chatty, friendly to the prisoners he had locked up in Bronson's shed. With this kid he was formal, cold, and flustered.

Doubtful that the kid even noticed. Or may have—the only sign being a small quick know-it-all kid's grin he flashed to Tom when the FBI finally came and took him away. Thus, the sheriff's inner world was already addled, a jigsaw puzzle trying to pull itself together after a wind had scattered it apart. And maybe some pieces lost. And maybe a few others changed in shape.

The windy season wasn't over, and there were surprises to come.

The American Public had come to Kennebec and who needed it? Newspaper reporters, TV crews, police officials from this state agency and that government agency took over both hotels; blocked traffic; made it impossible to get your second cup of coffee before the waitress snatched your plate at the Morning Star Restaurant; instituted roadblocks at the border and down 201 to the Maine Pike, so that nothing could get through without delay except another police car; interviewed half the town (magnifying the self-importance of half the citizens, while making the other half mad and jealous as hell); flew helicopters over the clouds, despite the undeniable fact that clouds and snow made it impossible to see anything as any-damn-fool-should-know, and called him Tom within ten minutes after they first made his acquaintance.

The first day he'd been obliging to the reporters and professional to the other police.

But when he stopped at the roadhouse before finally going home to bed, one of the reporters (who'd been calling him Tom) nudged him and said "Say, fella, where can you get a drink in this town, after hours?" The next day he started pushing the press back a little.

And when two of the federal police scared the beJesus out of Mrs. Watson and shoved her teenage son, he called the police together at the shed and said, "If you boys don't ease up and respect me and the people in my town, I'll personally crucify the next dodo who wanders out of line. I

will write a long letter to the Boston *Post* and the *New York
Times* complaining of the terrible police brutality of XYZ
and sign that letter, Sheriff Tom Holloway."

They didn't like it much. And Tom wouldn't have given
two cents for his chances of getting hired by any of those
famous agencies, but they did quiet down some. Professional courtesy.

He had it almost under control, when the wind dumped
the jigsaw on the floor again.

Little Patti Schlitzler. Miserable little girl. Waved him
over peremptorily and told him about Denny and Karen
and their strange guest.

Patti didn't say a word to her mother and father. Didn't
say a word to Mary Two Hat. Waited in the middle of the
damn night for him to come down the main street of Kennebec, with the damn snow falling, and her little bundled
up body, for him. Personal.

And the reporters picked it up. And instead of being the
"Sheriff Holloway, who lead the roadblock is seen at the far
left of the picture," he became "Sheriff Holloway, whose
detective work and faith in a little girl unearthed a Weatherman 'safe house' (see pp. 38–40 for an exclusive
interview)."

Patti Schlitzler's photo was on every TV station in
America, smiling like a star.

And *Life* almost used a photo of the two of them at
Denny's house for their cover photo. The photo did make
the centerfold.

And Tom Holloway was interviewed and interesting and
folksy and wise.

When they asked him what he believed, he spoke his
piece.

What could be wrong with that?

And if he had already thought over what he would say
when he was invited to the Johnny Carson show, who could
blame him?

Still, he was a little wary. He didn't flop over on his back with his legs apart, and afterward, when he thought about those days, he was thankful for all the pieces of himself he hadn't given to the press. He could think of a lot of things he'd said that made him blush, but only one thing he said or did made him ashamed.

Thursday night, when they were ready to move Denny and Karen to Bangor, he warned a few select reporters ahead of time.

He'd grown to like his two prisoners. The whole harboring-a-fugitive business didn't bother him much, because, in this part of Maine, who wouldn't? And anyway, they were going to pay and pay again if the State Prosecuting Attorney had his way.

Tom was a little shocked when he found their stash. Fifty pounds. Hank had always wanted to pull a midnight raid on those two, and Hank had been right. Tom would have busted them hard if he'd known. But he didn't hold it against them. They were people and fairly nice people, and when he remembered later what he did to them, he was slightly ashamed.

He finished his coffee and walked over to Snyder's to get the cruiser. Old Jacky Delion had checked the points and plugs, and since it was snowing pretty heavy by then, he'd put the chains on. So far, standard procedure for taking prisoners downstate.

But this time, there was a little switch in the routine.

Normally, Tom Holloway moved his prisoners without saying a word about it. He'd seen the prison in Portsmouth and decided that since his prisoners' destination was so grim, he'd at least spare them a carnival at their departure.

Usually, he moved his prisoners quick and secret.

This time, when Denny and Karen came out of the shed, flanked by Tom and an FBI man, there were cameras and flash bulbs and hollered questions and even a TV camera operating with a sungun, flaring against the falling snow.

Karen was crying when they got to the cruiser, and when Tom Holloway remembered this later, he was ashamed.

At the time, however, he just drove away pretty quick, so quick that the TV man lost his shot. Tom concentrated on his driving and the inane chatter of the FBI man blocked the sobs coming from the girl behind the partition.

Something in the FBI man's training hadn't stuck. He kept flashing back and forth between the courteous, intelligent, boring person Mr. Hoover had made and a bad kid from Jersey, who'd gotten his degree from Seton Hall and just barely.

The snowfall had him pretty nervous. So he talked. He talked about the FBI Academy and alluded to secret training he wasn't supposed to mention. He told Tom the names of three girls he'd laid. He informed Tom about a leftist conspiracy that was threatening what we hold dear.

Tom wished he'd shut up.

He told Tom his pistol scores at the academy.

They got stuck behind a snowplow. "Goddamned hick states that can't even keep traffic moving along," he said.

Tom was trying to think about his career. He just grunted at the guy, which didn't discourage him any.

They got stuck behind another snowplow.

"Goddamned thing, blocks the whole road. Why don't you goose them with the siren. Holy Christ, now he's stuck. Boy, some highway department. Some highway!"

Tom knew that to stay in politics he'd have to be nice to jerks like this every day. He was wondering if maybe he wasn't cut out for it when Caleb stuck his pistol through his window, fired, and put the jigsaw puzzle back together again.

Caleb's hand shook bad, and the pistol was jittering around a few inches above the sheriff's ear.

"Don't move," he said, unnecessarily.

The walk from the snowplow, casual towards the delayed cruiser, with his hair tucked into a red flannel cap and his hands on the pistol in his pocket—Caleb trying to look like a highway department worker coming to warn them of some obstacle ahead—that walk had quite unnerved Caleb. And what the walk hadn't done to his nerves, the roar of the pistol had done. In spades.

The driver's window rolled down, a star shaped hole in the passenger's window, and the concussion and smoke made Caleb feel like he had his hand in a foggy barrel of scorpions.

He would have killed anyone who moved; he was that frightened.

"Take it easy, son," Tom Holloway drawled. "You got us."

Caleb put the muzzle of Buckshot's pistol against the Sheriff's temple and that stopped the trembling.

The FBI man made a little move, coming out of his trance.

"Friend," the sheriff said, quietly, "If you reach for a cigarette, this boy is going to blow my brains out. We'll catch him later."

The FBI man let his muscles go slack.

Caleb reached around to open the prisoner's cage.

"Denny," he pleaded, "come around and get that guy's gun. Careful. Please be careful."

Denny hesitated. He gave Caleb a funny charming smile. It faded. He shrugged and his face gained five years. But he did get out and cautiously took the FBI man's .357 magnum from its official holster under his official FBI suit.

"Goddamn it," Caleb said. "Point the gun, Denny. Point the gun at them."

Slowly, like a pinball falling into a slot, Denny aimed the .357 at the FBI man, and Denny's face settled into the lines of a man who could shoot another man if he had to.

"You jerks are in bad trouble," the FBI man said.

"Shut up!" Caleb yelled.

He had the two men get out very slowly, and he had to use both hands to hold the gun steady. He took Tom Holloway's pistol from its holster, sliding up to the gun like it was a mean snake.

"Both of you get into the back," he said. Two guns in his hands and both guns nervous.

Karen slid out to give them room, but the FBI man had been thinking of what Mr. Hoover was going to say. He jumped Denny. Might have worked too, but Denny was so surprised that he dropped the gun in the snow and the two of them hugging and hitting each other.

Caleb fired both pistols at the middle of the rolling lashing and missed. Fortunately.

But the blast put an end to foolishness, and the FBI man loosed Denny's arm from the judo hold he halfway had on it.

"You punk son-of-a-bitch," FBI said to Caleb.

"In the back seat, pig," Caleb to FBI.

A new ballgame: Caleb, Denny and Karen in the front seat and the two tense angry policemen in the cage. Caleb pulled a cigarette from a pack on the dashboard and lit up.

He swore. "Menthol, goddamn."

The snow was falling thick. Blinking lights on the snowplow, twenty yards ahead. Caleb honked two shorts and a long and the snowplow pulled away. Karen was crying again and Denny had his arm around her, whispering in her ear.

"You really tore it this time, kid," the FBI man said. "Why don't you give it up before you get killed?"

"Shut up," Caleb said.

The cruiser following the snowplow and the wipers working hard against the snow and the hot air from the heater not quite enough to offset the icy air coming through the bullet hole in the window.

Despite the chains, the cruiser was skidding a lot. Caleb wrestling with the wheel; he didn't know the first thing about driving in the snow.

"Caleb," Karen asked, "why'd you do this?"

"Why not?" he said.

"We might have gotten off."

"Sure thing. Fifty pounds of dope."

"She's right," Sheriff Holloway said, quietly. "That harboring charge never did hold water. And with a smart lawyer, who knows?"

"Fifty pounds. That's possession with intent," Caleb said. "And with all the Weatherman static, they'd get ten years."

"What do you think it'll be now?" the sheriff asked. "Dead in some crappy shoot-out?"

Caleb braked the cruiser to a stop and turned in his seat.

"Okay, cop," he said. "I got a bank-robbery rap and an accessory-to-felony-murder rap hanging over me. Not to mention this and that. And I got enough to worry me without any cop bullshit jive from you. Dig?"

Tom Holloway didn't say anything, and the two of them stared at each other, testing resolve.

They both had a lot of resolve.

Caleb caught up with the snowplow and held his distance until it pulled off the road. Two highway department buildings: a corrugated-tin garage and a small frame office, with smoke rising from the stovepipe.

Kennebec County paid Tom Holloway $385 a month, and he bought his own uniforms. Most of the time he did nothing to earn his salary, cruising around in his car, drinking coffee, jawing with the citizens. He was paid for emergencies. He was paid to act unusually in unusual circumstances.

When he stepped on the low wooden step of the office, with the two men behind him, he pivoted and dove to the snow beside the doorway. A getaway! And his feet were chugging as he ran, crouched over, beside the frame office, across an open space, and past the tin snowplow garage. Then, he veered sharply, running back to the cruiser and the shotgun on the floorboards, and he was in full view of the lead slugs, lying slick in the barrels of Caleb's guns. No shots. Silence except for his footfalls.

Light gloss of new snow over the packed old snow. And some indiscernible hump in the snow lied to his feet and he pinwheeled and hit the ground rolling ass over teakettle.

It knocked the breath out of him, and when his vision cleared a few seconds later, that crazy kid was standing over him screaming: "You bastard cop, you son of a bitch. I ain't never killed anybody, but I ain't gonna spend the next ten years in some filthy slam. Try that again motherfucker and I'll kill you. I swear I'll kill you."

Tom looked at the kid's face, dead white as any of the faces on those other kids on the tarpaulins on the floor of Snyder's garage, and figured what the hell, he'd earned his $385.

Old Joe Derby, who'd been driving plow for years, was sitting tied up on the floor when they all came in. Joe greeted Tom Holloway quite cheerfully.

"Howdy Sheriff. Mercy. So he got you too, eh? This boy is a real terror, so he is. He's gonna have half the county in here before nightfall, like as not."

"You OK, Joe?"

"Well, I could use one of them portable TVs, and if somebody untied my hands so I could change the knobs, I'd be happy as a clam."

The old man's cheerful acceptance of whatever was to come calmed them all. They let themselves go easy. They became accomplices in the handcuffing and safe fastening that followed. A strange sort of grace came to them, even to the FBI man. They were correct and formal now, formal adversaries.

Caleb was gentle as he locked them up. And they sat where he told them to without complaint. The old man was making jokes and that helped too.

Caleb set the oil heater on "warm" before they left.

Outside, hurrying towards the car. Karen was the first one to notice the small figure squatting beside the cruiser.

It startled her. "Buckshot!" she exclaimed. "How did he get you involved in this?"

Buckshot grunted and rose to his feet, "It was my idea, honey. Hush, now. Don't use my name. I don't want them (he jerked his head toward the office) to know who was driving the snowplow."

"But why, Buckshot? You could get in a lot of trouble."

He smiled at her. "Phooey. Not much. I'm too old for them to do much to me. And I didn't want you to lose all your looks in jail. Give me a kiss before you go."

So Karen bent to kiss him, and for a moment, the old man was her baby in her arms.

"We'll be seeing you again," Denny said.

"Oh," Buckshot was a little disgruntled, "I don't expect you will." He bent over and started tieing his snowshoes. The snow was rising around them, blowing, hissing, cutting them off.

"You can keep my gun," Buckshot said to Caleb. "Don't shoot anybody you don't have to."

"OK."

He gave them a wave and was gone, vanished in the driving snow.

A minute later they all were gone. Delivered into the hands of the night, the blizzard, and the bright sparks of terror.

Denny drove and he had a tough time of it, though he'd logged a lot of miles in heavy snow. For twenty miles, they rode silent through a world of weird white half-shapes and gauze curtains of snow streaming around the car. Karen gasped once when the rear end of the car turned half around in the road and Denny gave her a quick nervous smile.

"I used to have a sports car when I was a preppy," he said.

"Please be careful," Karen said. "I hate this, Denny. I hate this."

Caleb asked about their arrest, and Denny told him, briefly. In short sentences. Bronson's shed had ice running like a thin frozen creek down the tar paper on one wall. He described the tar paper. He described the ice.

Caleb regretted asking.

The roadblocks were still up from the bank robbery. They hit the first one with their headlights on and Denny wearing Sheriff Holloway's smokey-bear hat. Lot of snow coming down and it's doubtful if the deputy at the road- block even saw the hat. He stayed inside his car and gave them a friendly wave as they went barreling by.

"One down," Denny said. "I sure wish I knew where we were going." Sweat on the palms of his hands and he wiped them on his pants.

"We could live with my sister," Karen suggested.

"They always come after your family," Caleb said.

"Yeah," Karen said. "But I'm the only one who knows where my sister is living. Her old man was a black cat. Mommy and Dada found out and really flipped out about it. They were trying to get her committed, so she split. She writes to me. She's living in some commune down in Virginia."

"I can hide you out in New York," Caleb said.

"Don't like New York," Denny said. "When I was going to school, we used to drive down from Boston every now and again. New York hurts my ears."

"Yeah. But it's easy to get lost there."

"How long you figure we have before they start looking for this car?"

"The next shift on that snowplow isn't due for another four hours."

"We can't make Boston by then."

"So maybe we'll stop somewhere along the way and take a bus."

Denny hit the siren every small town they passed through, and they'd shoot through, ignoring the red lights, the speedometer steady on 50.

A few people saw them ghost by. But most folks were staying home tonight and those that weren't were digging their cars out of the snow.

Cars on both sides of the road. Some skewed into snow- banks and abandoned. Some becoming snowbanks themselves beside the road. A few others, a very few others, crawling and skidding along, and the big Ford cruiser blasting by all of them riding on the ice and a rooster-tail of snow that spumed behind it.

The road had narrowed to one usable lane, with cars stuck on the left and right. More and more stalled cars as they left the mountains and entered more populated areas.

Caleb rolled a joint and offered it, but no takers, so he smoked it himself.

By rights, the next roadblock should have got them, but they were lucky tonight.

They blasted up this little hill outside of Aroostook, spraying snow on two . . . three abandoned cars, and on the other side of the hill, four cars were stopped in front of them, waiting in line.

Denny hit the siren and the cars grudgingly gave him enough room to squeeze by, but Denny had to slow down—40, 30, 20 MPH and the tires whining and the chains rattling and Sweet Jesus, dead ahead of them a state highway patrol car sideways in the road.

Blinking red light, turning around, hurting their eyes.

Caleb put a pistol in his lap.

Karen set her lips tight and American Gothic.

The trooper was out of his car pushing some dude in a Riviera who'd slid half off the road.

Embarrassed fatso driver. Trooper pushing so hard he'd better have hernia insurance.

Denny got on it.

Zig around the blockader, zag past the hind end of the Riviera, and gone. If the trooper had looked up, as close as he was, he couldn't have helped seeing that something was not kosher. But he heard the siren and was trusting. When he did raise his eyes, they were a fuzzy cloud going away from him.

He gave them a one-cold-cop-to-another wave, but they didn't see it.

"Wowee," Caleb said. "Amazing driving, Denny. Amazing."

Neither of them liked it much—Caleb's getting stoned just then—and Karen grunted short and Denny said, cold, "Yeah terrific."

Denny wiped his hands again and stretched his butt in the seat.

A few miles past Bangor, they left 201 and got on the Maine Pike.

Beside the entrance ramp a red-dot neon sign glowed: "Turnpike Closed," but they ignored it, doing 50 again. They slowed for the tollgate and the tollkeeper waved them through without leaving his chair.

The snow was deeper here, their headlights were dimmed, covered by ice, and every time they came up on one of the big semi rigs, they were blind for about ten seconds in its wake, as they tried to pass.

"You ever hot wire a car?" Caleb said.

"Christ no," Denny said.

"It's about time you learned. The Maine Pike goes right into the New Hampshire Pike. And the people on the New Hampshire side are going to think it's pretty weird for a Maine police car to go whipping into their state without even asking."

"Goddamn, goddamn!" A whine in Denny's voice.

Caleb broke the plastic of the map-light with his pistol butt, tugged two short pieces of wire loose, stripped the ends, and stuck them up on the dashboard.

A few miles past the Merrimacport exit, Denny spotted a VW stuck fast in the snow.

"VW's go pretty good in this kind of weather," Denny said.

No cars passed while they towed the little car back on the road, and Caleb fiddled around until it started.

Musty old VW with a baby carrier in the back seat and the smell of baby puke on the seat covers. When Denny started to get in, Caleb said, "Bring guns."

Denny hesitated. "Bring 'em," Caleb said. "If the cops got guns, I want one too."

He felt better with Buckshot's old Colt beside his feet.

The VW's legal owner had abandoned his toll ticket in the sun visor, and Caleb paid ninety cents at the end of the pike.

"Lousy weather," the toll collector said."I sure hope you folks get through alright."

"We're only going a few more miles," Caleb said.

"Well, good luck."

"Thanks."

They had to stop once in New Hampshire for another toll, and then they were on 495 heading south.

Denny looked at the little clock under the dashboard.

"They'll be after us pretty quick," he said.

"So? In this weather, what are they going to do?"

"They'll look for the cruiser. And they'll phone the toll-booths, I bet."

"Oh boy. I forgot about that."

"Super," Karen said.

At night, 495 is a dead, dull road. No lights or houses or human sign. A span of emptiness between turnpikes without even monotonous Howard Johnsons to break the monotony. Just dead, dark road and the odd sign now and then.

Caleb had Denny roll him a joint. The snowplow driver's relief was due to show at that frame office about now. Surprise.

Allow them ten–twenty minutes to get to a phone. Ten–twenty minutes for the police to get it together and fifteen minutes more before some trooper spotted their VW—the VW so carefully described by one of the tollbooth attendants.

"I wish we'd stuck to back roads," Denny said.

"We would have gotten lost," Caleb replied, mildly.

Half an hour later, just about the time that a toll collector was excitedly describing them to the New Hampshire

Highway Patrol (three freaks heading south on 495 in a black VW), said three freaks were boarding a crowded bus in Lowell, Mass.

Because the roads were so bad, the Greyhound was standing room only, and Caleb and Denny and Karen stood all the way to Boston. There seemed to be a lot of cop cars whizzing by them on the road.

Denny was pale, and despite his heavy jacket, he was shivering.

"You don't look so good," Caleb said. "You sick or something?"

"Yeah. Or something. Some kind of bug. I picked it up in that damn frozen storeroom."

Caleb grunted.

"Yeah, well maybe we'll stay with you for a day or so before we go south."

"OK by me."

They got off the bus in Boston, had a greasy breakfast, and an hour later they caught the New York bus.

Not so crowded. The three of them sat alone on the big back seat.

Denny stretched out across the seat with his head in Karen's lap, shivering and dozing. Caleb, against the window, watching the concrete go by and not feeling so hot himself. Tunnels. Concrete walls. Arches. Factory buildings and a glimpse of the Charles River, its blackness covered tonight by the snow. A strange, surreal beauty, but nothing warm.

Caleb lit a cigarette and put his feet up on the seat in front of them. After a while he said, "I'm sorry I got you involved in this."

Karen's voice from the dim profile beside him. "Yeah. So am I. But I guess there's no helping it now."

Outside of Boston. The engine of the old bus, roaring and clashing. The grey-white distances stretched away on both sides.

"Tell me what it's like, where we're going to stay," Karen said.

"Well," Caleb said, "I don't exactly know. When we get to the city, I'll see somebody and find out what I can. There's a loft on Twenty-ninth Street I can use if we can't get anything else."

"An artist's loft?"

"Naw. Just a big old room in a loft building. It's got a toilet, but it isn't fixed up any. The guy who has it is in California someplace, I think. I'm not real sure he's kept up on the rent, but if he has, I can get the keys."

"Do you like New York?"

"Yeah, sure. I guess so."

Caleb pulled out a joint and watched the driver's eyes in the big overhead mirror. Caleb shrugged and put the joint back in his pocket.

"You get stoned a lot," Karen said.

"Sure. It's an occupational hazard."

"I thought you guys were down on dope."

"What? Oh, the Weathermen? Oh yeah. They tried to ban drugs for a while. 'Drugs destroy the revolutionary consciousness.' Naturally, the kids stayed away in droves. No dope, no recruits. So the cadre decided that grass was alright after all." He laughed. "They decided that dope was good for you."

He shook his head. "Funny, funny, funny. All those stone-cold political heads sitting around puffing weed, do-ing their duty."

"You make them sound so serious," Karen demurred. "I always thought the Weathermen had a sense of humor."

"Yeah, maybe," Caleb said sourly. "Maybe I don't."

Caleb's affinity group had been formed in the frantic days before Weathermen went underground. His group was an afterthought, made up of people who'd made some of the actions, but not all of them, people who'd sometimes been there and sometimes hadn't. People like Caleb and

Sara who'd tried one of the communes and hadn't liked it much, but stayed in the movement anyway.

The Eleventh Street townhouse blew up, the Weathermen went underground, communications ceased between affinity groups, and Caleb's group fell apart.

It hadn't been much of a group to start with. Now, somebody was off in California. And somebody else had moved to the country. And Caleb was too busy dealing. And somebody else was too busy doing something else.

Originally, the group had six members. Of them all, only Jeff Svenigsun and Sara were unhappy at the turn of events.

Nobody even cared enough to dissolve the group formally.

The only political discussions they had, occurred when Jeff Svenigsun came over and argued that they ought to get back in touch, and Caleb argued that if the Weather Bureau wanted them, they could damn well call up.

Sara voted with Jeff, but did nothing more than vote.

The Weather Bureau was famous. Very big on the ten-most-wanted list. And a few of the other affinity groups within Weatherman had a few prominent members on post-office walls.

Caleb never hankered for a place of honor on a p.o. wall. He was quite content to lay back and forget the struggle.

Jeff upset things. Smart boy, Jeff. Jeff made a lot of phone calls and listened for what isn't said and did what none of America's cops could do: he located Weatherman.

One fine day, Caleb came home whistling. He rolled a joint, put on the "Joy of Cooking" and relaxed his mind:

> Daddy, all I ever did need
> was a good man's loving
> and a baby to feed.

The phone rang.

"Caleb, I've got good news," Sara said, too excited to

remember that Caleb wouldn't think it was so good. "Jeff Svenigsun made contact."

"Contact?"

"You know . . . with the people he was looking for."

"Oh. Good. Terrific."

"Anyway, there's something I've got to do."

"What? Blow up the Supreme Court?"

"This is a telephone, honey, remember."

"Oh balls," Caleb said.

"I just called to tell you I'd be gone for a while."

"How long?"

"I don't know."

"Don't come back," Caleb said, and hung up.

When it rang again, he picked up the phone.

"Caleb," she said, "I've got to talk to you."

"So, talk," he said.

"Not on the phone, dummy." Her voice softened. "Caleb, this is silly. Come up and talk to me."

"Alright. Alright." Rubbing his head. "Where?"

She muffled the phone, and Caleb heard disconnected underwater mutters at the other end. Loud voice when she came back.

"You know the Boondocks?"

"That bar across from Columbia? Sure."

"Meet you there in an hour."

"Half an hour. I'm too stoned to take the train."

Caleb had a little hit of cocaine and, elevated, got a taxi with no trouble.

They were sitting in a booth at the back of the bar; Sara and two men Caleb didn't know. He got himself a bottle of Heineken's and sat down with them.

Sara sitting next to a tall rangy young man. Balding, reddish hair and corduroy jacket. Looked like a graduate student worried about finishing his dissertation and two babies on too little money.

"I'm John," he said. "That's Willy." Spanish cat moodily nursing his beer.

Caleb flying on coke. "Always glad to meet a couple of co-revolutionaries," he said. "Can't be too many trying to topple the state."

Willy looked up from his beer and tapped him with his eyes.

John flashed a grin. Some people have a smile, some a laugh, but John had a grin. Bright, innocent, charming, honest, and twenty-four perfectly shaped tiny little teeth.

"You ever deal skag?" he asked.

"No," Caleb said.

John got off his grin, after holding it just a little too long, and hunched his elbows over his beer.

"When we first went underground, we lost touch with some of the affinity groups." He shrugged. "You know, there aren't any handbooks on 'Going Underground in Amerika.' "

"You could write one now," Sara said.

John gave her just a taste of that grin. "Yes, Sara," he said, "I expect we could."

Willy looked up from his beer. "You're funny," he said.

"Chinga tu madre," John said, pleasantly.

Willy shrugged and went back to his beer.

"We can't afford to lose people," John said. "We're not the United States Pig Army."

"Yeah. OK," Caleb said. "Jeff got in touch with you?"

"Uh-huh. There's something we need for you to do."

"The affinity group?"

"Uh-huh. Jeff says that the group is pretty much disintegrated. He said that he and Sara are the only ones who give a damn about changing this murderous government."

Caleb thought. "The boy's got a point there," he said.

"He also said that you were stoned out of your brains most of the time, and that he wouldn't trust you to take a ball bearing across to New Jersey."

"So that's what he said." Caleb waited a moment before he took a sip of beer. "Sara, let's split."

Caleb got up.

John shook his head, rueful, and settled a little deeper

into his corduroy jacket. "Some male chauvinist pig," talking to Sara. "Little lady, it's time for you to go home."

"I am staying," Sara said, quietly.

Caleb grunted and sat down again.

"What do you want?" he said.

"From you nothing. I just thought it would be a kindness to let you know what's going on so that you wouldn't get worried while you're stoned. The affinity group is merging with my group. Don't try to call Svenigsun, and it's been nice knowing you."

"I'll be out of town for a week," Sara said.

Caleb went up to the bar and bought another beer. He bought one for the Spanish dude who didn't bother to notice.

"Alright," he said. "What's happening?" And Willy smiled at him then.

"You're very curious," John said.

"Yeah, I'm very curious."

John shrugged and raised his mug in the air to signal a waiter. "I hear they've got a warrant for you in Detroit. Dope."

"Funny, I've heard that, too," Caleb said.

"You grow up in Grosse Pointe?"

"No."

John drank his beer, his adam's apple bobbing. "That's too bad. Some of our best people were raised in Grosse Pointe. 'Overcompensation' the *Times* calls it."

"Yeah," Caleb said. "They're always saying something like that."

"It doesn't matter where you're brought up," Sara said.

Willy burped.

"Are you stoned?" John asked Caleb.

"Sure."

"On what? I don't mean to pry, but I'm curious too."

"A little grass. A little coke."

"Ah. Cocaine makes me feel very powerful. Does it have that effect on you?"

"You're at the limit, John."

John sighed. "Perhaps so." Another gulp of beer. "It's a simple equation. Underground, we can't get contributions or hold jobs, and we need money. Banks have money. You need people to rob banks. I understand you did some stock-car racing once."

"Christ. That was years ago!"

"It isn't the sort of skill you forget."

Caleb lit a cigarette and dropped the match in the puddle of beer on the table top.

"OK," he said.

John reached over and squeezed his hand. Caleb noticed that John's hand was cold. Poor circulation.

"Wait a minute," Sara said.

"Go home, Sara," Caleb said. "I'll see you in a while."

Sara hit her fist on the table. "Listen, you male-chauvinist-pig bastards," she began.

"You listen," John snapped. "The Weather Bureau is one half men and one half women. It wants this. And you can't have a participatory democracy when you're at war."

Sara was too furious to talk. She made sounds from her mouth; but her rage was overrunning her syllables, and she rose up and turned and rock-ass walked out.

"This is silly," John said. He slapped his head. "Man, I'm such a dope." He stood up. "Wait for me." And he followed her.

Willy got up and brought two more beers back to the table.

"We only got three days to practice," Willy said.

The beer tasted flat.

"Is John wanted?" Caleb asked.

"Not yet. We been lucky so far. I think pretty soon. He knows a lot of people on the Weather Bureau."

"Terrific," Caleb said.

"I don't think he likes you," Willy said.

"I'm afraid he probably does," Caleb replied.

He could hardly remember Willy now. When he tried to picture him, he got a picture of Willy's torn, bright red throat and that picture he didn't need just now.

Caleb stared at the cold outside the bus, working to forget.

Bus moving through the snow toward the morning, white arc lights flanking the interstate. One parking lot after another, rising and falling with the roll of the land underneath.

Denny stirred in his sleep and Karen brushed the hair back on his forehead. "Hush," she said, quietly. "Hush now."

Caleb watched her face and wished there was enough light to see her eyes. Rustle of her body inside her clothing. She'd been locked up for a week and Caleb could smell her history. Soft smell and bitter sweat and the bottom of her, so near to the surface in her slow weariness, he could smell that, too. Right now, with most things gone, she was what she pretended to be.

"You have an old lady?" she asked.

"Uh-huh."

"You don't say much about yourself," she said.

"I don't like to talk," he said.

"What's she like?" Karen asked, quiet.

"Sara? Well, she's twenty. And she's political. And she's got a nice ass."

"Do you love her?"

He fired up a cigarette. "Sure," he said.

"Does she love you?"

Caleb turned to her face and wondered why she was asking.

"Beats me."

"Oh," Karen said. After a moment, she asked again softly, "Caleb, what's she like?"

Caleb laughed. "She's like General Giap," he said. "She's General Giap's double. At the Boston commune, there was this old tabby cat, General Giap. And she was this yellow and orange and black cat—and she'd Been There. Man, nobody messed with General Giap. Not other cats or dogs or people. When she got pissed, she'd bristle up to double size and stretch out her claws and stroll over to you, and you knew you were in for it." He paused. "I don't know if Sara loves anybody," he said.

He tapped on the window of the bus with his nails.

"That's New Haven," he said. "Junkie capitol of New England."

He crossed his legs and lit another cigarette. "I lived in New Haven once, with a couple of friends. It's hard not to get strung out there. The mafia brings a lot of junk through there, and it's a horrible place to live. Both dudes I was living with picked up habits, and I got real scared and split."

"Did you ever do junk?" Karen asked.

Caleb shrugged. "I've snorted it a couple times. But I decided a long time ago to draw the line at needles. I hate the goddamned things."

Karen shivered. "I can't understand people doing stuff that's going to really mess them up."

"Yeah, maybe. You ever do coke?"

"Not too often. I liked it though."

"So do I. But you can really get screwed up back of coke, too. I don't know. Maybe it's just a trade."

Slow talk, winding down, growing silent as the bus blasted through the shadowless light of false dawn.

The city. Before the bus hit One Hundred twenty-fifth Street, Caleb was paranoid again. Narrow dirty streets, garbage, and steel gates across the liquor stores.

"Karen," he said, "I think we better get off. The cops might be watching the Port Authority."

"Oh man. . ." she said.

"It isn't worth taking the chance."

"Oh hell."

So she woke Denny up and the three of them stumbled to the front of the bus.

The bus coming down Amsterdam in the Nineties. Wider streets, a little, and a few ancient rich people's apartment houses, standing out like politics in stone.

"Let us off at the next light," Caleb said.

Old bus driver. Hunched over the wheel and stared straight ahead.

"Can't," he said. "Against regulations."

"Oh come on, man. It wouldn't cost you a second and we live up here and why should we pay five bucks for a cab?"

The bus driver warmed to the subject and looked them over. "Listen," he said, "what if I was to make exceptions? Pretty soon everybody would be wanting to get off. And then, some of them would be asking me to drive them home: 'It's only a block out of the way.' Me driving up and down looking for street addresses, with eighty-seven other passengers who want to get where they're going. Can't do it."

Karen smiled at him shyly. "If you don't let us out, I'm going to take all my clothes off and then my old man will take his clothes off and we'll all have a good time, right here on your bus." She unbuckled the buckle on her belt.

At the next light, he let them out. "Goddamned perverts!" he yelled, as the door hissed shut.

Three refugees, they stood there watching the pigeon herds trying to dig yesterday's bread crumbs out of the snow.

5 / *The Fur District*

P.J. Black was a likable, ordinary man, mildly sociable, fastidious, with regular habits. P.J. dealt a lot of cocaine. He dealt a lot more hash.

He was a specialist and, perhaps, a bit of a snob. P.J. claimed that his selectivity was personal preference alone: "I don't do nothing but coke and hash. Why should I sell anything but coke and hash?"

But everyone was selling grass. Even in Queens.

And the dudes who sold scag (though very often highly stylized) were stylized grease. Like a day old hamburger with graceful moves.

And the lads who dealt pills were too religious for P.J.'s taste: either Tim Leary god trips or cynical great sinners. P.J. did not consider himself a religious man.

P.J. was a snob; there were certain types of people he didn't want to be taken for. But even in his snobbery, he was never graceless or demanding.

He was a man who valued order. And though he didn't aspire to order other people's lives, neither did he allow others to order his.

His loft was his cave, his place of privacy, his stand against the hurly-burly of the city.

He'd spent a lot of money on the loft, rebuilding it, installing a kitchen and bath, furnishing it with a mixture of stark modern furniture and plumped old couches.

On the advice of an artist friend, he'd purchased four contemporary paintings which had appealed to him, and which were already appreciating in value.

He wouldn't have bought the paintings if they hadn't pleased him. Nor would he have kept them if they hadn't increased their worth.

P.J. lived most of his life in his loft. Except for business, he rarely ventured out, and when he did go out, it was as a guerrilla behind enemy lines.

Perhaps twice a week he would have to do a little business. He would become brave. He would become resigned to it. He would accept his fate.

He'd spend the afternoon smoking hash, with J.J. Kale on his headphones.

Normally, the local deli brought him a vegetable or fish platter every day at six o'clock, but today he'd eat nothing for dinner.

He'd sit in silence until eight. Then, he'd snort a whole bunch of cocaine and old Chicago blues wailing through his headphones.

About midnight, he'd start drinking pernod and smoking hash again. Listening to Bob Dylan.

At 2:30 A.M., P.J. Black would take a pinch of his purest cocaine to his left nostril and quite elegant, Oxfordian, in his green British suit, grey waistcoat, and ebony walking stick, he'd dare the streets of New York.

A regular man, with unvarying habits.

He'd get down to the Village about three. An hour before the bars closed. The hour when rival suitors were awaiting the decision of the pretty little girls who came down to the Village to get laid. Often, P.J., fresh, startling, unrumpled, would interrupt the final round of these drunken decisions and have a girl to accompany him for the rest of the night and the morning. If not, P.J. was scarcely perturbed.

He usually carried four ounces of coke and perhaps a half pound of hash. He only dealt at the Great Auk, Pearl's, and the Leather House.

The Great Auk was a modest, run-of-the-mill dopers' bar. Pearl's was a bar for stylish middle-class blacks making a lot of money as photographers, advertising men, or TV execs. And the Leather House was a gay bar. P.J. balled men from time to time; but he wasn't gay, and the bouncer at the door only let him in as a special concession to the bar's clientele.

He only dealt with people he knew, and he was affable enough to keep his circle roughly constant in number, though continually shifting in membership.

He usually dealt for cash, but was very slightly flexible when necessary. He was, as has been said before, not religious.

From his business he made, on rough average, five hundred dollars a week. And was content.

P.J. was wanted somewhere, possibly California, but he was not wanted badly and a little extra caution was his only response to the routine legal efforts expended on his behalf by authorities two thousand miles away.

Police payoffs were about 50 percent of his protection.

His brother was the other 50 percent.

The precinct cost him two hundred dollars a month, plus the tacit understanding that he wouldn't deal scag.

His brother, Roy, was some kind of O.E.O. head-table black. Roy didn't have much pull, but he had a lot of names and lots of advance information.

Knowledge is protection in the city.

When the bars closed, P.J. stopped at a couple of after-hours joints.

When he'd had his last glass of wine and concluded his last deal, he'd stroll, still elegant, through the sleepy awakening Village and watch the uptown workers running to catch their trains.

He'd have breakfast at the Cockatoo, a soul-food restaurant on the West Side. Easy, slow breakfast, reading the *Times*.

Caleb slid onto the stool next to him and ordered bacon, eggs and grits.

"How you doin', man?" P.J. said. "I haven't seen you in a while." He flicked his eyes over Denny and Karen and dismissed them from consideration.

"Yeah," Caleb said, "I been out of town."

"L.A.?"

"No."

"Montreal?"

"No."

"Honey, would you bring me a spoon?" P.J. talking to the 250-pound black waitress. "I need sugar in my coffee so it'll be as sweet as me."

The waitress gave him a gold-toothed grin when she handed him the spoon, wondering if P.J. was a pimp.

Caleb went over to the phone booth and dialed his apartment. Fourteen rings and nothing, so he hung up. No Sara.

The coffee here was chicory coffee, and Caleb liked it, although it always upset his stomach.

"Anybody been asking for me?" he asked.

P.J. picked his teeth. "Well, Mike at the Great Auk was asking about you a couple of days ago. It seems you owe him some money. How come you never pay your bills?"

"Still running your old bourgeois jive?"

"My man, I am respectable. I value those little tokens of respect I've acquired through honest labor and the general charm of my personality. Cleanliness, too. Personal cleanliness."

He sniffed. "You been staying in some pretty rank Holiday Inns, Caleb."

"Yeah. I could use a shower."

"Caleb you have a knack for understatement."

Caleb sniffed his armpit loudly and drew in a heavy sniff. "If you were a girl, P.J., you'd be so overpowered by my glands that we'd be on our way to bed right now."

P.J. sighed. "Caleb, if I was a girl, I'd be on the train from Harlem to Seventh Avenue right now, just like my sister. And if I was here, pretty little thing, and ever got a whiff of you, I'd move two or three stools down this counter and whisper to the waitress."

"I didn't know you had a sister."

"Oh sure."

"Is she a good lay?"

"Caleb, all my family got those sweet little machines. And all my family know how to use them. One of these days I'll take you to bed and show you all about it."

"I don't dig men."

"Caleb, you're so sweet and naif. It'd be such a pleasure educating you."

"I'll bet. Have you seen Sara around?"

"No. No, I did see her about a week ago, two weeks. . . Naw, last time I saw her was the last time I saw you. Jesus." He paused. "What the hell happened to your hand?"

Caleb put his hand in his pocket. "It had an accident. You still got the keys to Slow Richard's loft?"

"Uh-huh. You gonna stay there?"

"I guess. Oh, these two people are my friends." P.J. nods to Karen, who's eating heavy, and Denny, who's nodding out, weaving on the stool. "But you never met them," Caleb said.

"OK," P.J. said. "You hot?"

Caleb touched his coffee cup and pulled back his finger jerky, quick, as if burnt.

"Oh, oh, oh," P.J. said. Last week he'd heard about a shipment of fine cocaine brought in by this Cuban dude. P.J. had thought that maybe Caleb and he could split a quarter. He stopped thinking that way.

"Do you know if Slow Richard's been paying the rent on that place?" Caleb asked.

"Do I consort with landlords? Am I a gypsy? Do I have occult powers?"

"No, but you're so sweet it's a wonder you don't get elected mayor. Of Boogaloo, maybe. Lemme have the keys."

P.J. carefully extracted two keys from his Morocco key case and handed them over.

"You need anything?" he asked.

Caleb thought. "No, I'm OK. Do you know where I can cop some tetracyclin?"

P.J. shrugged. "Well, there isn't a real big demand for that sort of merchandise, you know. Not too many people deal antibiotics. I suppose you could try Margaret. She's still working at Bellevue nights."

"You got her number?"

So Caleb wrote down the number and paid their check and left a twenty percent tip, since they were back in New York.

He picked up a *Times,* but the doings in Maine had missed the early edition.

Slow Richard's loft was a 80-by-100-foot shoebox, with a row of windows at one end, a row of heavy rusty iron shutters at the other end, and a door somewhere in the middle. A closet-sized john with old wooden box pullchain toilet, a couple of mattresses on the floor, and the usual ghosts of the Jewish seamstresses who'd given up their lives in that room years ago.

"Home sweet home," Caleb said.

"Welcome to New York," Denny said. "I'm going to crash."

It was pretty cold. Caleb felt the radiators. No heat. Karen draped her coat over Denny's shivering shoulders.

She sat down beside her old man on an historic mattress. Goosebumps on her arms. "Man, this is not going to be possible," she said. "It was warmer in Maine."

"It's colder in jail," Caleb said.

He drew the gun and put it on the floor.

"Man, those damned guns are a drag. Rubbed my back raw. Look, I got to call my old lady and a couple other folks. I'll stop on the way back and get you guys some blankets."

He bopped on down the stairs, a little giddy in his stride, and found a working pay-phone outside the Chock Full O' Nuts on Seventh Avenue.

He dialed a number and lit a cigarette while the phone was ringing. It rang maybe twenty times before the phone popped off the hook and hung up. He dropped another dime, and the phone jangled a long time before he got an answer.

"What?" A croak from the other end of the line.

"Long Jim, this is Caleb. . ."

"Oh man, you off your head? This is really outrageous. . . What time is it?"

"About nine o'clock. Look man, don't hang up."

"Alright, what'd you want?"

"Have you seen Sara?"

"Sara? Sara who?"

"My old lady Sara. Caleb's Sara. The Political Sara."

"Uhhh, yeah, last week."

"Did she say anything? Was she with anybody?"

"Oh man, I can't remember that crap. I only got to bed two hours ago. Now, goodnight."

"Jim, don't hang up. I just got back from out of town and I want to find her, that's all."

"Yeah, uh, she, huh. . . Man, I don't remember. She left a letter or something for you at the bar."

"Oh. Thanks. Man, I'm sorry I. . ."

"Up yours." And Long Jim hung up.

Caleb dialed Margaret's number, but no answer.

Caleb walked uptown through the fur district. Cadillacs double-parked; black men schlepping tall iron-pipe racks of fur coats; dead mink and muskrat in the little shop windows; and some small mimeographed posters which warned the little Jewish furriers that their livelihood was threatened by ecology zealots who were doubtless not aware, in their concern for the hair seal, leopard, and ocelot, that Jewish furriers had families of nice people who had to eat.

Caleb bought himself a pair of blue jeans, a lightweight green shirt, and six blankets at Macy's for $38.50.

The morning rush was over, the cabs were heading back downtown, and Caleb caught one easily, despite the three long bulky boxes he had in his arms.

"Where to?" the driver asked, hoping maybe Brooklyn.

"Twenty-ninth and Seventh Avenue," Caleb said.

The driver said something under his breath, but took him the four blocks to the loft.

Caleb gave him a buck to ease his feelings and hauled the blankets up the stairs. The heavy, awkward load left him panting and feeling the strain of the last twenty-four hours.

Denny was sound asleep. Mouth open. Flushed face. Baby snore.

"Did you get ahold of Sara?" Karen asked.

"Naw. I'm going to get Denny some medicine."

"You'd better be careful," she said. "The police have had a week to find out where you live."

"I never did have trouble being careful," Caleb said. "Besides, unless Chris talked, they don't know who I am."

"They took fingerprints at our house after they busted us."

"Well, that may give them a name, but it sure as hell ain't gonna give them no home address and zip code."

"Be careful," she said. "There's a lot of them."

"Sure. Look, if you want something to eat, there's a not bad deli down the street. The Jewish one; the Puerto Rican one is horrible."

He transferred some more cash from the money belt to his pockets and thought about taking the gun.

But his back was raw and Caleb was tired of playing cowboy. Besides, New York was usually safe enough in the morning. The rip-off artists slept late.

Downtown, Caleb had a second breakfast at Goldy's:

small, neat, slightly precious bagel shop on Christopher Street. Good breakfast, but expensive, and the portions a little on the skinny side.

The Village was sunny and cold. Soft midweek day. Not too many people on the street.

The commuters were uptown collecting ulcers, and the tourists were sleeping it off somewhere. Old Italian ladies pushing their beat-up, stolen shopping carts. Young, well-dressed girl-mothers, long hair bobbing over eighty-dollar dungaree jackets from Bergdorf's, marching their polite kids to play-group. The usual collection of black panhandlers and white-kid junkies hanging out in Sheridan Square.

Caleb paid a quarter toll to an old "God Bless You" wino and the other panhandlers let him alone.

For once, the air wasn't choked with gas and cinders. And a thin, shy, pale-blue light washed the sidewalks and shadowed the orange-drink cartons and cigarette butts in the gutters.

The light made Caleb feel free. He didn't think the cops knew his real name; they'd be looking for him in Detroit. He hadn't mentioned the Great Auk to any of the Weathermen.

And it was a good place for him to get a drink.

The Auk was a good West Side bar. Not a good-looker. Two rooms, end-to-end, in the basement of a brownstone. One window at the front which gave the Auk's regular patrons an unusual knowledge of shoe-and-sock fashions.

A long bar, a big jukebox, four tiny tables in the rear.

The two rooms had been painted stucco yellow by somebody's cousin four or five years ago. Pretty grimy now, but none of the regulars complained. The grime discouraged the out-of-town drunks.

A good bar. Old, and that's good because John Barleycorn ain't no whippersnapper and will not strut his stuff in any punk place.

The only similarities the Great Auk had with the bird of

the same name were a print of the bird over the back bar and the undeniable fact that, like its namesake, the Great Auk couldn't fly.

Rusty, who usually worked nights, was tending bar.

He and Caleb nodded to each other.

Couple of old Italian geezers sitting at the end of the bar, drinking beer.

"Gimme a rum and coke."

Rusty brought the drink and put his foot up on the sink behind the bar.

"You working mornings now?" Caleb asked.

Rusty is maybe twenty-five with a face somewhat the worse for wear. "Yeah. That son-of-a-bitch Michael."

"Anybody been asking about me?" Caleb asked.

Rusty had been ready to launch his story. "...Uh, you? No. Except Michael," he brightened. "He wants you to cover your tab."

Caleb sighed. "Man, I always pay my bar bills."

"Yeah, well, this is an old one and Michael said to put a two-hundred-dollar limit on you."

Rusty leaned over the bar and giggled. "He don't want to get burnt too bad when they take you away."

"Oh yeah. OK." Caleb laid a couple of hundreds on the bar. "Pay the man."

"It's too early man; I can't break those."

"OK," Caleb said. "I'll see Michael later." And stuffed the bills back in his pocket. Took a sip of rum.

"Uh, well, OK, man. I guess it'll be alright." He moved his head closer, confidential-like. "Michael said not to serve you unless you paid."

Caleb put the two hundreds back on the bar.

"I said OK." Rusty is annoyed. "But do me a favor and see Michael soon, OK?"

Caleb put the two bills back into his pocket.

"You got a letter for me back there?"

Rusty rummaged around behind the cash register, tossed a small envelope on the bar.

"Please hold for Caleb Smith" on the front in neat green ink.

Caleb finished his drink and rapped the bar with his glass for a refill.

"Dearest Caleb, I've been saved."

"Oh boy," Caleb said, under his breath.

"And it's the most amazing and beautiful thing that ever happened to me. I know you're going to be hurt and surprised, and I'm truly sorry for that. I wouldn't hurt you for the world!

"Last Tuesday, I was depressed because you were gone, and confused about my own life. Caleb, I was really down! Please listen to me, Caleb. Don't get all distant and vague! And if you're drunk and stoned, put this letter away and read it tomorrow. You mean a lot to me!

"I was standing down on the Morton Street pier, really low and unhappy. And this beautiful freak came over and talked to me. He had the most amazing childlike face I've ever seen. Caleb, he told me about Jesus.

"Now you know what I used to be. I never would have listened! But politics are wrong, Caleb. We've been hurting people! Love is the only way to make people change! God gave me grace on that day, and I listened. And Caleb, I believed!

"No, I didn't ball him. You don't have to be jealous. Jesus's love filled me up.

"Caleb I've been so unhappy.

"We prayed together on the pier and later we prayed in your apartment. (It never was Our apartment, you know.)

"I've been doing wrong, Caleb, and still I'm forgiven!

"But I can't go on the way we were. Dope is just a tiny, tiny high. Jesus is the greatest high there is!

"That's why I've moved out. Not to run away from you, but because it isn't right what we were doing.

"I love you, Caleb. Truly I do. I love you in Jesus.

"I want to see you again, very much.

"I've gone to Graniteville, Mass. The boy I talked to,

David Rollins, is part of a Christian commune up there, and I'm going to live there.

"Please come and see me. We can work it out.

"I would have stayed and talked to you face-to-face; but we would just have had a bitter argument, and this way you can have time to think about it before you come and see me.

"Love, Sara"

Rusty had been leaning over the bar watching Caleb read. "Bad news?" he asked.

Caleb crumpled up the letter and tossed it in the trash barrel under the bar.

"No," he said. "Not particularly. You still doin' scag?"

Rusty smiled softly. "You know how it is."

"Yeah, sure I do. Why don't you bring us a couple of hits."

Rusty poured Caleb another rum and made himself a martini.

"So why you working days?" Caleb asked.

"Man, that hardnose Michael. Every time he has a slow month, he thinks the world is coming to an end. Last Sunday he figures it all out and his percentage is not so good. Too many free drinks or somebody's stealin'. Christ," Rusty spat into the sink, "everybody's stealin'. He knows that. But nobody taking too much. He can afford it. We bring in a lot of trade to this joint. So he says it's me and puts me on days." Rusty ate the martini olive. "Screw him," he said. "I learned electronics in the army. Emilio is always after me to tap some phones for him." Rusty brightened. "Last time he was in here he wanted me to put a tap on this dude's phone. Seventy-five dollars for half an hour's work. I ought to do it. Screw Michael."

At two o'clock, Long Jim came in, and Rusty left to score himself some scag.

"You don't look so good," Long Jim said.

"Thanks, Jim."

"No, I don't mean to put you down or anything. But you

look like Spiro Agnew's bowels this afternoon. It's a nice afternoon too."

He poured Caleb another rum. "Do you mind if I turn on the TV? The Knicks have got a game."

"Yeah, Jim, I mind. Basketball is boring. Really boring."

He turned on the TV. "The trouble with you Caleb, is that you take everything too seriously. That's why you look like Spiro Agnew's bowels. You should learn to enjoy life more so you can fulfill your type and be a nice middle-class kid from the Midwest, who is going to go home to daddy when he grows up."

"Jim, why are you so rotten all the time?"

"I'm not rotten, Caleb. Being rotten isn't in my nature. Like Joey down there. It's his nature to come in here looking to hustle five bucks so he can blow his brains out. And it's your nature to live in the Midwest and sell cars. But my nature just demands that I comment on these and other aberrations of the human psyche whenever I come across them. I can't help myself any more than you and Joey can."

Jim watched the game for a minute, washing glasses.

"I also admit to some resentment towards you, Caleb. I used to think you were alright, but I was wrong about you and I'm not too proud to admit it. Anyone who phones me at nine o'clock in the morning isn't alright. He's no good, Caleb."

"I'm sorry, Jim. You got any speed?"

"Me, naw. Joey's probably got some though."

Caleb walks down to Joey who is hanging on the end of the bar, peering bug-eyed at his beer, and it turns out that, indeed, Joey has some methedrine which he swears is OK, and Caleb buys a nickel's worth.

He takes the small envelope into the women's john, locks the door, snorts, and finds out that the speed is OK, but not spectacular.

The weariness is gone. Flash.

"Lemme buy you a beer, Jim."

"Naw. If you don't want to watch the ball game, I don't want any of your booze. Besides, I get all my drinks free. Just leave it for me in the tip cup."

The speed straightened Caleb out. Halfway.

His head was clear and clean. Only his body betrayed him. Like a liner plowing through the China Sea in a typhoon, the captain bright-eyed and articulate, but the bridge-to-engine-room telephone broken, hopelessly.

The bar filled up, and Long Jim was performing an intricate Punch and Judy show behind his rostrum. He stopped his rap-show once to ask Caleb about his missing fingers, and Caleb said never mind; so Jim said the stumps looked horrible.

He leaned over close to Caleb's ear. "But I don't mind your horrible fingers, Caleb," he said and nonstop changed the subject.

"That kid from New Jersey was in the other night," he said. "And Izzy was down in his movie mogul outfit."

"Looking for me?" Caleb asked. "Has anybody else been looking for me?"

"Naw. Oh, some friend of Sara's was in here a couple of days ago."

"Who?"

"Tall, skinny cat. Red hair and balding. Snotty bastard."

"John."

"Yeah, that was his name. He was wondering if you'd been around."

"He's too sure about a lot of things. You know, Long Jim, it's easy to be too sure about a lot of things."

Jim sipped his Southern Comfort. "One of the nice things about speed freaks," he said, "is the way they lay their insights on you. Very exciting."

"Let me have another rum and coke, and put some rum in it this time."

Margaret Kelly came in with her new old man on her arm. She was a tall nurse lady who looked a little like Greta

Garbo. Her old man was a fattish, modish dude who looked like Margaret had made another mistake. "Hi Caleb," she said. "Jim, bring me a Bloody Mary."

"Margaret," Caleb said, "I need some antibiotics. Tetracyclin, maybe."

"You goin' into medicine?" she said.

"Naw. I got a sick friend."

"Are you going to deal them?" she asked, suspicious. (Greta Garbo squinting at you.) "I didn't know there were any tetracylin freaks."

Her old man spoke for the first time. "Hi," he said to Caleb, "I'm Jay Sokoloff. You know, you can get a lot of trouble stealing pills."

Caleb grunted and ignored him. "Really Margaret," he said. "Sick friend. Really."

"Well OK," she said. "I work tonight and I'll get you something."

"Bring a lot," Caleb said. "he's miserable to be around when he ain't feeling good. And he ain't feeling good."

"Won't it be dangerous?" Jay asked. He had an afternoon *Post* folded in front of him, and Caleb was trying to read the headlines.

Part friendly and part p.o.'d, Margaret patted Jay's fat hand. "Jay, save your advice for the writing where you get paid for it."

"Could I see your newspaper?" Caleb asked.

Jay gave him the paper and tried to touch Margaret with his glance, but she didn't care for him much, after all.

"Caleb," she said, "you been working in the sewers? You really smell bad."

"You should start smoking," he answered. "Smoking deadens the sense of smell."

Caleb found the picture on page three. Big photo of Karen and Denny and the Sheriff and the FBI cat.

Karen was crying and Denny, caught in the moment, was blank-faced, himself having gone away to Plonz.

The snow was grainy across their faces and it filled the

background with blurs. Caleb peered hard at the photograph, and he and his methedrine decided that Karen and Denny could not be recognized from any photograph so blurred, vague, and out-of-focus.

"Weathermen Escape." A blunt, unimaginative headline.

He read the article word by word. He reread it, sentence by sentence.

He found no mention of the name "Caleb Smith." He found no mention of his Detroit name. He found no mention of the name he'd given the Indian woman in Maine.

"Two gunmen stopped the sheriff's car. . ."

Caleb wasn't sure. With all that booze and speed in him, he might be hallucinating. He handed the paper to Long Jim.

"Long Jim," he said, "Do you see something weird about this?"

Long Jim leaned against the back bar and looked at the newspaper. Caleb watched his eyes. Steadily, they tracked across the page. They didn't freeze. Jim didn't grunt with recognition.

Jim put the paper down on the bar. "Sure it's weird," he said. "We live in troubled times."

"Yeah," Caleb said. "Uh, what did you think about the escape?"

Jim was annoyed. "I think you did too much speed," he said. "I think you should go home instead of bothering me with lame questions."

"Don't, Jim."

Long Jim stood back and asked, "What's wrong?"

Caleb wanted to tell him but the speed was standing in his paranoia like a guard with a shotgun.

He shook his head. "The escape, Jim?" he asked.

"OK, OK." He considered. "I'm glad they got away." He brightened. "It wasn't a very classy escape. It lacked finesse. That other dude. Now that was an escape."

"What other dude?"

Jim gave him a grin, "Man, you have been out of town. There was a Christopher Huptman who robbed a bank in Maine. Part of this same bunch. He got away from two G-men. They were taking him somewhere, and he grabbed the steering wheel and wrecked the car. I guess he's still running."

"Christopher? Are you sure?"

Long Jim was hurt. "Caleb, why don't you go home?" He sighed. Then he rang the tip bell hanging on the back bar.

"Got to prime the pump," he explained to Jay Sokoloff. "Bunch of cheap mothers in here this afternoon."

More people in the Auk and Jim had the jukebox bellowing, and Caleb drank a little more and couldn't think.

P.J. tapped him on the shoulder.

"What's this, P.J.? Man, it isn't even dark yet."

"The essence of regularity, Caleb, is knowing when to ignore it." He picked up the *Post* from the bar and pointed it at Caleb's face.

"Oh," Caleb said. "Oh, that."

P.J. ordered a Pernod with a water back.

He drank and made a face. "Terrible stuff," he said. He took a small glassine envelope from his jacket pocket and handed it to Caleb. Cocaine. "You'll need it, P.J. said.

"Thanks, P.J. We ought to do a deal again sometime," Caleb said.

P.J. smiled. "I should get involved with Pretty Boy Floyd? Caleb, we black folks got to be stealthy."

"I wasn't in the paper."

"I noticed. For whatever that means. Those friends of yours are big news though."

"No," Caleb said. "Nobody could recognize them from that picture. I'm sure."

"Keep smiling," P.J. said.

And the speed and booze and tired rose up in Caleb and broke his will.

He blacked out for a second.

Caught himself.

Said, "Going home."

Somehow, with his slyness pushing his legs to the street and a cab. He said, "Sara, bitch," once in the cab, and the cab driver turned around, looked at his face, and drove a little faster so Caleb wouldn't puke all over his cab.

Karen opened the loft door.

"I couldn't get your medicine," he said, and fell down.

It got late. The fur workers went home. It got dark.

Their building was empty except for the dust. And the ghosts of dead wolverines prowling the lofts, silent.

Odd smoky light, neither brown nor white nor grey, but an inconstant blending of the three, came pouring through the three 12-foot windows illuminating half the loft and abandoning the other half to whatever wanted it.

Karen sitting quiet and staring at the silent building across the street.

For hours she sat there, under the light which makes New York toss in its sleep. Sounds from the street below. A siren somewhere. The backfire of a big semi carrying something late, on its way to somewhere later.

Caleb snored and woke up enough to throw up three or four times.

Denny tossed in his sleep.

She was waiting for whatever comes next. Simply waiting. Wondering if she had the strength and her hopes slipping downward like leaves tumbling, drowning in the night mouth of the City.

She wasn't lonely. Other women have waited as she waited, and there were no terrors in it. The payment is the fact, and it's due and no more to fear. Honey, they're men.

Eleven o'clock the next morning she caught Caleb awake enough from puking to talk.

"Caleb," she asked, "what about the medicine?"

"Oh," Caleb said. And puked again.

"Caleb," she said, "I sent Denny down to the drugstore,

but all he can get is aspirin and he still has a fever."

"Oh, uh." Caleb said, and rolled flat on his stomach.

"Caleb, please. . . It's important."

Caleb fumbled through his pocket and found Margaret's phone number. "Ask her," he said.

So Karen went downstairs and phoned Margaret, and it turned out that Margaret had left the tetracyclin with Long Jim and wondered who Karen was.

Karen got Long Jim's number from Caleb, but nobody answered.

She bought a sponge mop at one of those nothing-more-than-$1.99 stores for $1.99 and carried it upstairs with her.

Caleb had the coke out, and he and Denny were getting stoned. Hands shaking, not one sober muscle between them, scattering the fine white powder, trying to snort it up.

Karen went downstairs and cried as she pushed through the ordinary folks, the fur workers bustling along the sidewalk.

She sat in a little Puerto Rican deli and had a white turkey on white with lettuce and mayo and a cup of Lipton tea.

But she did go back to the loft, after all, and sat there, listening to the two of them. The coke had eased Denny's fever and solved Caleb's hangover, and they were starting to tell stories and make promises again.

"I don't feel like I need that medicine now," Denny said. "But I'd like to see this Auk place you talk about. I'll go with you, I guess."

"Denny!" Karen was hurt, angry, surprised.

"Cocaine," he answered, "runnin' 'round my brain."

"I ain't sure you should go out," Caleb said.

Denny put on one of his tried-and-true charming expressions. "You said they couldn't recognize us from that picture," he said.

"Yeah, sure, but. . ."

"You said that nobody at the Auk would turn us in."

"I just don't want to be responsible for your getting hurt, man. There's a lot of stuff going on."

"You don't have to worry about me. Coming, Karen?"

Karen wanted to cry again, but figured it wasn't any use and that sooner or later she'd get Denny somewhere safe, and in the meantime, all she could do was hang on, anyway.

"OK," she said, "OK."

Denny picked up the FBI man's magnum and stuffed it under his jacket. When Caleb raised a curious eyebrow, Denny explained, "Muggers." Some explanation.

So they had dinner at Felline's on Thompson Street and a little after 8, full of pasta and easier at heart, they came to the Auk.

Michael McCarthy was an ex-marine from Pittsburg, who'd bought the Great Auk five years ago in hopes of making a living and a bohemian reputation. He thought he'd get laid a lot. He did. After five years, Michael McCarthy was sadder but wiser.

He and Long Jim were behind the bar. Long Jim jerked his head around to watch them come in, angry about something. Michael was adding up the register and tossed Caleb an indifferent wave.

Long Jim came down the bar, looked Caleb dead in the eyes, and said, "Go away. You crazy bastard. Get out of here."

Caleb thought he was covered tonight. Or, the cocaine was whispering to him. "Don't worry, Long Jim," he said.

Michael called Long Jim back to the calculations and Long Jim, after some hesitation, went. Michael called to Caleb, "Where's Sara?"

"Out of town."

"I wish I was out of town. I'm going to down to Bermuda on a charter flight." He came around the bar and sat next to Caleb. "I presume you'd like to help me finance my trip to sunnier climes."

"Sure," Caleb said. "How much?"

"Why don't we make it a deuce?"

"Sure." Caleb tossed two hundred-dollar bills on the bar.

"Jim," Michael said, "bring them a drink."

Long Jim brought three beers, and Caleb said, "Since Michael's buying, make mine a Remy." And Long Jim took one of the beers back and delivered the cognac.

"You ever been to France?" Michael asked.

"No," Caleb said. "I was in Montreal once, though."

"Real French cognac like you can get in the wine districts in France. . ." Michael smacked his lips.

Long Jim handed Caleb a lumpy envelope. "Margaret left it here for you," he said. Flat dead voice.

"I thought I told you no dealing in the bar," Michael said.

"These aren't dealing," Caleb said. "This is medicine." He opened the envelope. "My friend has the flu."

Michael was still steamed up. "Oh. OK." Pause. "I'm going to eighty-six P.J. some day. He's not leaving me much room."

"P.J. doesn't deal in here," Caleb said.

"Don't lie to me."

Caleb shrugged. "There's no reason to get all uptight. P.J. ain't ever gonna get busted."

"He's charmed, maybe? You tell me. If he gets busted in here, I lose my license and that license is worth twenty-five thou. If he deals in here and I catch him, out. You tell him."

"But Michael. . ."

"You too," he said. "I like you, Caleb. But I like my little business more than I like you. No dealing."

"Whatever you say. You de big boss man."

Michael was flushed above his Paul Sargent jacket. He tossed off his drink. "I'll see you later," he said. "Jim, make a call. That cigarette machine needs fixing again."

"He's the owner?" Karen asked.

"Oh yeah," Caleb said. "The owner, proprietor, founder, and bishop presiding."

"He seemed alright," she said. "I wouldn't want to run this place."

"He makes a good buck," Caleb said. "I have very little

pity in my heart for that stuffy son of a bitch."

Denny put his glass down. "Beer is expensive here. 'Gansett was only thirty-five cents in the bar in Kennebec."

"Yeah, but the city is where all the money is," Caleb said. "Maine has only had three individual dollars since 1804, and they move around so slow through the state that economists can trace their every move."

The jukebox blared suddenly, and Long Jim was standing close to them, looking grim.

"Man, what the hell do you think you're doing?" Real anger in his voice and his hands in fists at his side. "I got a car in the garage in Flatbush. You can have it."

The three of them sat silent. Caleb had known Long Jim for four years.

"Come on, stupid, don't be stupid. Take the car and get the hell out of here."

"The heat has been around?" Caleb asked.

"No. But don't count on 'em. They should have been here days ago. I read the *Post*. I also read the *Times* and the *News*. And so does every beat cop in the city. You two are prominent. Believe me. And you, Caleb, stupid, so long as you're with them, you're dead. Did you spring them?"

"Uh-huh."

"Now why'd you want to go and do a thing like that for?" Jim prided himself on his nonchalance. In four years, Caleb had never seen him this rattled. But he paused, and his dignity spoke to Denny and Karen. "No offense. But I know this dude, and you two I don't know."

"That's OK," Karen said. "Do you think it's dangerous?"

He exploded. "Hell yeah, it's dangerous." He eyeballed the customers in the bar; half a dozen regulars. "Man, the people who come in here ain't long on living, but they can read!"

"But they won't say anything," Caleb said.

"Not to the pigs, sure. But you know how the grapevine works. By tonight, half the old West Side faces will know that you're back, that you're Weathermen on the run. Oh

screw it. You damn fool." The way he said "fool" was an
indictment. Jim didn't like fools.

"Well, maybe," Caleb said.

"Could I have a glass of water?" Denny asked.

Karen watched him take the pills and her calm woman's
question: "What are we going to do?"

"I dunno. Go down to Virginia, I guess. Caleb, could we
hit you up for some money?"

"Sure. Whatever you need. The Weathermen can afford
it."

"Have you got your sister's address?" Denny asked.

"No. It's back in what used to be our happy home."

She took one of Caleb's cigarettes, lit it, and coughed.
"But, I remember that she's living somewhere outside of
Marion. I guess it wouldn't be too hard to find her."

"You want my car?" Long Jim asked.

"Like you said," Denny answered, "you don't know us."

"For a Cadillac, I don't know you," Long Jim smiled
(first time), "but wait'll you see this car. For this car, I know
you well enough. It's an old tin Renault."

"We could give you some money for it. We could buy it
from you," Denny offered.

"Naw." Long Jim laughed. "I'll steal a little more from
Michael on weekends and figure I'm helping the Revolution." He nodded to someone behind Caleb, and Caleb
turned to say hello to Izzy (Isadore Paelano), who he normally liked well enough, but not just now.

Izzy wore a dapper grey-suede pimp hat, art director's
sunglasses, a colored glass on a silver chain around his neck,
a gold-silk ascot, an ulcer, three packs of gauloises,
Shrieber's brown-leather logger boots, and the worst luck in
the world.

Izzy was a very talented, very unsuccessful moviemaker,
and his talent and his bad luck and all his pretentions bent
his body like an old man's.

"Howdy bub," he said, affable, standing in the circle of
his interruption. "Long time, no see, as they say."

"Hi Izzy."

"What's shakin'?"

"Not much. Can I buy you a drink?"

"Is the Pope Catholic?" He slid onto a vacant stool and let his pale-yellow cuff slip into view, ever so casually.

" 'Lo, Iz," Long Jim said. He brought out the bottle of Black Label without asking. "How's your porn flick doing?"

"So-so. Patricia, my little cabbagehead, let the batteries run down on the Nagra. You know," he confided, "at some point in any porn flick you just got to let the film roll. No more re-takes. Well, we were at such a point in my newest epic, with the camera rolling and six, count 'em, six beautiful maidens doing dirty things and carrying on; the Nagra quit. No sound. The biggest silence in the world."

"Tough," Jim said. "Any pretty girls?"

"Sure. There's this little girl from Forest Hills. A real gymnast. She really gets into it."

"When do I get to come up and watch?"

"Watch?"

They both laughed. An old joke.

"Where you been, Caleb?" Izzy looks at Caleb through his color glass, like peering through a lorgnette. "Any place exciting?"

"Nope. Just beating around."

"I would like to score a pound."

"No can do."

"Oh horse puckey. Me and a couple of other cats are going to shoot an homage to Brautigan and Artaud on Twenty-sixth Street, and how can we shoot that without dope? No dopey, no movie."

His mouth lost its disappointment, and quick: "Did I tell you I was getting into video tape? Software. Man, it's great! No editing costs, no processing costs, just shoot and see what you shot right away. And if it's no good, just shoot it over."

"I heard the quality was bad," Caleb said.

"It's not terrible. And they're bound to get better."

Caleb said, "Maybe."

"It's a gas, man. You shoot and shoot and shoot. And never have to worry about how much it's costing you. I got a compadre who teaches at Visual Arts, and he can get me a Sony camera any time I want it. And we've been shooting a lot."

Karen had her mouth close to Denny's ear, and he was nodding. Caleb watched her covertly and ordered another drink.

"It sounds good," he said, distracted. "Why don't you talk to P.J. about the dope?"

Izzy drummed his manicured fingertips on the bar. He drained his drink and stood up, abruptly.

"No can do," he said. "He keeps terrible hours." Izzy ogled a blond girl sitting alone in the back. "Ah-ha. Perhaps young Susie would like to be a star."

He faced Caleb directly and spoke seriously to Caleb's deaf ear. "It's funny. Making porn to make bread to make films for *Newsreel* to tear down the system that the porn films are based on."

When a man has no luck, he has no luck. But he can have convictions.

And, almost furiously, Isadore Paetano had political convictions. He shot films for *Newsreel;* he gave his time to rallies and marches and his soul to Goddard.

"Ah, Izzy. I didn't know you was a philosopher," Caleb said.

"Don't joke," he said. "I believe in some things." His voice became jovial and unsuccessful again. "See you in the movies, bub."

They had to wait until midnight, when Jim would go out to Flatbush and pick up his old car if it would start even, let alone run.

So they listened to the music and drank, spacious, loose, feathered with air. Caleb went into the women's john and took two thousand from his money belt and rolled a couple of joints with the last of Denny's dope. He ignored the pounding on the door and the woman's voice: "Come on, honey, get off the pot."

Caleb opened the door and slipped around her, quick as a mongoose. "Hi, Margaret," he said.

"Why don't you change your rag at home," she snarled, as she clumped into the Ladies.

Denny was grinning at him.

"Oops," Caleb said.

Long Jim leaned over the bar. "We'll miss you, Caleb," he said. "You put on a good show. Vulgar, you know, but funny."

"Thanks, Jim," Caleb said. "I try to suit my act to my audience. I have another, much classier act. It's too bad you'll never see it."

Denny took the money Caleb slipped him and passed it to Karen. He was very drunk and he didn't trust himself.

Margaret came steaming over, chafing and fussing, her Greta Garbo image gone, and instead of Garbo, Bette Davis.

She started with a sneer, dropped a few casual insults, built to a stream of invective louder and louder.

"What are you so mad about?" Caleb asked.

"Why were you so lousy to my old man?" she asked him back.

"He's lame," Caleb said.

"Jay's a writer for the *Voice*," Margaret observed. "He gets two hundred fifty dollars for one article. He did a picture exposé on state-hospital conditions in New York. Caleb, are you still dealing ounces for a living?"

Long Jim rescued Caleb from his sophistication.

Long Jim was holding the telephone receiver up and yelling, "Caleb Smith. On the hook."

Caleb quick said Excuse me to Margaret and fled to the phone.

The jukebox was too close and too loud. Caleb had to cup his ear to hear.

"Yeah?"

Calm voice. "Caleb Smith?"

"Uh-huh."

Political John: "Glad to hear you're back in town."

"Oh yeah. Me, too."

"When did you get in?"

"Couple days ago."

John sighed. "How I wish you'd called."

Caleb said nothing.

John again: "I understand you have some money for me."

"A little change."

John was hearty. "Fine, fine. I was afraid you might not have it."

"John, I hate your punk-ass games," Caleb said.

A slur on the other end of the line, acrid and smoky, "Yeah, so do I. But I see you made a couple of new friends. Are they OK?"

"OK how? OK, like an OK person, or OK meaning safe?"

"Are they safe? Can we help them?"

"John, this phone isn't the best phone in the city."

"Thank you. Very few drug-bar phones are really suitable for intimate conversation."

"That's true, John," Caleb said. "I gave them some money. They'll get clear, I think."

Genuine John. "That's good. It wasn't right that they should get tangled in this web."

"A web of sorrow, John," Caleb said.

"How are you feeling? I was worried."

"I have eight fingers, John," Caleb said.

Silence from John.

"That's two less than I entered life with. I am, John, forever incomplete."

"What happened?"

"Frostbite. It is very interesting country you sent us through, John."

Pause. "I liked Willy. I knew him a long time."

"Willy was a good cat," Caleb said.

"I never got to know Jeff, and I wish I had," John said, almost saying something more.

Caleb snapped, "A hero of the revolution, John."

Longer pause. John came back, soft as a girl. "I suppose. I suppose. Did you hear about Chris. . ."

"Yeah," Caleb said. "I'd like to talk to you about him."

John, bittersweet-delighted, "Good news, Caleb. I had hoped we might meet soon, and now, a suggestion from your very lips."

"You a fag, John?"

"No," John said. "And Caleb, you really bore me. You posture, and I don't care for your tough city-boy mannerisms."

"I am a city boy, John. Didn't you say you were born on a farm?"

Gently. "Not a farm, Caleb. A ranch. I was born precisely eighteen miles from Fargo, North Dakota, and exactly three miles from the U.P. tracks on a modest, but impoverished, homestead, inefficiently run by my alcoholic father. And where my disappointed mother, no doubt, still resides. Both her sons went bad, you see, and that's hard on an old widow woman. There's no need to tarry on that, is there?"

"I'm not much interested," Caleb said. "Though thousands may be."

"I hear Sara is out of town."

"So I understand."

"Too bad. I loved that girl. I really loved that girl. She phoned me, you know; some inchoate sermon about Jesus. Still, she's such a sweetheart."

"Yeah, I know," Caleb said. "But she never puts her legs down."

"What?"

"You know, John. When she's balling and writhing and twisting. She never puts her legs down."

"Uh, well. . . Meet me tomorrow at say . . . two o'clock, in the Boondocks?"

"Sure, John."

Honest John: "I'd like to talk to you, Caleb."

"Sure, John."

"Caleb, honestly, I'm glad to know you're alright."

Caleb hung up and listened to Bob Dylan sing, "Lay lady, lay/ Lay across my big brass bed."

He shrugged. He rejoined his drink and the thread of conversation.

Denny was very wrecked, and the fever was back again. It colored his cheeks and made his mouth clown-white. He was running it down to Long Jim, theorizing, universalizing himself, as if that could save him.

"You become a radical, Long Jim, when the facts of your own life push you into it. When you need to be a radical. You understand?"

So Caleb shut his ears and watched Karen's hands folded around her drink.

Caleb wondered how her fingernails would feel on his thighs. She looked like a scratcher. He cataloged his guesses about what she and Denny did in bed. He blushed and bought her a drink.

"You know, I like you better here," she said. "You seem easier."

"Yeah, sure," he said. "I like it here. I understand it. I have my place. I like it that most things are for sale and that it's off limits, usually, to cops. Besides, I'm a very happy alcoholic."

"In that case," Karen said, "I'll buy you a drink back."

"Why not?"

"You said Sara was out of town?" she asked.

"Yep."

"When's she coming back?"

"Beats me."

"Oh." Pause. "Do you mind me asking about her?"

"How long have you and Denny been together?" Caleb asked.

"I don't . . . uh, must be four years now."

"Where'd you meet?"

She looked at the tall rows of bottles through a golden haze, thinking; then spoke. "I was an unhappily married young suburban wife, with hubby an executive trainee for Prudential. I was just old enough to drink martinis, and Denny was working for the Audubon Society near where my folks had a summer cabin. Denny was the first freak I ever knew."

Caleb found himself wondering what she looked like then. Was she nervous, well-dressed, did she talk a lot?"

"To make a long story short," she went on, "I left hubby to his career and countless other satisfactions he'd be better off getting without me standing in his way, demanding what he couldn't give me anyway." She smiled. "It was Denny's soft, long brown hair that got me. I thought it would be like balling a fawn or a big furry mouse."

"We ought to make it sometime," Caleb said.

She kept her smile. "Now there's a bad idea," she said.

"Aw shucks, ma'am," Caleb drawled. "I thought you was one of them free-loving hippies, and I ain't had any free love in such a spell."

"Don't," she said.

She watched her drink, and since Caleb didn't see much going on in her bar glass, except a couple of ice cubes melting, he said "OK," and took his drink down the bar.

"Hi, P.J.," he said. "Two nights in a row? Once you lose that schedule you're gonna be just like the rest of us."

P.J. was elegant to the eyes, but it stopped there. Alligator boots, ruffed silk shirt, grey ascot, and brown eyes that had never seen a lynching, but had heard all about them.

Lounging, at ease, he was resting his chin in his hands and didn't budge for Caleb's greeting.

"Caleb," he said, acknowledging a fact of life.

"You're being friendly tonight," Caleb observed.

So P.J. straightened up and reluctantly looked Caleb over. His hand went back to his Pernod.

"Caleb you're a fool."

"Sure, P.J. Aren't we all?"

P.J. said "No."

Caleb walked back down the bar, but Margaret was still hanging over Karen's shoulder, and Denny was talking wild and drunk, so he went back and stood behind P.J. Just standing there, silent.

Under his breath, but audible, P.J. said, "Caleb Smith, who is a dangerous man. Ignorant. Do I want to know Caleb? Caleb who is hotter than a two-dollar pistol and still clowning around."

He set the stemmed glass dead center in front of him. He arranged his pack of Gauloises precisely beside his gold and enamel lighter.

P.J. sighed. He tossed a little envelope of coke on the bar, careless, out of the pattern.

Caleb scooped it up, quick.

"What's that for?" he asked.

P.J. wasn't about to see him. "Entertainment tax," he said, calm. Cold.

It had to be the best coke in the world to buy him off so easy, so Caleb shrugged, kept it, put two quarters in the box, and punched every Stones song he could find.

Twelve o'clock rolled around, and Long Jim grabbed his jacket; Michael was unhappy, but he got behind the bar to cover for him.

Caleb asked P.J. if he wanted to take a walk.

P.J. sipped the golden Pernod. "I'm holding weight," he said.

But Denny wanted more of whatever it was.

He and Caleb and Karen went out to get stoned.

An enormous number of cops in the Village and steady flashes of paranoia; flash, flash, flash. Them three doing their best to look normal. Which is to say they walked too stiffly or too loosely, or talked too loud or were suspiciously silent.

The police were the biggest fish swimming in the lagoon tonight, and their shapes and shadows made Karen start shivering.

"I'm scared," she said.

They were walking down Christopher Street, away from the mainstream, towards the Morton Street Pier.

A couple of gay paraders came by, giving Denny the eye.

"Please, Denny," she said, "let's go back to the bar."

But Denny had the night in him like a hook and was being pulled forward, helpless.

"No, Karen," he said. "You go back to the bar. I'll see you in a a few minutes."

Caleb smiled at Karen, but her eyes were asking him to take care of Denny and that made him a little angry, so he waved goodbye to her and caught Denny before the next corner.

Twisty streets. They were heading into the warehouse district which parallels the Hudson.

Closed wholesale meat markets.

Giant granite buildings for giant trucking firms.

One dim-yellow streetlight at every other corner and only the reflected cloud-light to guide their eyes and feet.

They turned off into a rubble-paved vacant lot where something had been torn down, and it looked like Berlin, 1944.

They had a couple or half a dozen hits of coke.

So both of them half-wrecked, half-stumbling down some ashy street and both of them lost inside themselves, locked in the usual mortal combat.

Denny was far-gone. The fever and the cocaine had broken his power. He was completely and unusually powerless. His body maintained itself while he watched the phantasms come to him. He was pure voyeur of his own life, with no power to change or direct anything.

Some part of Caleb, some puritan bedrock in him issued a warning: "You are very stoned. You aren't crazy. You will come out of it unchanged. You're stoned, that's all."

Caleb stopped walking. He slowly figured it out. They were just off Hudson Street, about three blocks north of a bar Caleb knew.

They weren't lost forever. They could get back.

The sweat rolling from his armpits.

He lit a joint and handed it to Denny. Denny was some-place bad. His eyes weren't focusing; they were rolling loosely in their sockets. Caleb lit a joint for himself. Denny was drowning. Out of reach. So Caleb picked up a couple of ash-can lids and slammed them together at top speed.

Enormous clang!

Denny's eyes jolted. A wisp of brown hair was falling over his forehead, and he brushed it back.

A cop stepped out of a shallow doorway about five feet in front of them.

Ordinary cop's face. Touch of priest Irish in it, and strange brown or green eyes. Caleb locked gazes with him.

"Oh," Denny said. And like a spikehorn started up, Denny spun and ran. Fast footfalls behind Caleb, a clatter of something metal. Cop and Caleb, eye to eye.

The cop took three steps closer, and Caleb could see that his eyes were green.

His uniform too often pressed, too shiny. The visor of his cap had small cracks in it. Gun sagging at his hip, un-necessary and half-hidden by his long winter coat.

"You don't want to get in trouble?" he asked.

"No."

The cop reached out and plucked the joint from Caleb's lips and tossed it away.

"That's good," he said. His breath smelled faintly of Sen-sen.

"You should go somewhere," the cop said.

"Sure," Caleb said. "OK."

"Two bits," the cop said. His shoes were cracked above his rubbers.

"What?" Caleb said.

"You ain't worth two bits," the cop said.

He cupped his hands and lit a cigarette. He smiled at Caleb—a short, puckish Irish boy's smile—and walked away. Around the corner and gone.

Caleb was released then, too late and hopeless.

His hand is hurting him.

He lets his breath out and starts down the dead street, click-click heel taps on the icy sidewalk, listening for Denny.

He gets to the end of the first block. No sign.

He starts to cross the street and the headlights pick him up.

He backs up obediently and stands on the curb.

Slow motor coming up on him. Squad car passes him slowly. They hit him once with the spotlight (contempt) and glide across the intersection.

The dark-blue uniforms inside. Caleb can see the light flaring on the uniform buttons.

Doesn't move.

Clatter ahead. Some noise. Not much noise. No louder than the noise a stray cat would make.

Squad car stops. Two cops get out of the car, casual.

One reaches through the window to direct the spot.

The light rushes across the high walls of the black stone warehouses.

Denny is crouched on the fire escape like a gargoyle.

The spot finds him, holds him, and makes him small.

Prodded, he gets to his feet. He stretches.

And pounce! He's flashing up the fire escape for the roof. Three steps at a time, even, unhurried, dancing, like a lovely girl; his feet soundless, though the fire escape is metal and must make some sound.

The spotlight follows him. Star!

The cops are, perhaps, shouting. But a hurricane is roaring in Caleb's ears, and he can hear nothing.

Denny is one foot striding up ahead of the other and his body curiously erect. He is one flight from the roof. Four flights up.

Black. Sudden black. Black. Black.

Goddamn them! They turned the spotlight off!

One. Two. Three. Four. Five.

When they snap the spotlight on again, Denny's lost in it. The light finds him broken, frightened, huddled, like a lost child.

The light prods him. What is he now, anyway?

Denny jerks. He explodes. Flurry of hair and hand and black magnum in his hand now, popping like firecrackers.

He is yelling something. He is yelling "Karen."

Not enough. The police bullets pock up dust from the brick beside him. They throw dust all over the fireworks display.

Denny walks calmly to the railing and folds over it like a burlap bag. He slides forward, slowly, into the night air.

His fall is graceful, deliberate. As polite as a Protestant falling into the fire.

His long, dark-brown hair streams back from his head, like a living parachute.

When Denny hit the sidewalk, he broke, like a rotten plank.

Caleb stook in the doorway of the Great Auk. Cold, so cold. He was shivering. He really wanted a drink, but he knew he couldn't.

Karen came over to him, looking past him, looking for Denny.

What could he say? That he wanted a drink? "Karen," he said. "The cops. The cops shot Denny."

She tried a little smile on him because she knew he was kidding; but he didn't respond, and her little smile faded.

"He's dead," Caleb said. "I couldn't ... I couldn't do anything."

P.J. brushed past them, in a hurry, not talking, not touching.

She opened her mouth to ask him a question, but a sound came out, half-moan and half-squawk. Her mouth moved and a bit of spittle trembled at the corner of her white floppy mouth.

She sat down. Heavily, like an old woman. The tears ran down her cheeks, simple and plain.

Caleb couldn't touch her. He had stolen too much from her.

She wouldn't stop looking at him.

Caleb turned away and asked Long Jim for the keys to his apartment, and Long Jim gave him the keys.

None of the people moved in the bar except to lift their drinks and set them down again, exactly and quietly.

Margaret went out in the street to get them a cab. Caleb held Karen's arm. He was afraid she'd fall down and hurt herself. She got into the back of the cab and pulled the door shut behind her.

Her cheeks were wet. She was homely with grief. She didn't want to be near him much.

Her mouth was shaping a word. Shaping, "No. No. No. No. No."

Caleb stood back, and the cab drove away. He could see the top of Karen's head through the rear window.

He didn't want a drink any more.

Long Jim's apartment was close, so he walked over there.

Under his front window, Long Jim had one of those slat Danish-modern tables, stacked with rock-and-roll records.

Caleb crawled under it and went to sleep.

6 / *Morningside Heights*

Sometime in the morning, Caleb woke up, threw up, and went into the kitchen to find something to clean up his mess.

He looked into the bedroom as he passed and Long Jim was sprawled across some chick, snoring. Caleb thought the other face on the pillow might have been Margaret, but he couldn't tell and didn't care.

He left Long Jim's keys on the table and got down the five flights of stairs and threw up in the street.

It was bitter cold and still. An off-duty cab passed him. "Ride Yellow for Safety" it had written on a sign on the back of it.

He thought he should get something to eat, though he wasn't hungry.

Rows of tacky Italian tenements. Red, green, and white flags hung from a few of the fire escapes, remnants of Mafia Solidarity Day a couple of months ago.

It was January. The first month in a new year.

Caleb stopped at the Hipster and had a Blue Note, a Mama Hipster's Sunshine, and a cup of Java. This eccentricity because the Hipster was a tourist spot with a jazz motif. Old brass instruments hanging from the walls and the menu kept the joke going. Caleb had ordered French toast, orange juice, and coffee. But Mama Hipster's Sunshine was more water than orange, and he didn't feel like drinking it, so he got up and left.

Uptown again. Nobody in the loft. He peeled off his money belt and thumbed through the stacks of bills.

He figured the Weathermen owed him a few bucks. He counted out five thousand dollars in hundreds and pulled up a piece of floor molding under the windows. Slow Richard's old dope stash.

Under the molding was a hole about six inches deep, broken lath and plaster. He banged his ruined hand on the broken plaster and vomited again. Bile.

After his belly stopped lurching, he stuck the money in the hole and closed it up.

Buckshot's old pistol was lying beside the mattress Denny had used.

"Christ," Caleb said. He stuck the pistol into the back of his pants and tugged his jacket down over the butt.

He tore a long strip off his shirttail and wrapped the rag around his ruined fingers.

The cab driver took the fast route uptown: Riverside Drive. Block after block of turn-of-the-century mansions facing the park and the strong grey Hudson. Caleb wondered if the people who dwelled in those mansions had nineteenth-century lives, with servants and manners and all.

The cabbie left Caleb off at the Boondocks. Three dollars and twenty-five cents on the meter. Caleb gave the cabbie four bucks, and the cabbie smiled.

No sign of John outside, and no sign of him inside, either.

Caleb set himself on a stool, lit a cigarette, coughed, and ordered a Michelob. The bar clock said two thirty.

A couple in the back studying together and nursing their beers. Two old dudes sitting at the bar, separated by as many stools as possible.

Young girl in a yellow scarf came in, peered around nervously until she found him. "Caleb Smith," she called out. "Where have you been keeping yourself?"

Perched herself next to him and big smile from a little Jewish girl's face.

Sotto voce: "Pretend that you know me, stupid."

She had long black hair and high-set breasts with hard nipples talking through the front of her blouse.

"Molly Goldberg," Caleb said. "I'll be damned. I haven't seen you since Grossinger's."

Her brown eyes flicked from off to on, and she gave him this even bigger grin. "Linda's the name," she said. "You still a bellhop?"

"Naw," Caleb said. "I'm a revolutionary now. A humdinger. You still peddling your ass?"

"Oh no," she kept on smiling through. She had long fingers with stubby, dirty, chewed fingernails. "I'm into Women's Lib now. You know, ferreting out male chauvinist pigs and making it with chicks. You know."

"I'd like to hold your tits again," Caleb said.

"Fat chance. Bartender, bring me a whiskey and soda."

She counted out the money from a little change purse she was carrying in her pea coat.

"What happened to your hand?" Linda asked. She made a face. "Why don't you get a clean bandage?"

"Snapping pussy," Caleb replied. He poured a long drink of beer down his throat and smacked his lips. "Lovely twenty-year-old virgin from Wellesley. Passionate, but dangerous."

Wan smile. "John said you were a jerk," she observed.

Caleb grunted. "Yeah, sure," he said. He pulled out a cigarette and, steadying his wrist with his good hand, managed to get it lit. "I'm tired," he said. "You from the Weather People?"

"Uh-huh."

"Why don't I just give you the money and go home?" He reached under his shirt for the money belt.

She put her hand on his arm. "No, Mr. Smith," she said. "John made it very clear he had to talk to you."

"Screw him," Caleb said.

She drank her whiskey and soda straight down and put a dime tip on the bar. "He said he had important news for you," she added.

"Oh yeah? What news do I need to hear?"

"I don't know," she said, standing up. "Let's go."

Caleb sighed, "You bewitch me honey, and I don't know what to do." He gulped his beer down and followed her.

Striding straight ahead through the citizens of upper West Side, New York. Kids playing. Mamas shopping. Newsstands with old coots and blind veterans making a living. Caleb trailed her at a half trot, watching her ass work inside her blue jeans.

He sang under his breath: "If you was a river, baby, and I was a diving duck, I'd dive to the bottom, and never come up."

She heard, but pretended she didn't.

Lines of force flickering in and out, like spider webs catching the light.

They caught the downtown train at One hundred tenth Street. She was looking around nervously, but nobody followed them onto the platform.

She motioned him to get off the train at the next stop, and they crossed the bridge to the uptown side. Nobody in the station except the token seller in his armored booth, and he didn't look up from his *Daily News.*

They got off at the Columbia stop and walked past the world's finest graffiti to the light again.

"You're very clever," Caleb said. "Want to get married?" He was giving her his best Mickey Rooney look, but maybe she never saw any Mickey Rooney movies.

John lived in a narrow red-stone apartment building, with the fire escapes trailing down the front of it and two stone gargoyles, which looked like inferior lions or superior dogs.

Both the gargoyles were snarling vacantly, so Caleb gave one of them a kick in the paw.

They rode upstairs in a chuffy elevator, with about two feet of floor space between them.

She was staring out of the iron cage, watching the floors go by, her neck twisted and a trickle of sweat running down it.

John heard the elevator stop at the landing and came out to greet them. Black turtleneck sweater, levis, and jump boots. His face floated above his feline outfit like a lighted billboard.

Caleb walked past him into the apartment, and since Denny was sitting on John's red brocade couch, he stopped dead in his tracks.

Caleb said, "Hello."

Caleb knew, of course, that the man sitting on the couch was Christopher. Denny was dead. Besides, Christopher had blond hair, and Denny's hair had been brownish, mouse-colored.

But the man's hair wasn't *exactly* blond, more a sorrel color, and Denny's hair had had some patches where the sun had bleached it light.

Caleb waited for the man to speak, because he didn't really remember what Denny looked like, and he didn't remember what Christopher looked like, either.

When Denny sat down, he used to sit sloppy, with some part of his body never quite contained by a chair or couch.

And this man sat prim. Graceful, but prim. A clue?

Caleb knew the guy was Christopher, but since there was a reasonable doubt, Caleb said, "I need a drink."

John came around from behind him and plucked a bottle of brandy from a heavy, plain oak bookcase.

John poured Caleb a good three inches. The brandy wasn't bad. Rather than inspecting the guy on the couch, Caleb ran his eyes over John's apartment.

Item: That Magritte print. The one with the gent wearing an apple in place of his head. Worth maybe forty-five dollars with a thin metal frame thrown in.

Item: One political poster. It had the silhouette of an AR-16 Rifle beside the slogan, "Oppose Reactionary Violence with Revolutionary Violence."

Item: A Sierra Club poster, with a picture of a lovely mountain meadow and the legend, "The Lost Cascades."

The man on the couch spoke. He used Chris's voice: "John, I oppose it. Seriously, I oppose it."

But ... but the last time Denny had spoken, when he cried for "Karen" as the bullets were hitting him, Denny's voice had been high and tight, like this man's voice.

Caleb tossed the money belt to the man. He started pulling bills out and counting them.

"I heard on the radio that Dennis Milanovich got killed last night," the man said.

Chris. The man was Chris. It was good the man was Chris.

Caleb felt a flush, a burning that started at his ankles and rose to his hairline. "Uh, yeah," he said. "Denny got shot."

"What happened to his wife?" John asked. John was standing a little too close to Caleb, and Caleb didn't like it.

"I dunno," Caleb said. His hands were shaking as he fumbled a cigarette out of a pack lying on the table.

"Where is she? Did she get away?"

"Goddamn it, John!" Caleb yelled. "Why don't you shut the fuck up! She's not Weather People. She ain't even fucking political! Leave her alone!"

"Thirty-two, seven, and change," Christopher announced.

John and Caleb were staring at each other, and Chris's voice wafted between them, cool and detached.

"The papers said we stole forty-one thousand. But," Chris sighed, "the papers always exaggerate the amount anyway."

Chris's voice had that enigmatic precison possessed by certain lunatic English movie stars. Caleb was impressed.

In that moment, Caleb decided that he liked Christopher very much. Christopher, whose eyes rode above his mask like a wary grey squirrel's eyes.

"We're lucky we got any of it, I suppose." John's cold voice.

Christopher started stuffing cash back into the belt; his hands weren't entirely calm, but he made neat piles of the bills and slipped them back into the money belt.

"John," Chris said, "you shouldn't do it. I..." Chris wanted to say something more, but he ate the words and swallowed.

Caleb wondered why Chris was so afraid.

John said, tightly, "It's time for you to go."

And Chris buckled the money belt and got up and shook his head, doleful as a mother and said, "John..." Asking, not telling.

John held the door open for Chris and patted his back as he passed. "Remember what I told you last night?" John asked. "Remember that long story about the chickens?"

Chris didn't reply.

Caleb wanted another drink.

Linda was sitting on the floor under a big bay window. She had her hands in her pea-coat pockets, though it was plenty warm.

"What about the chickens?" Caleb asked John.

John poured himself a glass of brandy. He took a swallow and looked out the window. "When I was a kid," he began, "I used to have to kill the chickens. I was the oldest kid, and about the time I was ten, I took over the slaughtering from my mother. Did you know that chickens still cluck after you cut their heads off?" He paused, politely, but Caleb didn't feel like saying anything just then. "I never let any of the other kids do the killing, even when they got old enough. And I hated it. You know, if you eat meat, ethically, you should be able to kill it, too. But sometimes, one person being ethical is enough."

"Oh," Caleb said. He turned around and noticed that Linda had a small black automatic clutched in her nail-bitten fingers. Linda was sweating more than usual.

"I'll trade you another drink for your gun," John said, softly.

Caleb took a look at Linda. "Alright," he said.

He gave Buckshot's pistol to John. The pistol was heavier than he remembered it being.

John poured Caleb another brandy. At least it was decent brandy.

"You have expensive tastes," Caleb said. He coughed and bent over a little.

"I'm an assistant professor at Columbia," John said. "They pay pretty well."

Caleb put down his empty glass. "You'd better run, John," he said. "The cops are going to be after you, too, baby."

John nodded.

"You have an informer, John. Somebody who knows you is telling everything he knows to the Feds."

Flicker of light behind John's eyes, like a door being opened and shut.

John's face flared red and puffy, and he shouted, "Who in the hell do you think I am, you ignorant son-of-a-bitch! There are three good people who are dead now and they shouldn't be dead. Willy's dead and Jeff's dead and this Dennis is dead, and you ... you want to keep playing ring-around-the-rosy. I'm sick of you, Caleb Smith. Here, have a drink!" Furiously, he pushed the bottle at Caleb.

"No thanks," Caleb said, quietly. A moment later, Caleb added, "I always drink from a glass."

John backed off. He stopped his temper. He took a breath. "I suppose you have a story," he said. "Tell it."

Linda scrambled to her feet and snatched a cigarette from John's pocket and fired up. One-handed. Quick, nervous puffs.

Caleb arrayed himself in what clarity he had on call.

"They were waiting for us. They knew ahead of time we were coming, and they set up their roadblock way before we got there. The phone lines had been out since before noon, and we didn't hit the Bangor bank until twelve thirty. The police in that part of Maine don't have radios in their cars. True. No radios. No phones. But they were waiting for us, anyway. You got an informer, John. Lucky you."

"Yes," John said. John had such little, perfect teeth. "Have you heard from Sara?" John asked, mildly curious.

Caleb waved that one away. "No." He gave himself space to let John's questions die away. He licked his lips, and in a voice as believable as he could make it, Caleb Smith said: "Christopher is an informer."

His words fell into the crack reserved for tired old jokes. John just kept on looking at him.

"OK," Caleb said. "Look, this other stuff isn't going to be very convincing, because you weren't there. You were still in New York talking." He watched John's throat to see if he'd scored.

No swallow. He hadn't.

"But the way it was," he continued, "Christopher *couldn't* have surrendered. The cops were all shooting. And us shooting back and total confusion. It would have gone against the grain to stop and surrender. Like being a Japanese pilot at Pearl Harbor and turning around without dropping your bombs. Not possible. Mob psychology, maybe, but I know I couldn't have surrendered, and I ain't exactly your number one revolutionary hero."

Caleb's neck was hurting from sitting so straight, being so reasonable.

"And, Christopher escaped. A known Weatherman, and he gets clean away from two, *two* FBI agents without a scratch. Now you can run all this hand-to-hand-combat crap you want, but nobody, not Mohammed Ali, is going to get away from two of Mr. Hoover's piglets when they're watching him hard."

Caleb could smell himself, and he smelled bad. A week's fears and excitements had commingled as residue on his skin.

Still, he had to talk. Had to keep on talking. "You know, John," he said, "I just figured it out. You're due to meet with the Weather Bureau pretty soon, right?"

John nodded, reluctantly it seemed.

"That's what the Feds are waiting for," Caleb said. "That's why they haven't busted you yet. They're waiting for you and the Weather Bureau to meet, and they'll take every single one of you all at once. And Christopher. . ."

John interrupted, a grunt of disgust. "That's enough, Caleb. That'll do. I don't need to hear anymore. And I am tired of playing at counterspy. You are the informer. You, Caleb Smith, are reporting to the FBI. You, Caleb Smith, caused the death of three men already. I'm tired of talking to you."

John slid a little deeper into his own body.

"John, I ain't the one you want."

"Would you like another drink, or something," John asked. "We've got some grass around here someplace."

"John. I am not the informer."

Far off, a horn was honking. Water was running through the pipes of the old building.

"Why'd you do it?" Linda asked. "I mean, I suppose I ought to hate you, but I just feel sorry and confused."

Caleb snorted. "If it'll make you feel better, hate me. It don't mean shit."

She continued, undismayed, "I mean, how did you get into this work?" she asked. "You must be very lonely."

"Oh, Jesus Christ."

Caleb got up and like he was a regular guest, headed for the door. Almost made it, too. He actually had his hand on the knob.

Click, click of a hammer being drawn back.

"I'll shoot you if you turn that knob," John said, quietly.

Caleb spared him a glance and he did have a pistol in his hand and he looked like he would shoot, so Caleb picked out a chair and sat down heavily.

"What now?" Caleb asked.

John pursed his lips—thin lips. "You know," he said.

"You schmuck," Caleb snapped. "You're going to be hitting one of your own people. Christopher has got you set up for murder number one."

"I don't think so," John said. "It's nothing personal. You understand that. I don't dislike you. Matter of fact, I even like you a little."

"Thanks a lot."

"I suppose you wouldn't like to tell us what you've passed on to the pigs?" John asked, not very hopefully. He paused. "I'm not very good at interrogations," he apologized.

"Don't worry about it," Caleb assured him. "You've got the knack. Just keep on killing and robbing for another couple years and you'll be able to hold you own with any SS man."

John ignored him. He poured himself a brandy. The bottle pinged against the glass.

"I'll make it short," John said. "I'm imposing on you anyway," he tapped his gun with his forefinger, "and I dislike cruelty."

Caleb believed him, but he said: "Sure, John. A regular bleeding heart."

"You probably don't know much about contemporary science. It isn't published in the vernacular." He lit a filter tip and his hands were still trembling and Caleb wondered if he ever did speed. "Basic physical and biological research are so sophisticated today that any really good work requires terribly expensive apparatus. And money for the apparatus comes, in eighty percent of the cases, from the government. They pay for research designed to answer their questions, and hence, through money allocations, they effectively direct scientific inquiry. If someone is pursuing inquiry that the government dislikes—no funding. Still, the control the government exercises is indirect, and a little sloppy."

"Get to the point, John." Caleb said.

"The world is going to end," John said.

"Terrific," Caleb said.

"The depletion of resources, population expansion, and effects of industrialization will mean the collapse of all life support systems, massive famine, and the death of the species by the year two thousand and twenty. According to MIT."

"Well," Caleb said, "why don't we all go on a hilltop and pray to de Lawd?"

John shrugged. "One more fact before your laughter overwhelms you. Unless the process is reversed—not studied—not investigated—not debated—*reversed*—by nineteen seventy-five, it will be impossible to stop. I suppose, in the last days, they'll use the nuclear bombs, too."

"You really believe this?" Caleb asked.

"The studies are quite clear. And, by extrapolation, the only quick way to seize power is revolution, no matter how slim its chance of success. And the chances are slim. And, by further extrapolation, all informers should be killed."

"I'm Caleb Smith," Caleb said. "Not INFORMER."

"I'm sorry," John said.

Caleb felt like throwing up. What do you do when you know where to say "yeah" in the music and when to pass the joint or the little bottle of coke? What do you do when your body knows all these attitudes and movements, impossible for any other body to duplicate? What do you do when you're precious, but you're dead. As yesterday's hamburger.

You feel like throwing up.

"You made a lot of mistakes," John said. "You underestimated us."

"I'm sorry if I underestimated you," Caleb said.

"There's a girl working as a go-go dancer on the East Side. Anyway, she makes it with a Captain in the Red Squad, sometimes. The captain knows she's got revolutionary sympathies, and he likes to brag to her. Flaunting his power." John shook his head to clear it. "She's a strong woman. That's how we found out about you. We found out too late to abort the robbery, but. . ." he paused again. "They were good people, Caleb. I liked Willy. He was a good sidewalk mechanic. A good, kind man."

"It was Christopher." Caleb said.

"Did you know the police aren't looking for you, Caleb? Aren't you lucky. There was a photograph in the *Times* of a pile of guns they took off our people. Didn't you touch one of those guns, Caleb? Don't you have fingerprints?"

"Yeah, sure, but the prints they have of me are from a dope bust under another name in Detroit. They're probably looking for me there."

"No, Caleb. They're not looking for you in Detroit. We checked."

"Oh boy," Caleb said.

"Christopher's on the fifteen most wanted list."

"Terrific."

"The Weather Bureau's on that list too."

"Maybe they ought to get together sometime, and while everybody is reminiscing happily about bombs exploded and banks robbed, Christopher can ease them all into the slam."

"The police aren't watching your apartment," John said.

"They're setting me up," Caleb said.

"Someone has to reverse this process. Someone has to turn it around. For the air, the earth, the other animals, the children all over the world. The process is a runaway engine with a dead hand on the controls. And there's hardly any time. Hardly any time."

"How much they pay you to give freshman lectures?" Caleb asked. "Boy, you really are smart."

"Uh-huh," John said. "Is the money counterfeit?"

"What?"

"The money you brought us. Is it counterfeit? I'm sure it's marked, but is it real?"

"It's real," Caleb grunted. "Straight from Maine to you."

John put his hands together. Almost like a suppliant. "I wish I believed you," he said. "We have to discount the money through the Mafia. And that hurts."

"I know somebody who'll give you a better rate," Caleb said.

John looked him over. "I'm sorry, Caleb," he said. "But

it's been decided. I joined the Weathermen of my own free volition. I knew what lay ahead. I knew I had to face the possibility that a bomb I made would kill some innocent chambermaid, or that one day I'd have to kill a pig. The Weather Bureau decided about you, but I agree with them. And I'm sorry for both of us. I've never killed anyone before."

"So don't start." Caleb pulled the bandage off his fingertips. Two blunt red mottled stubs. He waved the fingers at John.

"I see. Christopher said he may have hit you."

"Huh?"

"When you were angling around to get a shot at Willy. Before you blew the top of his head off. Christopher shot at you. Too bad he didn't hit more than your hand."

"It was frostbite," Caleb said. "You goddamned maniac! I had my two fingers chopped off by a crazy old man in a cabin in the woods. And Christopher is your informer. Not me. Look, you're such a just man. Such a smart mouth. All you have to do is ask Karen Milanovich. I know where she is, and it wouldn't take too long. I'm getting set up by Christopher and the pigs, and he's going to blow the whistle on you and the whole Weather Bureau. That's worth checking out anyway. It's worth checking."

"Caleb, Caleb, Caleb," John said like a mother. He came over and touched Caleb's arm. "My name is John Huptman. Chris is my brother."

So Caleb sat down again. "Oh boy," he may have said.

John offered him another shot, but Caleb's hand refused it.

"I'm sorry to be cruel," John said. "At first I thought we should shoot you as soon as you came in. But I thought better of it. You're a man. We should get to know each other."

Caleb's lips were parched. "That's no privilege."

"I know, Caleb. Not for me either. But you deserved some time to think. Camus once wrote for Combat, the

underground paper of the French partisans during the
Second World War. And he asked himself: 'What's the
difference, after all, between us and the Germans. They kill
Jews. We murder some eighteen-year-old German as he's
walking sentry duty at a bridge we wish to destroy?' And
Camus answered himself by saying: 'There is no difference
except that we know we are murderers.' I'm sorry, Caleb,
that you are making me a murderer."

"John," Caleb said. (Maybe water in his eyes.) "I'll bet
you beat off a lot."

"In a manner of speaking, perhaps I do," John said,
quietly. "I considered it for a long time, the method I would
use to murder you, and I thought you should have an
O.D. Shooting you or pushing you off some roof would
cause you a lot of unnecessary pain. But a big hit of high
quality junk and you'd just dream until you died. I think
that would be best. But," he said, intently, "if you have any
preferences. . ."

"Sure, John. Whatever you like. I never tried junk before,
anyway. Oh, I mean, I snorted it a couple of times but I
never shot up. Always meant to get around to it."

"OK," John said. "There's a tenement near here where
they find a lot of dead junkies. One more won't make any
difference. Caleb? Caleb?" John called Caleb back and
insisted on his presence. "Caleb, I'd like to have you tell me
about your informer career. I've always been straight with
you, and I won't torture you, because I don't approve of
torture. I would appreciate it if you told me how much the
pigs know."

"Jesus Christ," Caleb said. "John, you got a lot of balls."

"Please Caleb. You don't owe anything to the pigs. I
suspect they got you on a bad dope rap and agreed to let
you off if you informed on us. Correct?"

"John, I want to go home."

"OK," John sighed. "If that's how you feel about it."

Linda went into the kitchen, and a moment later, she and
her handbag came back.

Three in the tiny elevator was more claustrophobic than two.

As they passed the stoop gargoyles Caleb turned to John. "One question?"

"Sure," John said.

"Did you ever make it with Sara?"

"Yes, Caleb. I did."

"Dandy," Caleb said.

"The first time was when we were. . ."

"Shut up," Caleb said.

"I meant to ask you." John walked a little closer. "Was her religious conversion genuine? It's pretty hard to believe. Did she find out about you?"

"Shut up," Caleb said.

The light was getting strange. No shadows. The stream of force was flowing around them, and John in the middle of it, like a grey granite boulder.

Three pilgrims, all in a line. First, a young dark-haired girl. Normally, she would be quite pretty, but now she was using her face for a mask, and since her prettiness was not of bone, but rather a loveliness of pulse-flesh, she was ugly. And every wound she had ever taken was open and visible.

She had a brocade purse clutched under her breasts, pressed tight against her blue-black pea coat. The works: needle, syringe, spoon, elastic tubing, and a bag of junk. No bulges showed. Hardly detectable.

Her right hand was in her pocket, curled around a small automatic. There were cigarette scraps and two grocery lists in that pocket, too. The automatic wasn't much larger than a large cigarette lighter. It looked like one of those gag cigarette lighters advertised in the back of *Popular Mechanics,* a novelty to deceive your friends.

Caleb was in the center, too small for his clothes. His long, straight brown hair was too dirty to be soft, but looked soft in this light.

They passed an old Jewish woman on her way to the deli. She understood the pilgrims as "rebellion they'd get over some day." So no help for Caleb there.

Caleb had a week's growth on his face, mangy spots of hair, and patches of wind-burned flesh.

A cop, standing on the corner of One hundred tenth Street. Italian cop with his blue coat hung up on the big notebook in his back pocket and one of those battered walkie-talkies crackling from his shoulder. Madonna eyes and a quick wisecrack mouth.

Caleb knew that one word, one outcry, and John would kill him and the cop, too. John had decided. The cop was oblivious and no help there.

Three or a dozen people passing them, too far away, in another ocean altogether.

John had a dull red scarf wrapped around his neck, tossed over his shoulder. No fringe.

Caleb found something in a newsstand on the corner. Green, beat-up, enameled tin shed. *Post, Times, News,* on the narrow counter. Magazines like *Photoplay* on thin stand-up shelves on the back of the shed. Bulby, battered, Brooklyn, New York gent standing there, rocking on his heels, freezing his nuts off. A little something, not much. Death's steady grip on Caleb's shoulder, and maybe the "something" was a wiggle in his shoulder flesh, and maybe not.

Caleb stopped, "John, you got change for cigarettes?"

John's fist carrying the .357 magnum he'd bought after reading about handguns and considering his present and potential needs.

John's finger jumped, but iron will at the control board and no shot.

Tight voice: "Yes, Caleb. I believe I do."

Linda turned her head around, and her pace broke, like a freight train banging to a stop. She moved nearer to the newsstand and bracketed Caleb.

"What kind?" the newsy said. Cigarette hanging from his own lips.

"Gauloises," Caleb said.

Disgusted. "I don't carry no Gall-waseez."

"Sure you do," Caleb said.

Hands quivering around those primitive metal death blocks and Caleb riding the wire.

"What d'yuh mean? I told you I didn't carry 'em, didn't I?"

Caleb pointed at the green copper roof of a building across the street. "You know what that is?" he asked.

"Of course I know what it is. What's the matter with you?"

"It's Columbia University," Caleb said. "And you know what kind of people go to Columbia University?"

"Fags." The newsy plucked his cigarette out of his mouth. "Bunch of fags."

"Sure," Caleb agreed. "But in that collection of fags and pimps and whores, there is a big chunk which smoke Gauloises. Some businessman you are."

"Up yours, Mac." Caleb could go part way here, but this was a tickle, a jab and enough movement to wiggle a shoulder, no more.

"OK," Caleb said. "Gimme a pack of Camels."

Cold eye of contempt. "I ain't selling you nothing, you long-haired fag."

Caleb gave him a smile.

John said, "Let's go."

So they converted back into pilgrims and started up again.

Nothing in that young straight couple window shopping.

Nothing on One hundred eleventh Street.

Here comes the African Queen and maybe something there?

Tall, scrawny black dude, with a lump in the middle of his forehead, just above his eyes. His energy room was bursting out.

His glossy eyes casting tentacles across the street, all around him and whipping back, reeling in, like a fishing line. A tentacle found Caleb and, surprised, wrapped around Caleb's waist and tapped his flow. Burnt out. The black dude blinked and focused. He passed right by Linda and put out his arms to Caleb. "My man," he called out, elegant as green velvet.

One and eight tenths seconds later, John's gun hand jerked, but he didn't shoot. Not quite.

"Howdy, brother," Caleb said. "How you makin' it?"

The black dude gave him a sad smile. Too hip for gold in his teeth, but the caps were bright as noon: "You know how it is. You got expenses, you know?"

"Oh yeah, sure." A white-faced John was hovering near them. "Hey John," Caleb called. "This here revolutionary brother is a little down on his luck. How much money you make teaching?"

The black squeezed Caleb's shoulder, massaged it, and fell right into his part. "You one of those white boys who talks about Rev-o-lution?" he asked. "Man, the Panthers are revolution. They are IT. Dig it?"

Black patent leather boots underneath a long flowing African-style robe.

"How much those boots cost?" Caleb asked.

"I stole those boots," he said. "Spirited 'em away." Slight smell of lavender perfume? "I am the original phantom, prayer shawl and de-vine guidance. Can you dig it?"

"Did you ever kill anyone?" Caleb asked.

That took him back. He took his hand off Caleb's shoulder. "Mercy," he said. Deep dark eyes asking Caleb quick hard questions. "Whooee," he said. "Whooeee."

The black cat brought his arm around, like a semaphore signal, to point to John. To hold him apart from Caleb. "You a friend of his?" he demanded.

"Sure," John said.

"No," Caleb said.

Reflection. He dropped his arm. "You boys surely are confused," he stated. "You just gonna have to get your stuff together."

"No," Caleb said again.

John pulled a dollar bill out of his wallet and held it out.

"Wait a minute," the black said, gathering himself.

"Take it." John's will.

Hardly noticing, he brushed John aside with a wave of his ebony hand. On his index finger he was wearing a bright red-stone ring. Lowered eyebrows and his eyes having lost their slick. He asked: "You sure you two ain't just making it together?"

"We've never balled," Caleb said.

"OK." He sighed. He put his long fingers on Caleb's shoulder again and caressed. He carefully traced the line of Caleb's collarbone with his forefinger. Tapped him lightly, surrendering.

"OK," he said again. Swiveled his eyes to John and snapped his fingers. John held out for not quite long enough before handing the black the dollar. The black stuffed the dollar in Caleb's shirt pocket and fastened Caleb's eyes.

"I'll be seeing you," he stated, matter-of-fact.

"Sure." Caleb knows that he will.

Delicate as a giraffe, with no hands touching, the black inclined his head to Caleb and kissed his mouth. Deep, strong, he breathed into Caleb and moved him toward the circle of the blessed. Bit Caleb's lower lip with his sharp teeth and pulled back, watching until the trickle of blood crept out.

"Oh," he said, and the dark seeped from his face, going somewhere and taking the lavender perfume with it. He was suddenly, perhaps three years older. And he left them, brushing by John without a glance. Tired man going down the street, going home.

"Man," John said, angrily, "I should kill you right here."

But John didn't know these laws, and for the first time, John gave it away and the hand on Caleb's shoulder was unseated and precarious. "An O.D. is pleasanter than a bullet in the guts," John insisted. And Caleb smiled about as long as he should.

"Come on," Linda complained. "Where's the tenement? Let's get on with it."

They turned down a street, heading for the Hudson and not much time left.

Caleb had two of the ingredients, but without a little grace he'd never complete the spell. He knew it. And knew it enough to make his heart empty on the chance that a little of the precious stuff was floating around on this block of Puerto Ricans, Italians, and the stink of the sad mighty Hudson nipping his nose. Caleb emptied his heart and light as popcorn, barely touched the ground.

Linda was walking disjointed and awkward, as if she were walking along the side of a steep hill. And John, behind him, was panting, tossing away his precious breath to whatever wanted it.

Four Puerto Ricans shooting craps on a stoop, and Caleb gave them a wave, but needed nothing they could give.

An old (Polish?) woman was tossing breadcrumbs to the pigeons, and Caleb gave her a dazzling smile. Surprised, she smiled back. And her mouth snapped shut like a miser's purse, and she muttered to herself to compensate for her surprising smile.

Hudson very strong now. Caleb heard a freighter on the river. It was winter dusk, but the shadowless light was still holding on. Maybe another fifteen minutes at the outside.

Caleb's nostrils were wide and straining. The three of them climbing the last hill before Riverside Drive. The last block of tenements before the early streetlights on the Drive.

A girl.

At first glance, she seemed resolute; but the resolution was sham, and you could see the sham at once if you looked a second time: little girl, about sixteen. Field jacket and new hippy headband. Oh, it isn't what she dreamed it would be! Nice to sit stoned in the park all afternoon with those wild Spanish kids, but don't like it when they squeeze my breasts. Run away.

Hands deep in her pockets and wondering if there was a way out or if the taste in her mouth was permanent.

"OK," Caleb was thinking as they converged, "last chance but, oh what is required?"

A touch of that river wind muffled her fine blond hair. Mother's pride.

Sulky, lost, keeping to herself. If she hadn't run away, she would have become Doris Day or some bleary, hopeless, suburban drunk.

Still, only the psychotic are impervious, and she raised her eyes to Caleb.

Her voice used to know how to get what she wanted, and it hadn't learned yet that it wasn't enough.

"Hi, man," she said. "Like I just got into this city and I got no bread and I'm looking for a place to crash for a day or two until I get my head together."

Caleb stopped and loaned her a smile to hold her until his thoughts stood still. What is required?

"Where you from?" Caleb asked.

Impatient with him, "Oh man, like it doesn't matter where I'm *from*. I'm from noplace, man. But I sure could use a place to get stoned and fall out for a while."

John standing right at his back, broadcasting waves which pushed Caleb hard. Caleb resisted and felt the hot life returning to his right shoulder.

He smiled. "Yeah, but the place should be groovy, right? And good folks there, right?"

She smiled at him and cocked her head, forgiving him.

A strange chill was touching a couple of cavities in Caleb's teeth.

"There's a bar called the Great Auk down off Christopher and Seventh Avenue. The Greak Auk. And in there, sometime in the early morning you'll run into a black dude called P.J. And he is totally the best folks on the whole West Side, and you should tell him Caleb Smith sent you and that he should put you up."

She considered it.

"Take the Seventh Avenue train down there. Tell the bartender to put your drinks on my tab."

"OK," she said. "Why not? I'll do it. See you later man." (Did she skip down the hill?)

"No, you won't," Caleb said, but she didn't hear.

John prodded him. "Why the hell did you do that?" he asked. "They'll eat her alive down there."

"Sure, John." Caleb standing crooked, hipshot, with a slant of light lying across his forehead and his once-broken nose throwing a crooked shadow. "Sure, John. P.J.'ll probably put his dirty thing in her."

So John pushed him with the gun and up the hill toward the last tenement on the block. Red-stone stoop, four steps, wide arched vestibule with some kind of fake moorish carving overhead.

Linda went up the stoop and stuck her hand in her purse to make sure the needle was all right. Sun almost gone and with it, a particular phase of power. Hanging red and steamy over the Hudson.

All you need is time, luck, and anger.

Caleb walked right by the vestibule, turned the corner, and ran.

John was a highly rational man. He did not venerate his .357 Smith & Wesson as a religious object. He did not expect to merely flourish the pistol; perform magic; and obtain reverence, obedience, and fear.

No. Wrongly, he thought the gun was a tool, like a pipe wrench or a saw. A simple mechanical device that exploded a precise amount of smokeless powder to propel a projectile (the principle of equal and opposite reaction) along a furrowed tunnel, drilled out of bar steel, and then through the open air with diminishing efficiency and accuracy toward your intended.

Workmanlike, he read up on pistols. He cut small Xs in the heads of the copper-clad bullets because he read that dumdums, though illegal by the Geneva Convention, produced such horrible wounds that your target was rendered helpless on impact.

He practiced snapping his pistol until he had the feel of it. Then he joined a pistol club in Manhattan, and every Tuesday night for three months, he stood in line with identically serious businessmen, firing at paper targets with the club's .22's.

He considered a holster and decided against it because he knew he wouldn't need to carry a pistol all that often. But he did practice drawing his gun from his coat pocket, slick as you like, until he satisfied himself that the odds were, if not perfect, in his favor.

But right now, right now he was off-stride, exactly at two when he should be at three. Or a new rhythm was claiming his legs, and he ought to take three quick half steps, only he didn't know how. And he didn't shoot Caleb as he passed the door of the moorish death house, and he didn't shoot him when he ran around the corner. And the damn front sight caught in his coat pocket, and he ripped the pocket, dangling scrap of grey lining, when he did yank it out. And John yanked the trigger, and the roar rolled down that concrete canyon like a jet flying ten feet off the pavement. And a jumping haze in front of John's 20-20 eyes. Lines dancing, tormenting his vision, like a television set gone nuts.

And Caleb had changed direction a heartbeat before the blast and was scuttling along behind the rear end of a parked Pontiac. And Caleb was going across the street now, at nearly a perfect 45°, and the gun settled into John's hand like divine retribution; only it wasn't exactly, not exactly a perfect 45°—more like 46½°—and the bullet snapped past Caleb's spine and punched out a door pillar in the car in front of him. Green door pillar, buckled, smoking like it was sideswiped by a double-bitten axe.

And he was running low, behind the cars, and his knees tapping his chest, tap, tap, tap, tap. And Caleb seemed to

John like a streak drawn across the opposite side of the street with a child's quick blurred crayon.

More like a snake than a man. Undulant.

John lined up the sights, shaking, and heat risers coming off the barrel. Put the front sight between the two pillars of the back sight, and aimed the death machine at the back of a man who was a snake. At arm's length. And holding his breath. And John's heart kicking thirty-gallons-a-minute through a ten-quart hose. Bam.

Caleb was blitzing through three little Puerto Rican kids who were playing with those little red tops when the ruckus commenced. And John's bullet hits a building somewhere behind him, and it was kids and tops and Caleb, going all directions at once and wrapped around each other, and John didn't shoot anymore.

Caleb ran about ten blocks and sat down on the curb and held his sides and coughed. After a while, he went down into the Eighty-sixth Street subway station.

With his dollar, he bought a hot dog and a Coca Cola in a paper cup.

And still had thirty-five cents left for the token.

7 / *Allegheny County*

Drizzling rain on the Pennsylvania Turnpike, and whenever Caleb turned the heater on, exhaust fumes rose up through the floorboards. Thick layer of dust on the plastic dashboard of Long Jim's old Renault, and the ashtray was full and spilling over.

Tick, tick, of the wipers; they'd slow down when the old car climbed the long approaches to the tunnels through the mountains. Plaques beside the road told you which pioneers had killed which Indians near here, but traveling fast, you only caught a phrase or two: "Last Indian Raid in Wendish County" or "George Greeble's Ferry plied. . ."

The hills were dark muddy green, and the foggy haze hung close to the barren ridges and filled the hollows to the top.

The little four-cylinder engine was missing. Not enough to establish a beat. Odd miss, now and again. Little jerk at random. Just to keep Caleb awake.

It cost Caleb five hundred dollars and two favors to get out of the city. He caught Long Jim before the bartender went to work at the Great Auk. Long Jim was getting stoned in preparation for his seven hours behind the bar.

Long Jim's big KLH was translating a round piece of plastic and Geoff Muldaur was singing "Ginger Man" a little louder than he would have sung in person and Caleb stood in Long Jim's apartment, with one foot already crazy to be gone.

"I need some duds, Long Jim," Caleb was saying.

Long Jim sorting through his record pile, looking for a record to comment on his mood.

> Ginger man has come to town
> He don't care
> If you're white or brown.

"Long Jim, you got any dope?"

"Sure. I got a pound of good smoke I'm doing off in Zs. It's supposed to be Michuacán. Now I don't claim that it is Michuacán—what with the deception that surrounds us today. But it's good dope."

"Got any coke?"

"A little. I could let you have a spoon. I will also lend you some clothes. Normally, I would be reluctant to let you cover your body with my clothing, but the memory of how raunchy you are will cheer me when I'm down."

So Caleb bought a couple ounces of dope and a spoon of Coke from Long Jim and took a shower and gave Long Jim a hundred for the keys to his car. Caleb sat around after Long Jim left for work, waiting for Jim to score him a gun. Billy-the-cop showed up finally at the Great Auk and sold Long Jim a confiscated .38 for a hundred and a half.

Caleb was going south. A northern freak and paranoid. With a gun on the seat next to him, forty-five hundred dollars in the glove compartment, license plates he'd un-bolted from an Ohio tourist's car on Sullivan Street, with all that curious junk and Caleb wondering if he'd used up all his lifetime's luck.

What if the pistol didn't work. Caleb lit up a cigarette. What if he'd been burned?

There's enough illegal guns in New York to arm a South American revolution. Most of them have not had the best of care.

Suppose the firing pin was broken?

Caleb's delicate reasoning: Not a new gun, hence, not from some hijacked arms shipment or from an armory somewhere.

Billy-the-cop claimed that his guns were dependable; would he lie? The precinct cops had confiscated them from citizens who should have known better.

Perhaps Caleb's .38 had once huddled under the underwear of some executive's bureau in Cleveland. Who stuck it in his suitcase when he came to Mugger New York. Who took it out of his suitcase at the Americana. Who got drunk downtown, looking for hippy hookers. Who got noisy in some clip joint and was ejected, forthwith. Who was banging on the door of the clip joint, asserting his rights, while the bartender called the precinct house. And the cops shook him down. And came up with—aha—Deadly Weapon.

So the executive pays the cops fifty to let him go back to his respectability. And Billy gets the gun, which he offs at some slight profit to all. But what if Mr. Executive has let his gun rust inside? What if he broke the firing pin, quick-drawing the gun at some cocktail party?

Caleb couldn't think anymore. He pulled the Renault over at a rest area. He stopped the car, but left the engine running. He couldn't find the switch for the dome light.

Two semis parked nose to tail. Silent, dark; the drivers sacked out in their narrow bunks behind the cab.

Caleb lit a match and inspected the pistol. Spanish writing on top of the hexagonal barrel and fairly crude machining. He swung the cylinder out. Six bulbous slugs. He pulled the hammer back with his thumb and eased it forward again.

"Goddamn it," he said.

Roared out of the rest area with little tires spitting gravel.

Dark night. Stars and moon proceeding overhead.The world was a huge bowl with the Interstate bisecting it.

Lights were rare, faint, distant. Farming country and four o'clock and Guernseys lying dense and steamy in the thick hay.

Caleb rolled down the window. Ice blast of air and some vagrant odor of something alive sneaking past the smell of dead gasoline.

Caleb stuck his hand out the window and yanked the trigger.

Barooom! The blast of light scared him, and he almost lost control. The little Renault was weaving from one lane to the other like a drunk.

When he got her pointed right again, Caleb dropped the pistol back on the seat and wiped his hands on his pants and stretched his back muscles.

The engine was missing more often.

Not many other cars.

Caleb took a hit of coke.

It started getting light about six thirty, and the old car was rolling through the lush Shenandoah Valley. Breadbasket of the Confederacy during the war, and grey and blue cavalry rampaging up and down, colliding at this crossroads or this sleepy farming town.

Caleb was pretty well wired as he pulled into Marion, Virginia, early on a Sunday morning.

She was shut up tight as a drum. All the sidewalks were pulled in, and the bright American (Californian) mannequins in the shopwindows were the only citizens to welcome him.

He found a truckstop that was open, and along with his bacon, eggs, grits and coffee, the waitress gave him the information: "The people you're looking for might be living up in the mountains, in a big old place outside of Stamper's Draft."

Caleb asked, "Where's that?" And after some confusion, her assuming he knew more than he did, Caleb had enough directions to start off again.

As he was turning to go, she tapped him with a parting shot. "Of course, honey, if you want to, you could ask down at Jim Halsey's office. He's the sheriff, and he knows most everything."

So Caleb got back in the car, a little worried again.

Marion is a farming town. It's got a big livestock market, a couple of tractor dealerships, and two big grain elevators dominate the skyline.

But its got the usual string of split-levels and brick ranchers on the outskirts, because, after all, it doesn't want to be un-American or anything. It was quite a while before the ranked small developments became sparser and finally vanished altogether.

Starting to snow a bit and the flakes melted as they brushed his windshield. Only a few farmhouses beside the two-lane blacktop and the road twisty and dangerous. Caleb drove slow. Rising into the mountains and now some fairly heavy timber came down to the edge of the road.

About twenty miles out of Marion, Caleb saw a sign pointing to Stamper's Draft. Narrow one-lane asphalt with crumbly reddish cliffs on his right and a creek-river running through the valley on the driver's side.

Caleb drove slower.

Mr. Leyland Bob Mustoe runs the general store in Stamper's Draft. Mr. Leyland Bob Mustoe is seventy-three. He's got a five-year-old son. His wife (a well-liked, comely woman) died last year, and it's pretty hard for an old man to raise a contrary boy all by hisself.

If he retired, he could get ten grand for his store, mostly because he has the only two gas pumps in town. But he won't retire. He has no golden dreams of a golden-age community in Florida. He's said that if he retired, he'd die. He's noticed that most of the old folks who leave die within a year, and he don't count himself an exception to the general laws of men.

L.B. Mustoe is a man with enthusiasms. One of his most remarked enthusiasms is triggered whenever a good-looking, young girl comes into his store. In a flash, L.B.

straightens his bum leg, flushes his knobby old veins, and demonstrates that his last dental work occurred in 1938, when dentists were still fond of bright yellow gold.

Perhaps L.B.'s delight in the ladies is practicality, no more. Perhaps the pokes and prods which made Miss Albemarle complain, "He makes me feel like a side of beef" —perhaps they are no more than a desire to share the raising of the contrariest boy in the whole valley with another human soul.

But, probably not.

Although he's a registered Republican, one of his favorite maxims is: "Rich man never let the poor man get up, nohow."

When Caleb pushed the old wooden door open, he was uttering that simple maxim to Mister Joe Bailey, who owned the Stamper's Draft Post Office and was, hence, the postmaster.

Mister Mustoe went behind the counter and waited for Caleb to state his needs.

Caleb bought a Pepsi from an old cooler in front of the counter.

Funky old store—canned goods, no fresh vegetables, a wheel of cheese, snuff, and a big old oil-burning stove in the middle of the floor. Caleb bought himself a pack of Camels. The old man gave him his change.

"I'm looking for some friends of mine," Caleb began.

Mister Mustoe waited politely for him to finish, but he didn't. Queer fella.

Caleb started again: "Do you know if there's a commune near here?" he asked.

Mr. Mustoe considered. "Don't reckon as how I do," he said.

Joe Bailey came out of the back of the store, his belly hardly clearing the gap between the stove and the shelves lined with ancient canned soups and fruits. "Simon Piano told me once that those folks down Clearwater were trying to start a commune," he said. He chuckled. "He said they weren't having too much luck at it."

"Turn right, down there and follow the Jenny Mountain Road out past Peterson's place, the big log house. If them's those you're looking for," Mr. Mustoe said, helpfully.

"I'm a stranger here," Caleb said.

Mr. Mustoe waited for him to finish, again, and this time the boy did.

"And I don't know the Jenny Mountain Road."

"Only other road in Stamper's Draft," Mr. Mustoe told him.

Caleb felt foolish, though for no reason. So he said thank you and started to go, and Mr. Mustoe reminded him that it would be two cents deposit on the bottle if he was going to take it out, so he drained the Pepsi and left the bottle there.

"What do you think," Joe Bailey asked, after the Renault zipped away. "Does he or Mr. Piano have more hair?"

Mr. Leland Bob Mustoe shook his head. "Don't rightly know," he said. "Both of 'em got right smart of hair. My granddaddy had hair like that when he fought with J.E.B. Stuart. I seen pictures of him that my sister Harriet's got now," he concluded, vaguely.

"Bet you a quarter he don't get through."

"Done," Mr. Mustoe agreed, amiably. "Them little foreign cars go pretty good in the snow."

But Caleb's little foreign car had no tread left on its tires, and, Mr. Mustoe to the contrary, he was having a lot of trouble. Narrow dirt roads and bad visibility and when he maintained enough speed for the hills, he slid around the corners. Four, maybe five inches of snow on the road and Caleb slowing dangerously, because the snow was battering his windshield like a herd of suicidal moths and the wipers hardly keeping up.

Only two lighted farmhouses in three miles.

Looking for mailboxes, and some had names on them and some didn't, and not too many of either kind.

Doing fifteen miles an hour.

Just two miles past the point where Caleb began to doubt

the directions, the headlights picked up a Chinese ideo-
graph on a white board, hanging from a pole beside the
road.

He stopped, backed up, and after a little hesitation,
pointed the car down a narrow rocky road, downhill to the
right. More like a path than a road.

The pan touching bottom now and then, delicate bang
and too narrow to miss all the rocks.

The road leveled out finally, and Caleb pulled in and
parked between an old green and yellow school bus and an
older Chevy pickup truck, red.

Caleb shut down.

He could see the pilings of a rickety suspension bridge,
like narrow goalposts, behind the truck, and he supposed
that was where he should go.

He lit a cigarette and moved his foot off the gas pedal. It
felt like a brick on the end of his leg.

Most of the Renault's weather stripping had rotted years
ago, and the cold air walked right in.

He wondered what time it was.

He wondered if the sun would ever come out, or whether
this time its absence was permanent.

He wiggled into his jacket.

He crammed his Spanish pistol under the seat.

His legs loosened up, like suddenly becoming animal
again, and as he straightened up outside the car, he lost his
vision for a quarter second.

Too much blood.

The snow was four inches of fluff toppling over the toe of
his boot.

The water was roaring. Little river-creek, maybe twelve
feet wide. The bridge was maybe twenty feet long; the
water was boiling around the boulders below, and the
bridge not too sturdy. He crossed cautiously, with one hand
on the rope-handrail.

Through the falling snow, he saw a warm window; yel-
low-cream square.

Big two-story log building with that one lighted window,

which he guessed was the kitchen. He crunched around to the side of the house and banged on the door. It was one of those doors with a window in it, and the red polka dot curtains were open, so he eyeballed the place to see if anything lay in wait.

The emotional center of the short room was a giant white cookstove against the far wall. It was a battleship of stoves, a sacred white elephant of stoves. If stoves wore hats, this stove would have worn a hat with an imitation canary on it.

Three people sitting at the end of a long trestle table, which nearly filled the kitchen. On one wall, a cabinet filled with little bottles of spices and tea. Maybe a hundred different little bottles.

Caleb's knock. Startled, all three people flinched. Ghostey at the door?

The man was twenty-one/twenty-two, had roan-colored hair and a scraggly red beard, which was thick and wiry on his cheeks, but sparse on his chin. He opened the door for Caleb.

Eyes as deep green as new rye. You wouldn't expect eyes that color in such a homely face. He was taller than Caleb by two inches.

"Hi," Caleb said. "Is Karen here?"

"I'm Nelson," the kid said, "Bob Nelson."

"Caleb Smith."

Bob Nelson didn't budge from that doorway. Blocking it, quiet as a wall.

"Let him in, Bob," one of the women said. "It's drafty." She put her knitting down. It looked like she was knitting something small, for a baby.

She was no prize looker, either. Thick yellow braids piled on top of her head, heavy bones, except for her face which was a little wrong for her mass, somehow, too delicate.

Something in her flesh, some aura of genetic possibility prompted Caleb: "You Karen's sister?"

"Why don't you sit down?" she said. "It's cold out. Would you like some coffee?"

"Uh, yeah. Sure." Caleb sat down with a thump and

accompanying little smile of apology, which everyone smiled back to, but not with their eyes.

"Do you take milk?" she asked. "I'm sorry, but we only have dry milk. It isn't too bad in coffee. And here's the honey. We buy it up the valley at Mrs. Hiner's. Maybe you passed the place on the way in?"

The other woman, short, brown-haired, was reading a book and not looking up, which Caleb didn't understand. Out here, they must get about three visitors a month, and Caleb thought (nothing personal mind you) that she ought to be a mite more interested. She held out her cup to be filled when the coffee was being poured, and as soon as she had hers filled, she said "Excuse me," and left the kitchen.

"Sure," Caleb said.

The White Stove was smoking, and Caleb's eyes smarted.

"Sorry about the stove," Bob Nelson said, in his pleasant kid's voice. "The wood's wet, and the only way to get it hot enough to bake is to close the damper down all the way."

"Can't you get bottled gas out here?" Caleb asked.

The woman, who was maybe Karen's sister, said, "It's expensive."

Caleb picked up a sense of a long dispute hanging in the air, like gunsmoke from yesterday's battle. They were closing ranks.

"I want to see Karen," Caleb said.

"She may not want to see you," Bob Nelson said, still calm. He was wearing a pair of blue jeans more brown-grey than blue, and every fiber impacted with dirt.

The woodsmoke was really irritating Caleb's eyes. "That's true," he said, "but I guess she should decide that."

"I'll ask her, Bob," the woman said. "Why don't you and uh . . . Mr. Smith finish your coffee."

She left. Bob Nelson scratched his head, and Caleb scratched his head, too.

"Still snowing?" Nelson asked, politely.

"Yeah," Caleb grunted.

Despite the smoky stove, the room was cold and Caleb

kept his jacket on. He let his eyes drift around the kitchen as if he was interested.

The south wall had shelves on both sides of the sink. Unplaned 1 by 6s, rough cut, but sturdy enough. On both ends of the south wall, windows looked out at an afternoon as grey as the greyest Thanksgiving.

He waited. He saw two men in heavy red-checked wool jackets approaching the house. One had a chain saw dangling from his hand. The other one shoved him, and he sprawled into a snowbank. "Chain-saw" jumped up, hopping mad, and chased the transgressor to the door of the kitchen. The door burst open. The runaway laughed and slammed it behind him, bracing his back to hold it closed. Boom, boom, boom, on the door, and the door vibrated and shook.

Silence for five seconds and the first guy was just wiping a laugh tear from his eye when, with a terrific roar, the chain saw started up.

"Cameron, you running-dog-lackey-of-the-imperialist-pigs, if you don't open the door, I'm gonna cut her in half."

Deafening roar of the powerful little motor. Cameron made a face, and tiptoed away from the door and through the kitchen, like a stork with a hotfoot.

The door burst open again, and a fat dude was standing there, framed by the doorway, laughing and waving the chain saw around. Oil spraying off the chain and blue exhaust fumes shooting into the kitchen. "I'll cut him in half," the fat man bellowed. "And then I'll make a crowd of him."

The brown-haired lady came back to see what was.

"Jesus Christ," she shouted, "turn that damn thing off, Lang. You're stinking up the whole kitchen."

He turned it off and noticed Caleb sitting there. "Howdy," he said, not at all abashed; and to the woman, "We dropped six white oak and eight hickory. I'm hungry enough to eat a mud hen. You eat yet?" This to Caleb.

"No thanks."

"You sure?" he asked. "Anybody else?" He pulled a pan off the stove and poured hot water into a washbasin. "You heard. I'm Lang. Langtry Jeremiah Holter."

"This is Caleb Smith," Bob Nelson said.

Give Lang credit. He didn't say "Oh shit," though obviously he was thinking it. He gave Caleb a short nod and turned to his skillet. He mixed rice and the remnants of yesterday's vegetables, stirring them with a spatula.

"Karen's sister" came back into the kitchen and planted herself stage center. Except for her breasts which were pointed outwards, left to left and right to right, she looked like a German porcelain doll.

"Karen doesn't want to see you," she said, flat. The message wasn't from her; she was just an agent. Otherwise she'd apologize first. She'd still say it if it was from her, but she'd apologize first.

The fat man looked up from his cooking, assessed, grunted, and went back to watching his concoction steam.

The redhead nudged some mud off the heel of his boot with the toe of his other boot.

"She doesn't want to see you," she said again.

"You Karen's sister?" Caleb asked. "She told me a little about you. The family still hassling you?"

"I think maybe you should split," she said.

"You ever drive a police cruiser?" Caleb asked. "In the snow? They're really fast. A stone gas."

She had blue eyes and braids and she was somebody's big mama, but her jaw was quivering.

"Please go," she said.

The fat man clanged down his skillet on the iron of the stove. "God damn it," he said, softly and finally.

He spread his thick legs when he turned around, and Caleb saw it wasn't all fat. Not even mostly fat.

Maybe 225 pounds, pleading. "Friend, I don't know about you, and I don't want to know. Karen is real upset. Her old man is dead, and she's been crying since she got here. If she don't want to see you, then I 'spose you won't see her. Maybe we better get your car up the hill before the snow gets any worse."

"I'm Caleb Smith," Caleb said. His body weariness welled up and overflowed. He felt sick to his stomach. He felt dizzy. "I was there when Denny died. I couldn't help him. It's been a long trip, man. I can't screw around anymore. If Karen doesn't want to see me, I think she should tell me herself."

And either Caleb was crashing off the coke and twenty hours of exhaustion or (alternatively) he was faking it when he got up to face the fat man. His face went white, and he braced his hand against the wall because he was falling.

The fat dude had amazing suspenders. Christmas suspenders, red and green and bright brass buckles just above the yoke where it attached to the suspender buttons. The suspenders were streaked with oil and kerosene, and wood chips hung like burrs to the wool shirt under them. Big chest breathing.

"You alright man?" he heard.

Caleb said something.

The fat man got him by the armpits and sat him in a chair. A pressure on Caleb's neck. The fat man was pushing his head down between his knees.

And the blurry, spinning colors which filled his eyes stabilized, held still, and became objects again.

"Go away."

Caleb registered Karen's words. The foot of the trestle table was bruised from years of careless farm boots. It had been varnished once or twice. Caleb could see how the varnish had split away from the gouges.

She was standing behind her sister. Sister was wider than Karen, but Karen was taller by half a head.

Sister must have felt like a rowboat caught between a U-boat and a freighter. Very quick she got out of the line of fire.

Karen's white feet. Her white muslin nightshirt. Her face was white as white dust.

"What do you want?" she whispered. "What do you want from me?"

"Oh," Caleb said. "I thought . . . I guess I didn't think."

Lang, Karen's sister, Bob—none of them were breathing or seeing or anything.

"Oh, goddamn you," Karen said, and she had all her stash of tears running down her face. And her face was orange-pink; she looked like a turnip, and her face was wrinkling and getting smaller.

"Please, Caleb. . ."

So Caleb stole from his own troubles.

"Yeah," he said, smooth and plain as new pine. "I thought you wouldn't want to. I'm sorry, Karen. There's so many people trying to kill me, and I'm really afraid to die. It isn't the dying so much as being in the grave so long." He smiled at her, sweet as a child. "Denny. . ." he said. "I wish . . . I'm sorry. I would have swapped places with him if I could."

Karen's throat was swallowing or trembling and no words out.

Caleb got up to go. No weave or nothing. "I meant to say I love you, but here I'm saying good-bye," he muttered/sang, a little off-key. "Do you like Chicago blues?"

A roomful of absent people. Nobody was part of what was was between them. Caleb suddenly knew that the nervous chick wanted, very badly, to light a cigarette.

He sighed and went outside and the snow was finding its way down his collar and he was shivering.

For the first time in years, he wasn't going anywhere.

That interested him and he stopped this side of the bridge to puzzle.

He clutched his jacket closed.

He heard the fat man coming before he saw him, and turned, mildly curious.

Caleb really dug those suspenders.

"What?" Caleb asked.

And the fat man said Caleb should stay; there was a place

he could sleep in, and did he have a sleeping bag? Caleb said that he didn't, and the fat man detoured back into the house to fetch a huge pile of quilts, brightly colored crazy quilts, and blankets, too; and he took Caleb down to the woodshed, where Caleb scooped up both arms full of kindling—the fat man saying: "Take the ones in the back, they're drier." And off again, oddly merry, toward a tilting grey building, and them squeezing through a board door that wouldn't fully open, into what had been, and still smelled like, an old barn, and the fat man getting an oil-drum stove going, and piling the quilts in what used to be a horse stall, remnants of a pile of hay, and Caleb crawled under them and dropped so fast that his stomach lurched until he hit bottom somewhere safe.

It was one of those split-second sleeps, where you close your eyes when they count one and open them when they count two. And total black in between.

When Caleb woke up, it was morning.

Some lanky dude was standing in the warped doorway of the barn, his breath hanging in the frosty air.

"G'morning," the dude said, cheerfully. Levi jacket over three different colored shirts, Levi pants, and a pair of engineer boots. Hair a little short by New York freak standards, but, Caleb guessed, too long for here.

"Morning," Caleb muttered, and wiggled inside the pile of quilts.

"Simon Piano," the dude announced.

"Caleb Smith," Caleb grunted. He sat up and pulled a cigarette out of a forgotten rumpled pack. The cigarette tasted forgotten. "What time is it?"

"Must be seven-thirty," Simon said, more happily than was called for. "You slept a long time."

"I guess," Caleb said.

Simon shifted his weight from one foot to the other. "There's breakfast up at the house," he said. "Karen's gone into town with my old lady, but she said she wanted to talk to you when she came back."

So Caleb got up and gathered his sleeping robes and followed Simon Piano to the main house.

The air was clear. A magnifying glass. Snow bunched on the evergreens and they were white haystacks and the oak trees with their leaves gone were sad unfrocked priests.

The farm lay in a hollow, with misty hills surrounding it. The snow swallowed sound. It was dead quiet except for a few juncoes calling to each other.

"We got sixty acres here," Simon said. "That's the far line down there." He pointed to a fence which traversed a ridge to their east. Caleb had no idea how big an acre was, but the land Simon was describing with his finger was very big, maybe four square blocks.

He pointed at the mountains. "That's all government land," he said.

Caleb had the feeling he was getting the official tour, or part of it, and that made him feel good. Less uninvited.

"Our nearest neighbor is four miles from here," Simon said. "You can just see the corner of his barn over there."

Caleb could indeed see the corner of the neighbor's barn. He could also see the sun flashing on its tin roof. "Terrific," he said. "I like to be around a lot of people, know what I mean?"

"Really?" Simon took him seriously. "Not me, boy. I get claustrophobic."

They went into the kitchen, and Simon fried up some bacon and eggs, explaining that since there were eight grownups and two kids on the commune, breakfasts and lunches were do-it-yourself, and how did he like the eggs which their hens were still laying, it being a mild winter, and was the bacon OK? The bacon had once been an integral part of Herman, a porker they'd slaughtered in the fall.

It was pretty good bacon, though Caleb had tasted better, but Caleb didn't mention his reservations because he was hungry and wanted another couple slices.

These people hadn't known Denny. They weren't wanted

by anyone. Caleb envied Simon's enthusiasms, but couldn't share them.

"We grow almost all our own food," Simon continued. Innocent. "Except for rice and salt and that sort of thing. If we can get it together, we'll buy staples once a year in Washington and store the stuff as we use it. It's ridiculous trooping off to the store every other day if you can build a big enough storeroom."

Caleb agreed politely and asked if there was any coffee.

Simon handed him an old wooden coffee grinder and a bag of A&P coffee beans. He shifted a pot of hot water from the back of the stove.

The kitchen was warmer today, because it was warmer outside, no doubt. The coffee grinder was awkward to hold and tiring to work. Caleb wrestled with it until he had a heap of granulated coffee in a bowl.

"There are some advantages to instant coffee," Caleb said, peevishly.

Simon laughed. "You know, you're right," he said. "I've never seen a well-designed coffee grinder. They ought to make them so you could bolt them to something solid. The grain mill is a bitch, too." He pointed to a metal device which looked like an old-fashioned meat grinder. "You know," Simon said, very, very seriously, "I used to want to be hip. Babies, homemade bread, clean air, natural things —you know."

Funny nice grin he had.

"Well," Caleb said, politely, "it's nice to have something you want to do."

"Not always," Simon said, as if Caleb's politeness had given him a chance to show off the reverse of his enthusiasms. "It's awfully hard to decide things for yourself. Sometimes, it's really depressing."

The coffee was good, but, Caleb thought, not worth the effort of grinding it.

"How do you make a living?" Caleb asked.

"Tain't easy," Simon said. He stirred his coffee. "We sure

haven't got it together. You know, there's only three thousand people in this entire county, and I'll bet there aren't half that many paying jobs. Say, could I borrow one of your cigarettes? Roll-your-owns are a drag. Whenever a visitor shows up, it's like locusts on his cigarettes."

So Caleb gave him one. Simon ran down their economic status, and Caleb was waiting for Karen, so he gave him half an ear. Simon said they needed three hundred dollars a month, and he played piano in a roadhouse Thursday, Friday, and Saturday nights, which got them two hundred dollars of it, and Lang and Bob Nelson did carpentry or farmwork for the other hundred.

"And sometimes, one of the women does a little waitressing in Marion if we need a little extra," he concluded. "We'd like to make a living off the land, but our soil ain't red-hot, and besides, people who've been farming all their lives are having a tough time, let alone beginners like us."

"Grow dope," Caleb suggested.

Simon poured himself another cup of coffee, overfilled his blue-enameled tin cup, and some coffee splashed on the table. He rubbed it with his hand. "Dope?" he said. "We thought about it. Karen says you deal heavy."

Caleb said, "I do a little," and stretched. The warmth of the kitchen was making him sleepy.

"Hello." A soft woman's voice and Caleb turned to greet the newcomer.

"Hi, toots," Simon said. "How's Jason?"

"Oh, nothing serious. The doctor gave him a couple of shots and he cried and the doctor said that half the kids in the county have it, and he only charged me two dollars. I'm Annabelle," she said to Caleb.

Annabelle was an impossible, classically beautiful woman. Lean as a doe, and a sense of long muscles under her clothes. Lovely smoke-grey eyes and she knew all about her loveliness and carried herself accordingly.

"Annabelle is my old lady," Simon said. "We thought about growing pot," Simon persisted, "but that's the big fantasy trip of anybody who moves to the country. This isn't abandoned land. People go through it all the time. Berry pickers, coon hunters, or somebody looking for a stray cow. And if you hide the plants well enough so the neighbors don't find them, then it's pretty damn likely the deer will."

"Simon Piano," Annabelle said, with a smile, "hush up."

He gives her a grin and says: "Sure thing. But I got to say something, don't I?"

Little death silence until he tries to recover his fumble with: "I haven't had a chance to show a visitor how groovy we are for three weeks."

She touched Caleb's shoulder. "Karen's in the big room," she said.

So Caleb followed her into another part of the house.

Odd hodgepodge of a house. Doors and passageways and rooms and not much sense of a central purpose behind it. It was a farmhouse and, like many old farmhouses, had been designed and built and added on to by owners fifty years apart.

Some of the rooms were bright painted and Sierra Club posters, and some of the rooms still covered with the dull green Monkey Ward's paint that was there when the commune moved in. Hodgepodge.

Annabelle saw him noticing, and said: "It's a real drafty house, but it's a lot nicer here in the summer. You can swim in the river and everything."

"It's OK now," Caleb said, politely.

"Thank you," she said. "It's nice to have someone pleasant around here for a change, instead of all these grumps." Annabelle was a coquette.

She led him into the big room, and Karen was sitting on a cushion on the floor, looking not happy about seeing him.

Once upon a time, the room had been spacious. But now, there was a piano in it and a wood-stove and a couch and half a dozen chairs and half a dozen cushions. And paintings of indifferent quality and stereo speakers of superior quality hanging on the walls. All that junk might as well have been nonexistent. Karen's unhappiness filled the room.

Normally, Annabelle would have been the lovelier of the two women—a classic ideal of beauty vs. Karen's ruggeder, heavier good looks—a Leonardo face compared, say, with one of Degas' tough little dancers.

But now, Karen's face had a thousand years of simplicity in it and all the knowledge that accompanies death. Any comparison was unfair; Annabelle was a toy. Annabelle left quietly.

"Hullo," Karen said. Her voice was dull as pig iron. She patted a cushion beside her—not too close—and Caleb sat down and wrapped his arms around his knees.

"Did they hurt him?" she asked. "I meant to ask you before, but I forgot or something."

Her eyes were two shiny ball bearings.

"Did they hurt him?" she asked again, persistent, monotonic.

"No," Caleb said.

"Why are you men such tough guys?" she asked.

Caleb felt the sweat starting in his armpits and groin.

She was curious; she wanted to know why men were tough guys. Caleb couldn't think of an answer.

A black curtain hung directly back of her eyes, and Caleb could feel the light being absorbed in it.

"How's your hand?" she asked, not varying a syllable.

"OK."

"Let me see it."

Caleb's cushion was too far. Awkwardly he crawled over to Karen and presented his hand. Her fingers on the bandage were feathers of herons or ice clouds in the late afternoon.

The rag bandage fell away, and Caleb saw his fingers again.

Blunt. Swollen. Red. The whole hand was swollen. Infected.

The finger stubs were scabbed. Purple over the red.

"You haven't been keeping it clean," Karen said, not surprised.

"No. I guess not."

The feathers were tickling his hand.

"It's so easy to hurt," Karen said.

She didn't increase her grip one jot, but sweat was running down his forehead and into his eyes. Salty sweat. It hurt.

"It's easy to be a tough guy," she explained, patiently.

The bones in Caleb's hand were each being crucified separately. An intense and sexual excitement, the tension between him and his hand in the fire.

She and Denny had touched each other, and NOW HE'S GONE.

She began, finally, to cry and slow streaks dripping pat-pat onto her wrist, cooling it, damping the current.

The life coming back to Caleb's hand.

Karen's eyes changing color. The blackness washing away like the rain washes the thunderheads that gave them birth.

She pulled a beat-up handkerchief from behind her and blew her nose.

Caleb lay his hand on his lap. It felt cool.

"Well, I guess we might as well play it out," she said, brightly. Brightly, but underneath the brightly, she was OK.

Caleb ventured a just possible smile and watched her long hair and tried not to get hooked by her eyes again.

"Are you going to stay here?" he asked.

"For a while, I guess," she said. "I might go out to New Mexico. Denny's brother has a little place near Albuquerque. But I think I'll stay here until I get my head straight."

"They seem like nice people," Caleb said.

"They are. But they're really into the commune trip, and I don't think I can get into it. I really love my sister, but she's got her own life and her own old man. Jenny's with Bob Nelson, did you know?"

"How long have they been at it?"

"About six months. Oh, you mean the commune? About a year and a half, now."

He didn't trust her brightness. "Come on," he said, "why don't you show me around the place?"

And so they went out into that snowy morning, and after a while, Caleb gave her his hand again, and she smiled (flash), and they were holding hands like kids, and there was nothing odd about that at all.

Karen showed him the river and the pool where they swam in the summer. It was covered this January day with a thin film of ice, and Caleb saw what might have been a bass on the bottom.

They inspected the old barn, and Caleb poked at the huge chestnut timbers hewn when there still were huge trees and when there still were chestnuts.

They went into the chicken house, followed by fifty chickens who thought in their chicken brains that it was feeding time. Karen found two eggs.

They met Lang, who was whistling and talking to a window he was setting in a wall of the toolshed, and Lang said hello, but didn't take the nails out of his mouth.

The two kids, Jason and Katy, were having a snowball fight, ducking and dodging behind the snow-covered haystack, and Caleb said hello to them, and they ducked behind it and wouldn't come out, but giggled a lot.

Simon Piano and Nelson were working on the tractor engine and arguing with it and each other, so Karen and Caleb just waved from a distance.

"Is it for this my mommy and daddy scrimped and saved to send me through college?" the redhead yelled to them.

And Karen smiled and Caleb, seeing it, smiled, too.

They poked through every room in the big old house, from root cellar (pickled tomatoes) to the attic (mattresses and mouse droppings), and Caleb stood in the doorway of each room and said this or that, casual and wondering.

They stop, finally, in a narrow, tall bedroom, with a window overlooking the snow covered meadow.

"This is my sister's room," Karen said. "I've been sleeping here."

"It's pretty," Caleb said. Old, big pine bed with high sideboards. A cradle for adults. And a big circular hooked rug on the wide-board pine floor. A small fireplace. A chamberpot beside an old, big Empire walnut dresser. A small dressing table on which all the feminine accoutrements, times two.

"We might as well play it out," Karen said, quietly.

Warm air rising from the grate and Karen touching his arm.

Once, when Caleb was a novice dealer on the winter streets of New York, he owned a pair of deerskin gloves. Light-yellow, natural buckskin, with two snaps at the wrist and a small tightening strap over the back of the hand. It had been a young deer, or an unexceptionally strong older deer, or a deer magician. Some deer still in the deerskin. Some leap of deer. Some little jolt that spread from one of Caleb's fingers to the other. Some small grace that made his fingers a little more supple and swift and delicate as a flicker zipping through the cedar trees.

Caleb and Karen took off their clothes, and when he slid up into her, it was like that. Like putting on those deerskin gloves.

Sure, it's all motions up and down, from side to side. It's all chemicals churning electrodes into action and zipping those messages along the neurosympathetic twinge and the brain sorting them out like a busy accountant. Sure.

She wasn't sure she wanted to, but she finally said "hi," like a schoolkid. Caleb said hello back, not in his real voice.

So she invited him for sodas, and they got to know each other and grew a little older.

Caleb took her through the broken glass and rubble in the old brick alleys near the projects in Detroit. He took her into a blind pig. Night life. Where two incredibly ancient blacks, man and wife, were singing dark-blue blues.

She let him walk with her through a meadow in Con-

necticut on a bright, cold spring day with the green starting
to show, but frost-frozen.

She took him along the Kennebec in July to the pool
where she and Denny used to swim. High granite cliffs over
a deep pool in the blue water and the current tumbling you
and rolling you and retrieving you into a natural eddy.
Denny oined them there, and was naked, too. The sky
changed then and went purple-blue. Denny was in Caleb's
arms for a minute, and then, all three, not speaking over the
roar of the water, lay down under a hot August sun on a slab
of granite to dry.

Caleb lay with his head on her breast, not sleeping, just
free-floating and easy. She stroking the back of his neck.

They must have balled three or four more times that
afternoon, working out their memories and making
promises.

Sometime in between, lying under a down quilt and the
fire crackling, Caleb told her about John and the corner he
was in. She must have held him closer then, her body of
yeast, her skin sweet as new bread.

Some of the things Caleb had wished they'd do, they did,
and some not. Cold and bright outside the window, with the
snow scattering and swooping.

Nobody knocked at their door. No footsteps came down
the long hall. Still, everybody knew, and that night three
other beds shook in the old farmhouse. Even Lang's. Lang
was usually a male solitary, but Dot, the nervous chick,
visited his room that night and eased his pain.

Sometimes when Karen moved, she was moving to
Denny, and for those sometimes, Caleb simply stayed with
her, letting her sadness drain.

But mostly, she tossed and heaved for him, for them, and
Caleb quite dissolved.

They had found their warm burrow, and outside, the
west wind—the weather wind—pushing the snow around a
little, shoving it under the woodshed, banking it against the

trunks of the black walnuts, and letting it slide along the house.

The two of them lying there, watching the sun bowing his farewell behind a line of spare grey willows. Caleb cupped around Karen like two nesting spoons.

"I'm hungry," she said, and got up and turned on the beside lamp, and Caleb watching her cover herself, wanting her again; but she was setting herself for the others, and he got up and dressed, too, and both of them went downstairs.

Kitchen very smoky. Lang clattering skillets and whirling around to dice some carrots on a chopping block on the table. Red-headed Bob Nelson was rolling joints; Simon and Annabelle were puzzling over the *I Ching*. Karen's sister, Jenny, sipping tea from a fancy red private cup.

"Karen," she said, affectionately, "you're outrageous."

Caleb saw that Jenny's nipples were distended and pretty good size under her sweatshirt, and he wondered what her breasts did when she was balling, not wanting her particularly at this moment, but just wondering.

Karen blushed and said something like: "You're pretty outrageous yourself." Something like that.

Lang clanged his skillets louder and said, "Goddamn this thing." And smoke pouring from a huge hole in the top of the stove and Lang looking for the stove-plate that covered it.

Bob Nelson laughed. "What was your grade-point when you were in college?" he asked.

"All C's," Lang said, still clattering. "When I wasn't too drunk to go. Ah, yes, my boys, a great English critic was lost to the world when I got too wrecked, finally, to go to class at all." He took a heavy drag on a joint and kept it. "I was bound for that old professional life, but Devil Dope got me first. Think of it, now." He pointed to Annabelle. "Some little, quiet, green campus, just outside of Provo, or Denver. Here you are, hanging around, maybe not a full professor, but at least halfway and nobody gonna can your ass because you got tenure. Man, you could be drunk all the time! And teeny-boppers in the front row, flashing that sweet stuff at you!"

Dot came into the kitchen. "How's the stew?" she asked.

Lang stuck a curious finger into one of the pots on the stove and sucked on it. "Good boogie," he pronounced.

"I wish you wouldn't stick your fingers in the food," Dot said. "Or that you'd wash your hands before you cook. One or the other."

"Flavors the venison," Lang said. "Mr. Smith, you are about to taste genuine Allegheny deer flesh. Dead deer is better than dead cow, anytime."

"Caleb," Jenny asked, "What's going to happen to my sister?"

Lang tiptoeing around in the background. Dot lit a cigarette. A store-bought cigarette.

Caleb turned to Karen. "How much do they know?" he asked.

"Everything that happened in Maine. I haven't said anything about what you told me about John and Chris and the informer stuff."

Caleb scratched his head.

"Wait a minute," Simon said. "Before you say anything, you should know where we're at, because . . . well, because this is more serious political business than we usually get involved in. Augh . . . ," he slapped himself on the head. "I'm such a muddlehead," he explained. "Look. We talked it all over last night. About you and Karen being on the run and all. And it would only be fair if I told you where we were at before you confided in us any more than Karen has." He thought for a moment. He wrinkled his face. "A couple of years ago," he began, "Weatherman politics were a lot more appealing than they seem now. I was at the Chicago convention; Lang was in SDS; most of us, at one time or another, made the marches and tangled with the cops. But now, we don't do much of that sort of thing anymore. You're a ghost, sort of. Do you understand?"

Caleb made a face.

Simon turned a little red in the face. "I mean ... I mean that both you and Karen can stay here for a couple of months anyway. Because we don't want to turn you out and besides, who knows, you might be doing the right thing. Maybe our little farm here is one collosal copout." He moved his hands apart, dismissing the subject, and said, "Where's that stew?"

And their talk was suspended while plates were passed around, and somebody poured glasses of water, and somebody else dipped the stew with a big iron ladle.

The stew was really good, and Caleb was hungry.

While they ate, Caleb explained things to people who seemed more interested in stew than his information.

He told them about John, about the Weather Bureau. He told them about Chris the informer. Nobody looked up from their plate.

"I don't know what I'm going to do now," Caleb said. "I try not to think about it. Karen'll be OK, probably. If she can stay low for a couple of months. The cops ran all that "harboring a Weatherman fugitive" crap, but nobody is going to buy that nonsense except the newspapers. The only thing they're likely to stay mad about is the dope. I don't think they'll stay mad too long. The cops are really busy these days, and they ain't got time for wild-goose chases. Not when even if they caught you, you'd probably get off with a year's probation. I mean, if they'd got Karen to jail in Maine when public feelings were high and Denny was still alive—sorry babe; I mean that it's going to blow over, with a little time."

Caleb was tired of talking. "Pass the bread," he said.

They ate heavy and steady.

Finally, Lang pushed his plate away from him, belched like an old bear, and asked, "How about yourself? You're pretty hot, aren' you?"

"Yeah," Caleb said, slow, "I suppose so."

Caleb didn't like to talk about himself. Biography had an

unpleasant way of becoming evidence. But they had offered to let him stay. And he couldn't gracefully say nothing.

Blunt Caleb: "It's a box. The FBI is looking for me because of Maine. The Weathermen are looking for me because they think I'm an FBI informer. If either one gets me, I suppose the other one will quit looking." He shrugged.

Lang was picking his teeth with a wood splinter.

Bob, the redhead, was rolling one careful joint after another.

Karen was watching his face.

"I ain't too worried about the FBI," Caleb said, finally. "A long time ago, I got busted bad in Detroit for dope." He grinned, "I had another name then." He reached into his pocket for a Camel and found nothing but a rumpled empty pack. "I figure that if they couldn't hang onto me then, they can't catch me now. Besides," he argued, "look at all the people the FBI hasn't been able to catch. It took 'em months to catch Berrigan, and they never did get Cleaver, and for that matter, they haven't caught the Weather Bureau, yet." He paused. "Not yet, anyway."

Bob Nelson was passing out joints, one to a customer.

"But Goddamn it," Caleb said, "I really don't like to be running from the Weathermen. I'm not so scared that they're going to hit me; John might do it, but the Weatherpeople aren't going to make Caleb Smith 'Weather Enemy Number One'—it's just that . . ."

Caleb crumpled up his empty pack of cigarettes and stuffed it into the ashtray. "I just don't want to be an informer," he said. "I ain't one, and I don't want to be one. Ah, screw it. Anybody got a cigarette?"

Wordlessly, Lang handed him a can of tobacco and some rolling papers.

Everyone was quiet for a minute while Caleb fumbled with the tobacco until Annabelle said, "It's a bitch, alright. Anybody want some coffee?"

Lang washed the dishes, while they sat drinking coffee,

and Jenny asked Simon whether he'd had any luck offering to trade their surplus eggs for soap and matches at Mr. Mustoe's store, and he said he'd ask tomorrow. And Lang wondered whether the little oil leaks around the tractor's oil gasket would prove fatal, and nobody had an answer for that one either.

Caleb tossed his cocaine on the table, and Lang, nose twitching like a rabbit, cried happily, "The Amazing White Peruvian. Christ A'mighty."

And the envelope went all around the table; bang, bang, bang, bang.

Funny bright light in the kitchen. Everybody glowed.

"Man, this stuff is ILLEGAL," Simon said, outraged.

"You ought to be illegal," Lang observed. "Want to make some music?"

And so they took their coffee up and migrated to the big room, and Caleb took the can of rolling tobacco with him.

"Let's try 'Cocaine,'" Lang said. "Let's thank the Lord."

Lang had a big old Martin Dreadnaut, made maybe in 1935, and the wood mellowing every day thereafter. He started flat-picking the basic progression:

> Every time me-and-my-baby
> Go downtown
> Police come
> And they knock me down.
> Cocaine. Running round my brain.

Not bad flat-picking. But the tempo was too slow, and Simon picked it up on the piano, a little ragtimey.

Annabelle shook the tambourine off-beat. She stopped, set her mouth, tapped her foot until she had the beat, and then came in loud.

> Come here baby, come here quick
> Old cocaine 'bout to make me sick.
> Cocaine, all 'round my brain.

Lang was grinning at Simon because they'd been on, and so, when they were coming around for another verse, Simon started a long tinkley run, held it longer, longer (while Lang strummed along, obediently), and then stopped dead. Half a tick before Lang was supposed to start singing again.

In that space, Lang hit three bell-like notes on the old Martin. Lang then smiled at Simon.

Simon said, "You prick."

And they wailed into the verse:

> Reached in my pocket
> Grabbed my poke
> Note in my pocket said:
> 'No more coke.' Co-
> caaaaaaaaaaaaaaine.
> Run all 'round my brain.

They made music. They sang the song so you could hear it.

Caleb lay beside Karen on the floor, stoned and his mind flickering over the choices he'd made. So slight at the time, but they'd formed him, every one. He felt Karen's ribs breathing and the scent of her body made a circle wherein he lay.

They made music for a medium-long time and were marvelous together. Caleb? Caleb? He was tapping his foot.

Karen nudged him finally and they went upstairs together and undressed each other and Caleb said, "Where's your sister going to sleep?"

And Karen said her sister would sleep with the redhead, and the old bed bounced on the wood floor again, and if anyone heard it, they just smiled and went back to sleep.

Caleb woke up early, hungry, and rolled out of the circle of Karen's sweet stink, dressed quick because his feet were cold on the floor and, with unlaced boots, stepped outside to take a piss.

He went back into the house long enough to lace his boots and grab his jacket and somebody's pair of green work gloves.

He crossed the bridge and walked down the road, thinking.

He'd worried and puzzled all night. He thought he'd found an answer, but now, in the morning, he wasn't so sure.

It was very cold, but walking faster kept him warm.

His plan seemed shaky to him, nearly impossible, vulnerable at every junction. But it was a plan. He was a little proud of himself for thinking about it even though it might not work.

And he couldn't think of any better ideas. And he didn't like running from EVERYBODY. So he tossed himself into his scheme like a Schlitz can tossed into the river.

Bob Nelson was in the kitchen working on the fire. Through the kitchen window Caleb watched Simon and Lang crawling under the tractor on a great square of patched tarpaulin.

"There's bacon and eggs in the icebox," Bob said. "Jump in."

So Caleb cooked his breakfast, the eggs cooking slow on the wood stove.

Caleb told Bob he wanted to work today. On something very hard. Bob gave him a look, but said, "Sure. But I don't know why you want to work when you don't have to. I wouldn't." He stuck another piece of wood in the firebox and asked Caleb if he'd found any more cigarettes.

Caleb said no, so Bob make a little face and started pouring tobacco from the can in the center of the table into a creased paper.

"Today," Bob said, "would be a grand day to sit in front of the fire. And the two things of absolute priority which got to be done are miserable and not for the likes of us literate folk. Let the rock-pickers work today. Today is a day for the triumph of New Jersey. Let the longshoremen from Jersey

City and the sandhogs from Newark have today. Let them do the work."

He blushed like a teenager when Caleb cocked his head, quizzical.

Caleb asked Bob if he was from New York, and Bob said that he'd lived in the city for a year, but his original home was in Connecticut.

After Caleb ate, they both went outside to work on the chimney. The kitchen chimney wasn't drawing right. That meant the stove wasn't heating up. That cold stove was inciting rebellion, spearheaded by the women (who shared the cooking, but baked all the bread).

Bob and Caleb got the extension ladder, hauled two buckets of mortar onto the tin roof, and set to.

The old mortar was rotten, and air was slipping between the bricks and confusing the draft. They had to tear the old bricks off down to where the mortar was solid. And then build the whole shebang back up again.

Caleb was afraid he'd fall off the roof.

They were standing two stories above the bare snowy lilac bushes. Standing on rotten planks nailed through the tin skin of the steep roof to the rafters below.

Cold.

Can't move from the waist down.

Wind.

Wind.

They worked in silence. Rustle of their clothing and the thump of the bricks as they stacked them on the uphill side of the chimney and bap, bap, of their hammers breaking mortar scraps, cleaning the bricks.

"You know," Bob said, "you got yourself in quite a pickle."

"Oh yeah?"

"Well," Bob said, "I had to start somewhere. Do you mind my talking about it?"

"What did you say?" Caleb yelled. "This wind. . ."

"I said '*I had to start somewhere,*' " Bob yelled.

Caleb extracted a brick and chipped a piece of clinging mortar off the end of it.

Caleb cut his palm against a scrap of brick.

"Does it bother you?" Bob said, loudly. "Your fingers, I mean."

"Sure," Caleb said. "It's like I'm three years old in that hand."

Bob pulled the last brick and tested the mortar and pronounced it solid enough and splashed a little water on a clean brick and laid the first repair on the chimney.

They were working closer together, and Bob didn't need to raise his voice. "Caleb," he said, "I don't know if this'll do you any good, but last night I was thinking and an incident came to me and I thought I'd tell it to you, though God knows why, since I couldn't figure out how or what it meant."

Caleb raised his eyebrows politely and laid a brick.

Bob was undaunted. "It happened when we were tearing down the old spring house. When those old carpenters put something together, they couldn't afford a lot of nails; so they did a lot of their joining with mortises and tenons. The effect is . . . well, it's like each part of the building is resting on each other part. Really strong. Really hard to tear down."

Caleb splashed too much mortar on his brick. He scraped it with the trowel.

Bob hurried his gait: "Anyway, I meant to say that your problem is that everything rests on everything else. When we tore down that spring house, we had to take out one wood prop after another until the whole thing fell in. You know what I mean?"

"No," Caleb said. "Hand me another brick."

The chimney grew back up layer by layer. Simon came over and asked if Bob'd come down and look at the tractor because now the damn voltage regulator was acting up. Caleb continued laying bricks as the wind got colder and the snow came.

From time to time a wisp of clammy dead flue gas rose up the chimney like a vice-president's breath.

The Alleghenies dipped in fog. Fog-snow clouds rolling down the draws and laying in the hollows.

Bob came back and announced he was knocking off for the day, and Caleb should, too, but Caleb said "No thanks," and Bob said he was a damn fool and went inside, where it was warm.

One by one, one brick chasing the next, buttered with mortar and butted up tight. And the aluminum level laid on each brick to keep it in conformation with the brick underneath.

Karen came out and asked him to come inside, and when he said he wouldn't, she got mad and took herself out of the storm.

He cut his hands, and his blood in the mortar gave it body.

The storm came in, the mountains were lost, and when he started a new row, he brushed the last row clear of snow.

Delicate, straight work. When he went wrong, he took the mislaid brick out and laid down a new bed for it. But he didn't go wrong too often.

He kept blinking to keep the snow off his eyeballs, and his cheeks were wet with tears.

Little shake in his muscles and he shifted his weight, easing himself on the fragile foothold.

The snow brought the dark early, and Caleb climbed down the ladder, leaving three bricks for someone to finish tomorrow.

He washed off the mortar bucket and trowels. He washed his hands, and the lime had dried his skin and made it papery to the touch. Annabelle told him to use some hand cream on them, and he did.

He ate the dinner Annabelle had cooked. Croakers, brown rice, butter collards, and it was pretty good. He told them all thank you, because he'd had a good time there, but he had to leave for a while. He told Karen she could either come with him or stay, and he'd come back and get her. She said, after some argument, that she didn't want to come to New York, and Caleb said that was probably for the best. When he was outside the kitchen door, he gave Bob twenty dollars for his share of the food he'd eaten, but Bob would only take ten. Simon and Bob pushed the little Renault up the hill with their pickup after they'd loaded the pickup box with timbers to give it traction.

The Renault went alright until Caleb reached New Hope, Pennsylvania about three o'clock the next morning. It quit, and Caleb rolled it off the shoulder, threw away the plates, and hitched a ride into New Hope with an eighteen-year-old freak who'd started driving on speed in California three days ago.

Caleb got off at the bus station. The first bus to New York was at eight o'clock, and Caleb was on it.

He called P.J. from a phone booth in the Port Authority.

P.J. wasn't happy about being awakened so early.

Caleb didn't seem to care. "P.J., I need a favor," he said. "Find somebody who's hiding from the FBI. Before the FBI does."

8 / Avenue A

"My last name may be spade, Caleb. But my first name is not Sam," P.J. said, sweetly. "What you talking about? I ain't no detective."

"It's worth a grand," Caleb said. "Hard cash. And all you have to do is find them for me; get me an address."

P.J. was suspicious. "Where'd you get a thou? Man, what you been sniffing?"

"I robbed a bank, remember? Besides, P.J., why should I lie to you? I got the bread. If you deliver, I'll deliver."

"I don't know Caleb. You'll pardon me for my skepticism, but you are really in a box. And while I, naturally, don't doubt your ethical sense or ability to pay off, if I was in the box you is in, I might be willing to mislead old friends. I might be willing to say most anything. Dig?"

"A grand, man. One thousand dollars. And not too much work for it."

"Oh yeah. If I do the impossible, I maybe get a thou, and if I don't manage to be a slicker detective than the entire FBI, I wasted a lot of time I could be spending making my precarious living."

"Ah, come on P.J. Don't hustle me. Look, I know it's hard, but this dude is political, and you know everybody political. You ought to be able to find him. Hell, ask your brother."

A harried commuter was tapping on the door of the phone booth with his neatly rolled brolly, so Caleb gave him the gesture and the sour mouth that goes with it, and the commuter went away.

"I also need a good healthy radical journalist, one who'll promise not to write anything unless I say OK."

"Sweetheart," P.J. said, disgusted, "you know how expensive it is to buy a man who'll stay bought?"

"I figure five hundred. He doesn't have to do anything either, but he's got to be a name."

"He'll cost you a thousand," P.J. said. "Delivered."

A tired-looking woman with a couple of young kids was waiting grimly outside Caleb's telephone booth.

"Who am I supposed to find?" P.J. asked.

"Two dudes, both Weathermen—John and Christopher Huptman. They've both gone underground, I guess. But you shouldn't have any trouble finding them. John Huptman is looking for me."

"And you want to find him first? I heard someone was asking after you. This Huptman dude? Caleb, I am your good buddy and all, but I don't want to set up no Weatherman."

"Oh, Christ, P.J. I'm a pacifist, you know that."

"A grand is not very much money for endangering my business," P.J. said, "messing with the Weathermen."

Caleb recalled a few favors he'd done for P.J., and P.J. ran a counterlist back at him, and Caleb made a few vague promises, and P.J. doubted his ability to perform on his promises (what can you do from the grave?), and Caleb tugged at the strings of long acquaintance, and P.J. reminded him that he, P.J., was black while Caleb was white, and they settled, finally, on nineteen and a half—a special package price.

"OK," Caleb said. "I need them fast. The journalist can wait, but I need the Huptmans very soon."

"They getting a little close to you, Caleb?" P.J. asked. "I know where you can get a dynamite gun."

"Yeah, P.J. So do I. I already got one of those."

The woman was rubbing her green coat against Caleb's telephone booth like a cat in heat.

"That girl you sent me was a dud," P.J. said. "She didn't know how to move at all."

"That's life, Casanova. Don't change the subject. I'm impressing on you the danger I'm in and how, if you don't come across, I will be one dead pussycat."

"Man, this is really a bummer," P.J. replied. "I would really hate to see you laid out cold and white. I would miss your kind spirit as I make my rounds through nasty inhospitable New York. You better have the money, Caleb."

So Caleb said he had the money and P.J. should leave word with Long Jim at the Great Auk when he had some information, and please make it fast. P.J. said that he wanted a little up front, so he'd have some enthusiasm, and Caleb said OK, he'd leave an envelope for him with a little enthusiasm, and P.J. said it should contain a lot of enthusiasm, and Caleb called him a greedy nigger and hung up.

The green-cloth-coat lady smiled nicely at him when he opened the booth door and asked, "You one of the Manson gang?"

Caleb smiled back at her and rumpled her little girl's hair.

She bundled both the kids into the booth with her. Caleb shrugged and into New York haze on Times Square, nearly noon. January sometime.

He ate at Nathan's Famous. A couple of hot dogs with a Rheingold to wash them down.

He watched the apprentice pimps who hang out there. They weren't doing much.

He couldn't catch Izzy until five o'clock, so he wandered

down Forty-second Street looking at the movie marquees.

Last month's big movies. Porn flicks with black strips painted over the genitals of the performers.

He sat through most of a film called *The French Connection,* which was about an honest reactionary cop tracking down big-time pushers in New York. This cop was running around and beating on people and that, Caleb supposed, was what made the film "realistic." But the cop wouldn't take a payoff, no matter how much, and Caleb had never met a New York cop like that.

The film bored him after a while, and he walked out and found a movie house which promised to show him really dirty things if he parted with $3.50 for the privilege.

Lots of middle-aged Americans inside, each sitting as far from the others as was humanly possible, given the difficulty that everyone was also sitting as close to the screen as possible.

Newspapers in their laps and Caleb wondered how many Americans were flagging their robins inside their Brooks Brothers suits.

A couple characters in the front row were laughing out loud, talking about how ridiculous the flick was, and everybody else resenting the hell out of them, but not able to say anything because the two loud-mouths were right, and everybody ought to feel like they did.

The critics were seated. Caleb noticed, front row, center.

Lot of pretty long-haired girls getting stuck by a lot of long-haired males. A little dirt under every fingernail.

Caleb once made it with a girl from a Berkeley commune who paid the rent by action in sex flicks. She was a pretty good lay, and Caleb half-hoped she'd show up on the screen for memory's sake. But no such luck.

Short porn. Man and woman or sometimes two women. All jaybird naked at the opening and ending when the man reached his climax. Lots of jump-cutting when the man lost it.

It was all meat after a while, and though Caleb would have liked to ball one of those girls, he didn't really approve of their means of livelihood.

He left before the rush hour filled the theater and the prices went up.

The Pleades was not Caleb Smith's favorite bar. He'd done a little business there in the past, but he never hung out there.

The place was too perfect, too designed. Old oak bar, stripped and sanded so the grain showed soft and yellow. Big oak back bar. A good box with not one record that wasn't hip. A little Charlie Parker, a little Muddy Waters. Some Stones cuts. The Pleades was so hip that during the heyday of *Hair,* they hadn't put "Let the Sun Shine In" on their Wurlitzer. In the back was a restaurant with good wine, fairly good food, attentive service, and a staggering tab.

A few slick freaks hung out there. And ad men who dressed like freaks. And some of the moviemakers from Visual Arts.

A few terrible avant-garde paintings on exhibit, for sale. Lit in the best of taste. And natural brick walls. And pretzels in wooden bowls on the bar.

Izzy was sitting with a couple of dudes Caleb didn't know. Caleb brought his beer over to the table. Nodded to Izzy, who gave him a "Howdy, Bub" and kept on talking.

The two strangers were, Caleb guessed, students at Visual Arts, and Izzy was doing his big-frog-in-a-small-pond routine, slashing some director who was overrated, filmically unimaginative, famous, rich, and not Izzy. So Caleb sipped on his beer and watched the waitress, who was sleek as a mink and worth watching.

"Poop. *Joe* is pure poop," Izzy was saying. "An emotional exploitation film. What did it tell you? I mean, what did it really 'tell' you that you didn't already know?"

"Sarris says. . ." one of the students began a defense.

"Sarris?" Izzy was incredulous. "Do you know how old

Andrew Sarris is? He saw *Birth of a Nation* when it was a first-run flick. Who is Andrew Sarris?"

"Izzy, I got to talk to you," Caleb said.

Izzy clapped his hands together. "Aha," he exclaimed, "the dope man cometh."

" 'Fraid not. I got to talk to you about something else."

Izzy was disappointed, but the Visual Arts kids were too easy, so he said, "Sure thing," and "Later, gents."

Caleb ordered drinks, and while they waited, Izzy pressed him for a promise on the dope he wanted.

The drinks came, and Caleb said "Thankee" to the waitress and got a smile from her, who couldn't be twenty-two yet and nice body in skintight blue jeans and not bad nipples.

"I want you to make a movie for me," he said. He described exactly what he wanted.

"That's sick, old buddy. Sickee," Izzy said. "Besides, you don't need film for that, you need video tape."

So Caleb told him why he needed the movie and said he'd pay for it. Izzy was impressed with Caleb's troubles, but not enough.

"No, amigo," Izzy said. "I ain't gonna do that to some poor unsuspecting woman. I done a lot of things I'm ashamed of, but that is really rotten."

So Caleb said there were two kinds of revolutionaries: those who talked about it and those who lived it, like Che and George Jackson. He said he'd pay Izzy a grand for the film.

Izzy said that you couldn't have a revolution unless you respected human dignity.

"You can't separate the means from the ends," he said. He also said that expenses, airfare, and crew would eat up most of the thousand, and what kind of jerk would work for nothing?

"How many films you made?" Caleb asked. He held his beer stein in the air, like the Statue of Liberty play, until the waitress exchanged it for a full one, and he bought another scotch and soda for Izzy and gave the waitress his best profile.

"How many movies, Iz?" he asked again. "You did that short about the Barrio, and you and Peter Bowen shot a thing about his life as a junkie. What else?"

"The horse trainers at the circus. Mekas liked it." He tapped his fingers on the table, a drum roll.

Caleb was soothing and pushing at the same time. "I don't mean to run the dozens on you. But you're what now. Thirty?"

"Brakhage wasn't so young when he started," Izzy answered.

"Yeah? Well I don't know about him. Look, this film. If it does the trick, it's stone cold certain *Newsreel* will be interested. Maybe you can even get a distributor. It could be an amazing movie."

Iz hadn't touched his drink. "Yeah, Caleb," he said, "but it's really dirty. I mean, I do skin flicks, but Jesus Christ. . ."

"Izzy," Caleb said, seriously, "if you don't shoot this flick, the Weather People gonna shoot me. And that ain't very nice either."

"Oh balls." Izzy picked up his drink, and the light caught his ruby ring and a tiny red flash in the early evening light.

He said he couldn't get the equipment, and Caleb reminded him that he could borrow gear from Visual Arts, and if he shot over the weekend, he'd be back before they missed it.

So they drank a little more. Izzy drinking fairly hard and Caleb nursing his beer, and about seven o'clock Izzy said it would cost twenty-five hundred, plus expenses, and Caleb went into his pocket with all the dinner crowd hanging around and a well-dressed, expensive couple glaring at them because they were hogging a table, and he counted out five hundred dollars.

Those who saw the cash change hands probably thought it was a big-time dope deal. The waitress asked Caleb his name when she came over again.

"P.J. Black," Caleb said. "Who are you?"

"Rachel," she said. And though they weren't quite finished, she gathered the glasses and handed Caleb a check.

Caleb looked at it and sighed.

"On me," he said. "Iz, will it be a good movie?"

A lame question. Izzy got up to go. "Does a bear shit in the woods?" he answered.

Pretty crowded. Martini and Bullshot crowd. Caleb abandoned his bar table for one in the restaurant and rested his boots on the chair opposite him.

He had $3900 and change in his money belt. Between P.J. and Izzy, he owed $350 he didn't have, so he figured, things being what they are, he might as well eat good anyway.

Caleb had a steak with mushrooms and a baked potato with sour cream and a chef's salad and a bottle of Bardolino and a brandy and three cups of coffee.

The waiter wasn't much older than he was and must have pulled down fifteen a year. Caleb left him a modest tip, but no tip for the waitress, though his drinks were on the same tab: $35.45 and tax.

She was at the front of the bar cleaning a table. Two dapper, grey-suited fags waiting for it.

Caleb tapped her on the shoulder, and she had a little interest in her eyes when she looked at him.

"I didn't leave you a tip," Caleb said.

"Terrific," she said. "Super."

"Do you ever do coke?" he asked.

The two fags listening politely. In no hurry.

She had one of those triangular black-haired Indian–Eurasian faces. "I've done it."

One of the fags nudges the other one and says in a deep English accent: "So have I."

Caleb ignores him and puts the little envelope with maybe a dime of coke in her hand.

"I used to do a lot of this," Caleb said, pleasantly, "but it made me horny and mean, so I quit."

He caught a cab outside and was already at Fourteenth Street when he remembered his trouble and told the driver that he didn't want the Great Auk after all; he wanted to make a phone call first. He found a phone inside Your Father's Moustache. A bunch of dudes from Omaha with these straw hats were singing "Swing Low Sweet Chariot" slightly louder than the place's tired ragtime band.

"Yeah!" Agitated voice on the phone.

"Is Long Jim there?"

Some muttering and hand scraping. "Yeah, what'd you want?"

"Long Jim? Caleb."

Little pause and the voice on the other end snuggles up to the phone, "Friend, you should be in L.A."

"Anyone looking for me?"

"Yep. Right now in fact."

"Can he hear you?"

"I wouldn't want to take the chance."

"OK." Look, I can't explain anything, but I'm going to send you a sandwich. And inside the bag will be something for P.J. It's important he gets it. OK?"

"Sure. I got friends in L.A. They'd put you up for a while. My friends are very heavy, very muscular dudes. They ain't hippies, friend."

"I got to get myself out of this, Jim. I got to stay and work it, one way or another. Look, what kind of sandwich do you want?"

"Salami on rye with plenty of mustard," Jim said. "And a pickle."

Caleb bought his sandwich in a deli around the corner on Bleecker. While the deli guy was getting it together, Caleb stepped between the rows of soup cans and counted out another thousand, quick. Outside, he slipped the money into the sandwich bag, careful, so none of the passersby could see what he was doing.

He picked out a young kid panhandler.

The kid, sensing a quarter, walked toward him, like Caleb was a magnet.

"Five bucks if you deliver this to the bartender at the Great Auk." Caleb pointed at the Great Auk.

The kid was dubious. "What's in it? Dope?"

"No. The bartender's sandwich and some money. There's some guys in there I don't want to see. Ten bucks." Caleb drew back his coat a little so the kid could see his gun.

The kid shrugged. "What the hell," he said. "Twenty."

The kid took the twenty and the bag and came back outside fast enough so he couldn't have stolen any money out of the bag unless he was Harry Houdini.

Caleb waved to him, and the kid gave him a theatrical bow, which made Caleb think for just a moment that maybe the kid *was* Harry Houdini.

The loft was about as grim as Caleb remembered it. Mattresses on the bare floor. The huge unseeing square eye of the window.

Caleb got to sleep about four o'clock. About three o'clock he thought about his mother. He wondered if she was still alive.

He stayed in the loft for three days until P.J. answered Caleb's routine afternoon telephone query with good news. He'd found John. He'd found Chris. It had cost him a lot of money. He'd found a corruptible radical journalist: Jay Sokoloff.

Caleb groaned and carried on and called P.J. a lazy nigger, but P.J. was Sokoloff's connection and knew a lot of things about the fat journalist that Sokoloff wouldn't want known, so Caleb said OK.

Caleb phoned Izzy, and Izzy had the video tape movie and was excited about it and was going to stay up all night editing. Izzy asked Caleb about money, and Caleb became vague.

On the way back to the loft, Caleb stopped at a liquor store and bought himself a bottle of fifteen-year-old Scotch, because he'd never tasted really good Scotch before, and he figured he might as well get it in while he could.

It didn't take Benny-the-mechanic five minutes to get through Christopher's front door, and he could have done it in forty seconds if Caleb hadn't insisted: "No scars."

Benny was one of those Cuban refugee uptown burglars, and he didn't much like coming down to the lower East Side, where he might get mugged by some crude junkie. But Caleb had promised him a deuce just to get the door open, and so Benny and his picklocks had come downtown. A cautious little man, he kept his cab waiting downstairs, doors locked and windows rolled up tight.

The three of them standing in that dingy one light bulb hallway: Caleb, Benny, and Rusty, who was getting nervous because he couldn't stand a burglary rap.

P.J. had taken more of Caleb's money than Caleb could afford, handed him the info, wished him luck, and politely declined Caleb's invitation to be part of the proceedings.

The door swung open.

Caleb gave Benny-the-mechanic his deuce, and Benny scurried down the tenement stairs, watching warily at each landing.

Little apartment. Bedroom with a couch and TV and a plastic coffee table. On the table, a couple of Marcuse's books and Christopher's spiral notebook. Kitchenette with instant coffee beside the tiny gas stove and not too many cockroaches.

Spare. Spartan. A room where what lived?

A couple windows facing the street and one window which looked out on the air shaft and into the apartment opposite. Caleb's apartment. For a few hours, anyway.

Getting the old Polish gent out of the apartment across the way had cost Caleb twenty, and the promise that if the cops caught them, they'd say they broke in.

Caleb had sworn they weren't burglars, oh no. The old Pole seemed to need the assurance.

Rusty ran a tap on Chris's phone. Nothing elaborate, just

an extra wire going to the junction box under the table.

"How long did you study this stuff?" Caleb asked.

Rusty had the cardboard back off Chris's TV. "I dunno. Months. I joined this correspondence school, using Michael McCarthy's name, and I kept sending them letters promising to pay, and they were sending me lessons for a year. They had collection agents after Michael, and he went nuts."

"You sure you know what you're doing?" Caleb asked.

Rusty was offended. "I told you. Anytime I want I can have a full-time gig tapping phones. Why don't you shut up and let me work?"

Caleb went and sat on the windowsill.

Rusty, whistling, made the connections, and put the set back together. "I know how to fix stereo systems, too," he announced. "If you ever have any trouble with yours, let me know."

"Sure."

Rusty ran a thin coaxial cable along the moulding and turned the edge of the linoleum over it so it wouldn't show. He bored a modest hole in Chris's wall below the air shaft window and snaked the cable outside.

"Done," he said.

"Aren't you going to check it?" Caleb asked.

"Can't," Rusty said. "Not until the video machine is hooked up. It should work, though."

He stood there looking at the installation for a minute, and Caleb worried.

What the hell. Life depends on an enormous number of things not failing. The roof beams don't usually rot; the brakes don't usually fail.

Caleb gave Rusty a hundred, and Rusty thanked him and went looking for his connection.

Cabs don't often cruise through the lower East Side, and Caleb had to walk halfway to the Pleades before a yellow answered his hail and took him the rest of the way.

He was tired. He supposed he should be excited, nervous,

swift. But his adrenalin had been used up and he was more comfortable nursing a rum and coke than making the motions that just might save his life.

Izzy had gone straight over to the Polish apartment. Caleb didn't have enough, now, to pay him, but another drink was enough worries for one man to hassle.

Cold, grey, overcast afternoon giving nothing to you and taking what it could. Caleb put a quarter in the box and listened to Tina Turner singing something her husband had put her up to. Had a little more booze and it was pretty much the same.

Karen came in. Still dressed in heavy country clothes. She had a couple burrs on the sleeve of her jacket. Face tired, and a little too soft for her own good.

"Hi," she said, quietly. "Will you buy me a drink?"

Caleb signaled the bartender. "Why aren't you in Virginia?" he asked.

She looked at him.

"This ain't no time and no place, honey," Caleb said. "You got bread. Take your buns up to the Port Authority and get on a bus."

She said no, she didn't want to do that and that he didn't own her, and why was he so mad for christsake?

He picked one of the burrs off her coat sleeve. It came away with a tiny ball of green fuzz. He rolled it between his fingers.

"Long Jim told me where I could find you," she said. "I called him up."

"The FBI isn't looking for me," Caleb said. "Not yet, anyway. They're looking for you though. They'd like to put you in jail. Why couldn't you wait a few months, stay low until this thing blew over? Why did you decide to come to New York, just now? You don't really want to see the Empire State Building, do you? Come on. I'll go with you."

Karen was confused. "Where?"

"To the Port Authority. Come on. Let's go get a cab."

"No," she said.

"Why in hell are you following me around? I said I'd come back for you."

Karen put her hand on his arm. Face close to his. Big eyes. "Don't be nasty, Caleb. I know you're tough."

He wanted to hit her, but he didn't. He slammed his glass down, and an ice cube bounced out and skittered down the bar.

The bar clock said four o'clock, and it was time to make his phone call. Mad. Too many demands at once. Turning like a bear in a cage.

"Goddamn it," he said. "Oh man, this is such bullshit." He pushed back his high stool and put his feet down.

"I got to make a phone call," he said. "Do us a favor. Do us *both* a favor and get the hell out of here. Karen . . . agh, what's the use."

Downstairs. Little cubicle for the phone outside the men's room. Nobody close enough to overhear and probably not all that much to overhear if they could. Still, Caleb hunched himself over the phone, protecting his secrets with his body.

It rang half a dozen times before John Huptman picked it up.

"Hi, John," Caleb said. "How's the old anarchist revolutionary?"

John paused, placing the voice. "Oh," he said, "it's you."

"Sure. Caleb Smith. Your favorite sitting duck. How's one of the world's most miserable human beings doing today?"

"Where are you?" Dead, cold voice.

"Well, John. That's what I called to tell you."

"How'd you get this number?" A bit of bitter fear, an aroma, over the line.

"John, come off it. Would I tell you?"

Silence on the other end of the line and mumbling. Was that a girl's voice in the background? Did John ask her to see if there were squad cars outside?

"Hey, John. Is that Linda there? Is that your little matzo-ball?"

The hand off the phone and a clearer rush of sound.

"What's going on?"

"Well. That's really a long story, John. I just wanted you to get another shot at me, that's all."

"No games," John said. "No games, Mr. Smith."

Caleb backed off a little from the phone and leaned his elbow on the phone box. "John, if I was your informer, you'd be in jail right now."

"What do you want?"

"Well," Caleb drawled, "I just thought that since you're such a big-time ethical cat, you'd like to know that it ain't me you should be shooting at. And I'd like to prove it to you. You being so moral and all."

"Specifics," John snapped. "I don't like you particularly, Mr. Smith. Clearly, I distrust your motives. You know I'd murder you if given another chance."

"Sure you would," Caleb agreed, cheerfully. "But I'd have to be standing very close and very, very still."

"Specifics."

"I'll be at Twenty-nine Avenue A at six o'clock tonight. Nine B," Caleb said. "Meet me there."

"Why?"

"John, I remind you that if I have your phone number and am a cop, I've got your address. If I could bust you, I wouldn't have to drag you down to Avenue A. If you want to find out what I have in mind, meet me. If you're not satisfied, I'll go with you anywhere you might want to go. Bring somebody else from the Weather People. Bring guns. Bring all your implements of destruction."

"I'll think about it," John said, and Caleb thought that he would do that.

"Tell your brother to meet you at his place at seven tonight. Tell him, also, to watch the news on Channel Seven. The six o'clock news."

"Why should I help you?"

The only hard part. Caleb had thought about it for hours, turned it over, and asked all the questions he could think of. No help. He tossed it back to John and hoped the percentages were OK: "Oh John. There's just an off-chance that your brother is a pig. There's just an off-chance that he wants to betray you and all the people you've worked with. It won't cost you much to find out."

Caleb hung up then, because the nut would be harder to crack if he kept on talking.

He'd had five drinks, but Mr. Barleycorn being the prankster he is, Caleb wasn't getting drunk. He ordered another one.

Karen hadn't finished hers. "You hungry?" he asked her.

She shook her head no; but Caleb insisted, and the two of them went into the back-room restaurant. As they were leaving the bar, Rachel came in for the evening shift. Saw Caleb, saw Karen, gave Caleb a look. Not unlike the way a Kansas kid might have watched, from a very great distance, the Wabash Cannonball.

Little bit of spring had entered the early evening air and the cold day warmed and small promise of fruiting plants to come later in the year.

The restaurant, which had seemed antagonistic, an enemy to be met and challenged, now seemed friendlier and even, perhaps, a bit romantic.

"I'm glad you came," Caleb said.

Karen with her little girl grin and the two of them at a small table and the waiter not too harassed tonight and liking Karen. The service was more than usual.

At her suggestion, they had ham steak and a not too expensive California white wine. Salad, sweet potato, whatever. It was pretty good, and some strange shyness crept into them both, like high-school kids at their first fancy place.

For a brief time in the forties, Bing Crosby owned New York City, and Fred Astaire and his friends had a hot time, and the blacks knew their places. A fragment of that period

surfaced in the restaurant tonight, and for the time they ate
and talked, all the junkies slept and all the gunfighters
declared a cease fire.

Caleb and Karen talked. Oh, about things past. About
the odd gymnastics they'd gone through in high school.
About Karen's prom. About Caleb's D.A.

Nothing spectacular. Learning each other as much as the
other would permit. Less afraid, though death sat inside
both of them and made them talk faster to cram it in.

Karen told Caleb that the first time she met him she
thought he was crazy, hard, and dangerous. And they
smiled together. Caleb told Karen he'd wanted her ever
since he first laid eyes on her in faraway Maine.

Shadow of Denny came in and they were quiet for a
moment, letting him take his due.

Little pieces of time. Self-contained chunks, each with its
own aroma and one after another.

They had coffee after dinner and Karen made the usual
joke about drinking it black. "I had an uncle," she said,
"Uncle Frank. I was something of a tomboy, and he was an
old boozer, but I really liked him. I used to follow him
around. He told me once that the sugar and milk and coffee
I was drinking wasn't coffee at all, and if I really wanted
coffee candy, I should be more honest about it. Old tough
guy. I started drinking mine black and haven't changed."
She regarded her small cup of black coffee dubiously. "I
don't even think I really like the stuff," she said. "Tea is
much easier on you."

Caleb poured a little milk in his own cup and offered it to
her. She laughed.

Talk. Food. Warmth. Maybe they became lovers.

Outside, it was another chunk of time, labeled "Christopher." Caleb slipped right into that time before they
caught a cab.

He was good-natured from wine and a little old for
soldiering.

Too good-natured to push Karen away. Too friendly to make her abandon him tonight.

Caleb had the old Spanish .38 slid into the back of his pants. He wondered if it still worked. He was dead sure it was ridiculous: grown man weaving through the city with his archaic metal death machine stuffed in his pants, ready to strike like the Green Hornet. Phooey. Ridiculous.

The cab driver was one of the shaggy freaks the cab companies had started employing when their wages became inadequate for any man with a family or rent to pay.

Freak running it down about a Grand Funk concert he'd caught last night, stoned on Soma, which Caleb knew was a horse tranquilizer. Freak blasting through traffic disguised as NEW YORK CITY HACKIE, seeking every quarter-inch advantage.

Normally it was a good game, whipping through the streets with a really good driver, but today the game bored Caleb and made him nervous.

When their cab scraped by a bus so close you couldn't whistle in between, Caleb said, "Grand Funk is a promotor's ripoff. They couldn't play good music if they married the Stones. Why don't you slow down?"

Freak shot a glare and shut up and slowed down.

Caleb gave him an average tip when they got out of the cab, and the driver gave him an average sneer.

Couple Puerto Rican kids playing outside. Big black woman across the street, balancing her grocery bag while she fumbled for her key. Gutter full of trash. Two old cars, an Olds and a Bonneville, half-gutted beside the curb. No lock on the door of the tenement and Caleb put his hand on the butt of his pistol, because there were a lot of landings between him and the fourth floor.

The stairwell was no man's land. As they walked upstairs, past the graffiti and the bags of garbage, Caleb sensed the denizens of that slum listening to his footsteps and breathing easier when he'd passed their door.

Smell of evening meal. Stink of piss and the melancholy reek of small hopes that almost never came off.

Simple survival.

No different in their caves than woodchucks cowering in their holes.

There's a joke in New York. When one of the Rockefeller kids reached twenty-one, his father gave him a set of blocks to play with: the blocks on Fifty-second Street between Third and Fifth Avenues.

Caleb thought it would be nice if the kings could live as slaves for a year or so. Or long enough, anyway, for them to get robbed and raped a couple of times. He thought that the lower East Side would be leveled by the survivors of his little experiment. But, probably, he was wrong. Probably the survivors would never look back.

Izzy opened the door for them and they stepped in upon a green ocean of green linoleum, wall-to-wall. There was also a couch, a stove, a sink, a tub in the kitchen, and a picture of J. Christ on the wall, with huge red heart and transsexual expression.

Izzy was excited, "Man, did we get some footage!"

Jay Sokoloff was on the couch and one of Izzy's disciples was tinkering with a video tape unit. Spinning knobs and making adjustments.

Caleb said hello to Sokoloff, who gave him minimum hello in return. He was wearing a pair of elephant bells he'd obviously worn all week.

"Who else is coming?" Izzy asked. Without waiting for an answer he went over to the video recorder and corrected a dial his assistant had just set. "Man, we got some unbelievable stuff."

"You can interfere with Chris' set whenever you want?" Caleb asked.

Karen poured herself a glass of water and sniffed it and poured it in the sink and got a glass of orange drink from the refrigerator.

"Yeah, sure," Izzy said. "All I have to do is throw these two switches." Pointing to a dial and a toggle switch labeled "remote." "I called up the station, and they said they're going to have their special report at six twenty-five. They'll run a couple of thirty-second spots after the city news, and then the anchorman will introduce the special report. I think we should cut in right after the spots."

Caleb shrugged. "You know what you're doing. You do it."

Izzy shoved the couch over, so they all could sit and look across the airshaft into Christopher's apartment. Caleb thought that unless they turned the lights on, Chris wouldn't be able to see the audience watching him.

"Is he home?" Caleb asked.

"Yeah." Izzy picked up the phone tap line. "Do you want to play the phone tap through the video machine's speakers, or do you want the tap to play through the headset?"

"Make it public," Caleb said.

Izzy's assistant looked up from his plugging and unplugging.

"Your boy came in twenty minutes ago. I think he's taking a shower now."

They could see Chris's chair and the TV set they'd wired. The rest of Christopher's apartment was invisible. Caleb lit a cigarette and offered one to Karen.

She smiled and shook her head "no" and sat on a chair away from the action and pulled some knitting from her purse and started working on it. Sokoloff moved over and hunkered down next to her and watched her knit. Caleb figured she could take care of herself.

Izzy tugged Caleb's sleeve, and Caleb followed him to a quiet corner. Caleb leaned against the wall under the picture of J. Christ.

Izzy was earnest and worried. "I spent a lot of bread on this," he said, whispering.

"Sure," Caleb said. "You'll get it back."

Izzy's relieved nervous smile. "I'm going to need it tonight," he said. "I got to pay the guys who worked with me. And if I don't stick some cash in my checking account tomorrow, all the checks I wrote for airfare are going to bounce higher than a Seven forty-seven."

"You'll get your money," Caleb said. "Sokoloff writes for the *Voice.*"

"Oh yeah? Good news. Maybe a little review in the film section. Maybe a little notoriety."

Caleb smiled. "I don't know. Why don't you ask him."

"Your boy is back," Izzy's assistant announced. "What time is it?"

"Nearly six." Sokoloff checking a big gold watch set in a wide leather watchband.

Christopher. Caleb could see him through the window, and he was Christopher, alright. Wearing a white terry-cloth bathrobe and a fluffy towel draped around his neck. Like a college kid. Chris had bony shins.

Caleb stared at him through all the distance between them. Neat, well-educated Chris. Pretty Chris, who looked like a fraternity kid before a heavy date. Caleb wondered if he hated Chris and decided he didn't.

Caleb turned his eyes away, suddenly afraid that the weight of all that vision would touch Chris's antenna and make him uneasy and quick to run.

So here's what it looks like before the knock on the door: there's this small lower east side apartment with green swirly linoleum on the floor and white painted walls. Not much space. No bathroom. That's in the hall. The old man who rents the place has set his seal upon it, but the weight of an old man's fussy neatness is hardly enough to alter the fact that anybody could be living there and will be when the old man dies.

A video tape recorder is standing in front of a small window which faces another small window across the air shaft. The recorder is strange here, like an artifact from another planet. Sleek. Metal and plastic. An oblong box with the eye of the monitor screen facing them and switches and dials around the screen. Izzy's assistant is crouched beside the set, mothering it. He's a young man who's been cared for. He is, perhaps, easily led. He has, at any rate, an eager face. With his eagerness tempered by too much flesh in the body, too fat wrists, and the certainty that he won't ever get much of what he vaguely hopes for.

Izzy is standing beside him, the DIRECTOR. The HIRED GUN. He's watching the man he's been paid to hit, hands on hips, calm professional interest.

Sokoloff is beside Karen. A little too close for Karen and not close enough for him.

She's wearing blue jeans, which were dirty a week ago, and a heavy sweatshirt, which slopes over the rise of her breasts. Her green plaid jacket is draped across her shoulders, and she's knitting a baby blanket for one of her friends in Virginia.

Sokoloff is trying to say something witty and interesting, but he isn't making much of a dent. His references seem odd to Karen, sophisticated, grotesque. He's about ready to start asking her questions about her life, so he'll know where to go.

Across the way, Chris bends over his TV set and the terrycloth robe rises to show another four inches of skinny shins. Flickering light on Chris's set. Izzy's assistant throws a switch and the monitor imitates Chris's TV: a girl running through the surf with a tube of shampoo supered over her.

Three sharp raps at the door.

Shot of chemicals hit Caleb's brain, and his muscles jerk. Tremor, but a brief one. He gets his pistol out and stands beside the door with it hanging loose in his hand. Izzy opens up. Linda and John, like callers or dinner guests except that instead of a bottle of wine, both have pistols and both pistols centered on the middle of Izzy's directorial paunch.

"What the hell," he says.

John, calm and cold. "We are expected, I believe."

So they walk in, pushing Izzy before them, and Caleb

levels his pistol and John and he eyeball at each other ready to shoot.

Blue eyes to green eyes, and not much showing in either set.

"Hi, John," Caleb says. His arm is straight out in front of him.

Linda is waiting for a cue. Short, dark chick. Sensible shoes. On her own hook, she decides that John has Caleb covered and picks out Sokoloff for herself. She aims her gun at the journalist, who promptly turns white and tries to become one with the wall behind him.

"As you see, John," Caleb says, "it isn't a trap."

John thinks on it for a moment. "Who are these people?" he asks. His pistol still rock-steady.

"Karen's the girl from Maine. The one who got busted for helping me. Izzy made the movie we're about to see, and the other dude helped him. The slick gent is Jay Sokoloff, who writes for the *Voice* and the *Guardian*. And I'm Caleb Smith, who is getting tired of holding a gun on you when I don't want to shoot you, but can't put it down until you put yours down because, sweetie, I don't trust you much."

John's eyes. He could have been some poker player. "OK," he said. He lowered his gun, but didn't put it away. Linda sat down in a kitchen chair, prim as a spinster, with her little automatic in her lap.

"Explanations." John said.

Caleb put his pistol in his pocket. "That's Chris's place." He pointed to the window. "We've got a video tap on his TV. Tonight, some of his programming is going to come from right here. You can see his phone. We've got a tap on it, too."

Perhaps, John, for the first time, began to suspect that his brother was a wrong one. His face went one shade lighter and his eyes seemed more prominent.

"Chris knows better than to use his phone," he said. "We've been tapped before."

"He'll forget," Caleb said. "He's gonna be in an awful hurry."

John deliberated. "I don't believe you," he said.

A little sugar voice from Caleb: "That's been your trouble all along, John. No faith. When's your big meeting?"

John was wearing a scarlet tie with his same old corduroy jacket. The tie said no less than he did.

Caleb nodded. "OK," he said. "Someday—I'd guess soon—all the heavy Weather People (yourself included) are going to be in one room. And if the police come busting into that one room, there won't be any revolution. Zero. John, if you have a little patience, you might be able to stop the police from charging into that room." Caleb shrugged. "Besides, if I'm lying, you can always kill me."

But despite his offer, Caleb wasn't putting his pistol down, and John knew it.

John and Chris never had been very close. Chris had stayed in North Dakota five years longer than he did. And even when they both joined the Weathermen, their relationship had been formal. Considerate, but formal. They each had their own lives, and some brotherly pride made them determined to keep those lives apart.

Still, John could see Chris's familiar body across the way, and he was suddenly more precious to him than he'd ever thought possible.

Childhood scene: a muddy river outside of Fargo and the two of them with an old tire swing. Chris swings out over the pool and yelling hell-bent-for-leather and the flash of his brown body in the air and the white water explosion when he hit the river.

Suddenly, John didn't care much about Caleb's pistol. "Alright." Him speaking soft, without any of the coldness his voice usually held. "You know what I'll do if you're lying."

"Sure, John." No mockery. Caleb understood.

Izzy's assistant turned up the sound.

". . .Jamaica, Trinidad, Puerto Rico, the Bahamas. This year, put a little sun into your winter. Fly the American way."

A chorus of girl's voices sang, "Fly the American way."

Caleb watched the picture of a big plane winging over a sunset somewhere and wished he was on it.

They all drew in close around the monitor. Chris's set still had the same picture: one of those flickering imitation movie marquees with lines and dots and intercuts of news-worthy people and the repeated slogan: "WABC Six O'clock Report."

The camera cuts to this concerned, but affable, dude, sitting at a table big enough for the War Room. Behind him are a bunch of clocks which show the time in half a dozen cities—in case anyone should want to know.

"John Berdue," he announces, sonorously. "This is the six o'clock report. A new turn in the war, a king overthrown in Jordan, school strife in Georgia, and, later, a special report on man in today's complicated world."

They all watched. They didn't have anything to say to each other, so they all watched.

The announcer shows a bunch of film clips of the war and, voiceover, tells us all that in somebody's opinion, the war is winding down and all the soldiers you see here will be home one day. The soldiers are shown marching through the mud and shooting at something (someone?). The an-nouncer says that according to the administration, the best way to get the reds to the conference table is with high-ex-plosive bombs. Linda made a rude noise.

They see planes taking off aircraft carriers and movies taken from the nose cameras of the planes. New explosions on drab, pockmarked hills.

The announcer remarks (wryly) that Americans have been bombing those hills for seven years now, without the noticeable winding down of anything.

The camera shows half a dozen refugees who look pretty much like any people who've had everything taken from

them. Then there's a commerical for a dishwashing deter-
gent which keeps your hands so soft and lovely, your husband will want to commit unspeakable perversions upon
you ten minutes after the evening dishes are done.

A couple more commercials, filled with odd and gratui-
tous advice.

Chris gets up from his chair and returns with a Pepsi.

Caleb edges slowly back. He wants to have the wall
behind him. He wants to get in a good shot if he has to.

John notices and slips Caleb a ghastly, deadly smile.
Teeth.

The announcer comes back on and shows a slide of a map
of the middle east. A blinking arrow points to Jordan. News
photos of milling crowds and a couple of the King of Jordan, missing and believed defunct. The announcer notes
that the coup which toppled him was led by pro-Russian
elements.

Cut to a short interview with a pretty girl who's some sort
of princess, in school in Switzerland. She starts crying and
carrying-on when the interviewer asks her about her father.

Cut to studio announcer. "Not only Princess Izhad
wonders," he says. "Tonight the whole world is asking,
'What has happened to the King?' "

Cut. We see a Buick moving serenely through Death
Valley. A lovely windblown model is at the helm, and
someone is saying really weird things, while she pilots this
huge car through the desert.

The voiceover declares that "some people think the
Buick is a sign of status."

Apparently, this is not correct because he goes on to
inform us that it is a reward you've earned, because you've
made your pile the hard way, relying only on ruthlessness
and will.

The voiceover insinuates that girls very much like the
nutty model (who is apparently lost in Death Valley) will be
yours by the carloadful if you spring for a Buick.

Cut: A school bus with not one pane of glass unbroken.

"In Tuscaloosa, Georgia, violence flared for the fourth day as federal marshals began to implement Judge Cohen's controversial busing decision."

The camera went on to show some black kids, obviously scared, being escorted into a once-white school. Big white teenagers were hulking around, like the last survivors of the blackboard jungle, and the black kids were all slight and appealing.

The announcer said something more about it and expressed (wryly) moral indignation, but not so much that even George Wallace could be offended by it.

Cut back to the studio. Caleb knows the time in Paris, Istanbul, London, Moscow, Cairo and Tokyo. Dynamite.

Christopher finishes his Pepsi and vanishes again, and Caleb starts to sweat. Corrosive visions flame through his head: Chris remaining in the kitchen making, possibly, a ham sandwich, while their bogus "Special Report" played to an empty room. Death by commercial interruption and ham on rye.

Caleb set his right arm to come up quick and start the mayhem, but no good. No good at all.

For the first time he could remember, Linda was smiling at him. Fondly. She was facing him direct, not even watching the monitor, and had herself so braced that nothing short of an elephant gun was going to knock her down before she got off a couple of shots.

She knew. John was watching his brother's room and the monitor, but Linda knew Caleb. She had her tiny little automatic pointed right at his balls. And that big, fond smile.

So Caleb sweats, waiting for Chris, and some female voice is talking on the tube. "Soft, pleasing Crystalique. It's the feminine way to solve feminine problems." The picture is another chick splashing through the surf, obviously she is feminine and not just another broad.

The spot ends, and on the monitor, the "Special Report" titles make their appearance. Izzie is hunched over his dials, for him, this whole schmeer is just a technical problem.

"Hit it," he snaps. His assistant, quickest hand Caleb ever saw, hits the remote toggle and the reels of video tape start spinning. The monitor goes grey.

Quick adjustment and the title Izzy shot comes in sharper: "WABC Special Report—Two Brothers a Long Way From Home."

Caleb watching the room and Chris is standing behind the chair, watching the screen and scratching himself.

Watching the footage Izzy shot in Fargo.

Slow pan across incredibly vast wheatfields. A combine coming very slowly towards you.

"Watch the contrast," Izzy says, and his assistant moves two knobs two clicks to the left.

The combine roars by and a bunch of straw thrown over the lens to dissolve to a deserted prairie town, with a funky old pickup rumbling by.

Izzy's voice on the tube. Caleb knew better, but he twitched anyway, as if Izzy had suddenly become famous.

"North Dakota grows more wheat than all but two states," TV Izzy said. "But in this modern industrial age, the age of mechanized farming, there isn't much need for the farmer. One man with machines can do the work of twenty, and farm towns all over the county literally vanish from existence."

Cut to a rutted dirt road. The camera traveling along, and the prairie on both sides like a sea of grain dividing before them.

"All the kids leave. There's nothing to hold them. No work. And the land is too expensive for a small farmer."

We're moving around the edge of a grey shed of some sort, on foot now, and the camera sees a dilapidated house and a barn with rust flecks in the tin roof and a decided tilt to its northern corner.

"This is the Huptman farm, where John and Christopher Huptman grew up."

An old bowl with a few scraps of grain in it outside the

chicken house. An old cast-iron pump over a wooden well cap.

Someone like John Huptman is saying things in another world, and oh, his face—oh, his face. But the TV man is telling us a story, and we listen to that instead.

"Two brothers. Farm boys. Local folks remember them as a little smarter than average."

Camera passing under an old apple tree, winter scabby and grey, and we walk towards the house; our boots crunching through the snow.

"John Huptman was the oldest of them, and by all accounts, the brightest. Christopher was a quiet kid. Mannerly."

A last slow look around the yard.

"Two kids who left home and took different paths. John Huptman became a revolutionary. A radical. John joined the Weathermen."

So we turn around on our axis and face this old lady. Grey hair pinned up so tight her cheeks are pulled flat and taut.

A few blotches on her bare forehead that once (when she was a belle) were freckles. She must have been beautiful, once. No, not beautiful, but pretty, buxom, a lot of fun. And married too young to a man increasingly too old and him gone, now, these last five years, and she is weathered now, like a locust fencepost. Her body is fatty. She has a bank of fat to draw on because who knows?

"Christopher Huptman grew up slower and more thoughtfully than his older brother. We can't guess his motives, perhaps no more than a great respect for order."

The old weathered woman is smiling now, inviting us to come near.

"Christopher, like his brother John, joined the Weathermen. But Christopher Huptman joined as a police agent. A spy. This afternoon, in a rare gesture, the President of the United States awarded him, *in absentia,* the Distinguished

Service Medal. The highest medal the United States can bestow on a civilian.

"Christopher Huptman is still underground, still pursuing his dangerous mission. But at this moment, as you're watching this program, raids are being carried out against those Weatherman cells that Christopher Huptman uncovered. Hundreds of G-men, secret servicemen, and the police of five major cities are striking against those radicals J. Edgar Hoover described as 'the most potent, dangerous conspiracy in America today.' "

A microphone is shoved in front of the old woman.

"What do you think of the news, Mrs. Huptman?"

She wasn't excited, impressed. She faced the question as calm as a graceful day in spring. "I'm right proud of Chris," she said. "He never told me what he was doing, but I suppose he wasn't able to. Chris was a good boy. Quiet. Never did know what he was thinking about."

We're tight on her face, and a smile is rippling the surface of her skin, but not showing, just giving evidence. "I'm proud that the President gave him that medal, but I'd sooner he came home for a visit."

She laughed. Boys will be boys. Then her face went softer than it often did. "I pray for John," she says, simply. "I pray he won't get himself hurt, and I pray that God will touch his heart, so he understands. God don't like communism."

The camera pulls back from the porch and the figure on the monitor shrinks slow and TV Izzy is saying, "Two boys: one a hero and the other a fugitive. Both are a long way from home."

"Cut." Izzy's assistant snaps the remote toggle and breathing fills the room.

Christopher is watching his TV: a commercial for Bloomingdale's with a lot of kicky people dancing around in some discotheque.

His hand snakes out, slow, slow to the phone. Drawn to it.

Izzy's tech throws another switch, and Christopher's own

breathing comes into the room. Harsh breathing. Strangled.

He dials. We hear the clicks. The buzz of the phone is very loud.

It rings twice and the connection clicks open. No one speaks on the other end of the line.

Chris talks. And between the hard efficient syllables are all the soft places he didn't know he had: "Fishbowl, this is Red Ferret. Mayday. I repeat, Mayday. I'm coming in. Get somebody over here to cover me."

He held the phone for a moment, though it remained silent and impenetrable. He was tearing off his bathrobe as he disappeared from view.

John started to cry, and Linda went over to him, trying to hold him, give comfort. She still had her automatic in her hand, and she was thumping his back with it.

And so Karen got up, pale as a young Irish nun, and left the apartment. Caleb followed her. And Sokoloff tagged along behind.

She stopped, stock-still, beside a small, sidewalk fruit stand. Three bulky women in babushkas and the smell of overripe fruit and some thin guy in a white apron watching to see no apple vanished into a purse unreported. At least it was too cold for flies.

She looked directly beyond Caleb. "Don't touch me," she said.

"Karen. . ."

So she did look at him, and he wished she hadn't. "You killed that woman, Caleb," she said. "When she finds out she betrayed her son, she'll die. You lied to her. You lied to me and Denny in Maine. You take too much from people. You know, I'll bet you lied to me about Denny, too. I'll bet you had Denny killed just so you could ball me." Like someone announcing a simple mathematical truth she said, "You're no good Caleb. I don't want you."

Sweat on his forehead. "Karen, I had to do it."

"No," she said. "You liked doing it, Caleb. You didn't have to use that poor woman. You didn't have to use Denny. You didn't have to do that."

Sokoloff standing close-by, but far enough away to be almost polite. Big dude in gaudy, dirty clothes.

She turned to him. "You," she said. "Would you take me to the bus station?"

He said, "Certainly," in a voice that had finished college.

Caleb reached out for her, his hand not his but an agent of him.

"No," she said. Oh, she had fine long eyelashes that waved like corn tassles in the slight breeze. "If you drag me, I'll come with you, and when you're asleep, I'll cut your throat."

So she went over and stood next to Sokoloff and even put her hand on his arm.

"Thanks for the story," Sokoloff said.

Caleb watched him.

He watched them until Sokoloff managed to wave down a cab, yelling "Taxi" and waving his arms.

He watched them get in the cab. Sokoloff was very clumsy.

He watched them for some time after the cab was gone.

A yell, he heard the thin man from the vegetable stand: "Hey stupid, you gonna buy something, or you gonna block traffic all afternoon?"

Caleb gave him the finger, and the thin man threatened to call a cop, and Caleb walked away.

The Great Auk was quiet and very nearly deserted. An uptown businessman with his live-in teenybopper sat at a back table and the candle flickering on their faces.

Long Jim said hello, and Caleb ordered a double bar whiskey.

After tonight he could never come back here again, Caleb knew. Christopher had been his protection. He thought about telling Long Jim about it and decided not to.

The jukebox was playing the Stones: "Wild, wild horses couldn't drag me away..."

Long Jim brought him his drink and asked, "Did you see Sara? She was in this afternoon. She said ... let's see..." He scratched his head. "Well, I can't remember exactly, but she said that the Jesus-Freak thing was all a big mistake and she wanted to talk to you."

Caleb downed his drink and ordered another.

"Screw her," he said.

He sat sideways on the stool, watching the couple in the back until they got nervous and left.

After a while he changed to gin and tonics, because it was going to be summer again someday.

Sometime later, Izzy came in and asked Caleb for money. Caleb gave him some and said he'd get the rest next week. Izzy was very upset; so Caleb let him see the handle of his .38, and Izzy said that next week would be OK, but put him in quite a bind. Caleb offered to buy him a drink, but Izzy didn't want one. Apparently he had an engagement elsewhere.

Sometime later he wondered whether John would kill Chris and decided he didn't care much one way or another.

Sometime later still, he went uptown to the Port Authority to look for her.

But among the thousands and thousands of travelers' faces he found there, none of them was hers.

Epilogue / Aroostook County

Ice out. The slabs of ice from the northern rivers sliding like rafts to the sea. Breath of broken ice and crocus poking their heads through the snow.

His sleeping bag was tied on top of the pack.

The cheap canvas pack rode a little awkward on his shoulders and still smelling of new canvas.

It held:

Three pairs of socks.

A hand line and hooks.

Extra shoelaces.

A new hunting knife with no edge on it.

A pocket stone.

A shirt.

A pair of blue jeans.

A compass.

A frying pan.

A bag of brown rice (five pounds).

Two film containers stuffed with dope.

Two bottles of rum.

His first ride got him as far as Boston. His second ride was lucky; a college kid in a brown Mustang ran him all the way to 201.

A log truck returning empty from the mill dropped him off outside of Kennebec. The driver explained he wasn't supposed to pick up riders.

The sand they'd used on the winter roads lay in small banks at the edge of the highway.

The air had a bite to it. Caleb settled the skinny pack on a new part of his shoulders and sniffed the overwhelming smell of new growing pine. He got lost a couple of times, and his boots were soaked clear through from the melting snow; but he got to the landing before nightfall.

He built a bough lean-to beside his fire and sat under the boughs and watched the river: brilliant blue, milky white, and green.

He found some beetle grubs under a log and baited his hook with them.

Caught two small chubs from a boulder at the edge of the white water, those chubs selecting his bait from a torrent of food washed downriver.

The fish were mostly bones, but brown rice is pretty boring alone, and he sucked the flesh from each backbone, scrap by scrap.

The next day he didn't catch any fish, so the brown rice was boring.

Buckshot paddled in the next morning about nine, and Caleb went down and caught the bow of the canoe when it came in.

Buckshot said howdy, and Caleb said the same thing.

Caleb opened the bottle of rum and took a long swallow. The bottle upended and the light dancing on the glass. Passed it to the old man.

"I was thinkin' on goin' to town," the old man said.

Caleb wriggled his toes inside his boots. The boots were dry this morning.

"I got more rum in my pack," he said. Recovered the bottle and took another deep swallow.

"Way you're hittin' on it, we're gonna need more rum," Buckshot observed.

They passed the bottle back and forth.

The old man said, "I heard what happened to Denny. It's real tragic." He meant to say "sad," but he said "tragic" instead.

"It was a bummer," Caleb said. He looked at the old man's face. "It was a real bad time," he said.

Buckshot took another swallow and sneezed. Wiped his nose on his coat sleeve. "Mercy," he said. "They still hunting you?"

"Uh-huh. I mean, I'm not on any post-office walls. But they're looking for me alright." He paused. "I hate it," he said. "I thought it wouldn't bother me, but it does."

Buckshot nodded. "How's Karen?" he asked.

"Alright, I expect," Caleb said.

"Where is she?"

"I don't know."

Buckshot cocked his head quizzical and through a couple days of stubble he asked: "What happened? You and her. . . ?"

Scudding white gunboats of clouds overhead and swift as the river below. The forest is mostly birch and white pine and descends thick to the river. And Caleb has his right boot on a rock which is sticking its black head out of the brown mud on the shore.

Something is tickling him behind the eyes and water dancing around behind them, he can feel it . . . hear it.

But something tickling his chest, too, and the two tickles collide and he says "Whoooooooooooooooooooop!"

And the laughter makes him speechless, and it doubles

him over, and he turns his red blasted guffawing face up to
Buckshot and says: "You talk too much."

After they stop laughing-sputtering, they get into Buckshot's canoe, Buckshot getting in first and Caleb shoving
her out and one foot wet jumping into the prow.

And Buckshot turned the bow of the canoe upstream.

And they went somewhere different.